Mouthwatering Pra...

Deat...
"Personable chara...
—...

Forever Fudge
"Nancy Coco paints us a pretty picture of this charming island setting where the main mode of transportation is a horse-drawn vehicle. She also gives us a delicious mystery complete with doses of her homemade fudge . . . a perfect read to wrap up your summer!" —***Wonder Women Sixty***

Oh, Fudge!
"*Oh, Fudge!* is a charming cozy, the sixth in the Candy-Coated Mystery series. But be warned: there's a candy recipe at the end of each chapter, so don't read this one when you're hungry!" —***Suspense Magazine***

Oh Say Can You Fudge
"Beautiful Mackinac Island provides the setting for a puzzling series of crimes. Now that Allie McMurphy has taken over her grandparents' hotel and fudge shop, life on Mackinac is good, although her little dog, Mal, does tend to nose out trouble. . . . Allie's third offers plenty of plausible suspects and mouthwatering fudge recipes."—***Kirkus Reviews***

"WOW. This is a great book. I loved the series from the beginning, and this book just makes me love it even more. No one can make me feel like I am in Mackinac Island better than Nancy Coco. She draws the reader in and makes you feel like you are part of the story. I cannot wait to read more. FANTASTIC is the only thing I can say further about this book." —**Bookschellves.com**

To Fudge or Not to Fudge
"*To Fudge or Not to Fudge* is a superbly crafted, classic, culinary cozy mystery. If you enjoy them as much as I do,

you are in for a real treat. The setting of Mackinac Island immediately drew me to the book as it is an amazing location. The only problem I had with the book was reading about all the mouthwatering fudge made me hungry."
—**Examiner.com** (5 stars)

"We LOVED it! This mystery is a vacation between the pages of a book. If you've never been to Mackinac Island, you will long to visit, and if you have, the story will help you to recall all of your wonderful memories."
—*Melissa's Mochas, Mysteries and Meows*

"A five-star delicious mystery that has great characters, a good plot, and a surprise ending. If you like a good mystery with more than one suspect and a surprise ending, then rush out to get this book and read it, but be sure you have the time, since once you start, you won't want to put it down. I give this 5 Stars and a Wow Factor of 5+. The fudge recipes included in the book all sound wonderful. I am thinking that a gift basket filled with the fudge from the recipes in this book, along with a copy of the book, some hot chocolate mix and/or coffee, and a nice mug would be a great Christmas gift." —**Mystery Reading Nook**

"A charming and funny culinary mystery that parodies reality-show competitions and is led by a sweet heroine, eccentric but likable characters, and a skillfully crafted plot that speeds toward an unpredictable conclusion. Allie stands out as a likable and engaging character. Delectable fudge recipes are interspersed throughout the novel."
—*Kings River Life*

All Fudged Up

"A sweet treat with memorable characters, a charming locale, and satisfying mystery." —**Barbara Allan**, author of the Trash 'n' Treasures Mystery Series

"A fun book with a lively plot, and it's set in one of America's most interesting resorts. All this plus fudge!"
—**JoAnna Carl**, author of the Chocoholic Mystery Series

Also by Nancy Coco

The Oregon Honeycomb Mystery Series
Death Bee Comes Her

The Candy-Coated Mystery Series
All Fudged Up
To Fudge or Not to Fudge
Oh Say Can You Fudge
All I Want for Christmas Is Fudge
All You Need Is Fudge
Oh, Fudge!
Deck the Halls with Fudge
Forever Fudge
Fudge Bites
Have Yourself a Fudgy Little Christmas
Here Comes the Fudge

A MATTER OF HIVE AND DEATH

An Oregon Honeycomb Mystery

Nancy Coco

Kensington Publishing Corp.

www.kensingtonbooks.com

KENSINGTON BOOKS are published by

Kensington Publishing Corp.
119 West 40th Street
New York, NY 10018

All Kensington titles, imprints, and distributed lines are available at special quantity discounts for bulk purchases for sales promotion, premiums, fund-raising, educational, or institutional use.

Special book excerpts or customized printings can also be created to fit specific needs. For details, write or phone the office of the Kensington Sales Manager: Attn.: Sales Department. Kensington Publishing Corp., 119 West 40th Street, New York, NY 10018. Phone: 1-800-221-2647.

The K and Teapot logo is a trademark of Kensington Publishing Corp

Kensington Mass Market Edition: April 2022
ISBN: 978-1-4967-3562-1

ISBN: 978-1-4967-3179-1 (ebook)

10 9 8 7 6 5 4 3 2

Printed in the United States of America

This one is for Phyllis, who believed in me and shared her generous heart. You bolstered me and always spoke your mind. I will try to be more like you. The world is not the same without you.

Chapter 1

"Oh, Wren, what do you think?" Aunt Eloise asked as she walked into my shop, Let It Bee. She held out her Havana Brown cat, Elton, dressed in a green alien costume.

"That costume really brings out the color of his eyes," I said. My cat, Everett, meowed his agreement. Elton was Everett's uncle. My aunt had bred Havana Brown cats for years until after Everett's mother died. Then she decided that encouraging people to adopt cats was a better way to go and started a Havana Brown rescue group.

"It's for the McMinnville UFO festival," Aunt Eloise said. "You're going, right?"

I winced. "I forgot about it. But in my defense, all my time has been taken up by the Let It Bee second-anniversary celebration this weekend."

"It's only Monday, and the festival doesn't start until

next Wednesday. So you have plenty of time to get ready. I'm sure Everett is looking forward to it." My only living relative and near and dear to my heart, Aunt Eloise was a tall woman with the large bones of our pioneering ancestors. At least, that's how I liked to think of it. Anyone who's played Oregon Trail, the computer game, knows it took hardy stock to make it all the way out to the Oregon coast.

Eloise had grown up in Oceanview, Oregon, along with my mother. I, myself, had spent only three years in town before going away to college. But over two years ago, I returned and started Let It Bee, a shop featuring honey and bees in a 1920s building just off Main Street and a few blocks from the beach. "I'm bringing Emma and Evangeline. You know how Everett gets jealous when his sisters get to do fun things and he's left out."

Everett meowed his thoughts on the matter. I sighed. It had been years since I'd been to the UFO festival. Based on a UFO sighting in McMinnville in the 1950s, the festival was equal parts campy, with parades and vendors selling alien souvenirs, and serious, with speakers discussing the science behind sightings.

"Fine," I said. "We'll go for the parade and shopping, but I'm not dressing up."

"Oh, goody." Aunt Eloise pulled a silver costume out of the pocket of her long cardigan sweater. "I made him this! What do you think, Everett?" She held up the metallic spacesuit.

He jumped down from the cashier counter and walked to her. Aunt Eloise bent down, and Everett sniffed the suit delicately, then meowed and rubbed up against her leg.

"He likes it!" She straightened. The smile was wide in her strong face. Her gray hair was held in a bun on top of her head, and I caught a whiff of her orange-blossom perfume. "Now we can all watch the parade in style. Wait until you see my costume. I have a necklace that looks like a collar. The cats are the owner, and I'm the pet!"

"Well, that's certainly true of all cats," I teased. "But I'm not wearing a costume."

"You said that already," she pouted a moment, then broke into a wide smile. "Is it okay if I ask Sally Hendrickson to come with us? She would wear a costume. She's into cosplay."

"Yes, that's fine," I said.

The bells on the door to the shop jangled, and my sales manager, Porsche Allen, stepped inside the door. She shook off her umbrella, folded it, and walked into the shop. "Not busy today?" She looked around the currently customer-free store.

"We had a nice rush this morning, but between the rain and school getting out soon, there's a bit of a lull," I said.

"Typical Monday," Porsche said as she put her umbrella into the holder behind the cashier stand and pulled off her raincoat. Porsche was tall and thin, with gorgeous black hair from her Korean mother and sparkling blue eyes from her American father. Today she wore jeans, black booties, and a green sweater. "Hey, Eloise, what's up?"

"We're going to the UFO festival in McMinnville this weekend," Eloise said. "Isn't Elton cute in his little green costume?" She held up her kitty and placed the silver metallic costume on the counter. "I brought this one for Everett."

At the sound of his name, Everett jumped up on the counter and brushed by Porsche so that she could stroke his brown fur.

"Nice," Porsche said. "I took the kids to that festival last year. They had a blast."

I grabbed a zippered hoody sweatshirt off the coat tree near the counter, slid it on, and then grabbed my purse. "Please tell me you didn't dress up."

"We didn't," Porsche confirmed. "But the boys want to this year."

"Oh, good, we can all go together," Aunt Eloise said.

"Well, I'll let you two figure things out. I have an appointment. Thanks for coming in a bit early and covering for me, Porsche. Is someone picking the kids up from school?"

Porsche had two boys, River and Phoenix, who were ten and eight years old, respectively. "Jason worked from home today, so he can get them." Her husband, Jason, worked for a local tech company and was able to work from home whenever he wasn't traveling.

"Great, thanks. I've got to go see a bee wrangler about the fruit-tree honey," I headed toward the door.

"Tell Elias we said hi," Aunt Eloise said.

"I will." I waved my goodbye and pulled the hood up over my curly hair to keep it from frizzing too much in the soft rain. It rained a lot in spring on the Oregon coast. Unlike Porsche and her umbrella, most natives simply put on a hooded sweatshirt and stepped out, hood up. I guess we were used to being damp.

Elias Bentwood was a bee wrangler who lived in an old house on the edge of town. He'd trained me in the art of beekeeping and was my go-to guy for local honey. If Elias didn't have it, he could point me to where to get it.

I got into my car and drove the mile or so it took to get there. The house was a one-bedroom shotgun style, which meant you could open the front door and shoot a gun straight through the house and kill someone in the backyard. Aunt Eloise said that a bachelor lumberjack had built it in the 1920s, and it had been neglected until Elias bought it in the 1980s.

The tiny home was painted white and had sea-blue shutters. Elias maintained it well. I'd known him ever since I'd gotten out of college. Most of his hives were hired out at the moment to the farmers near Mount Hood. It was fruit-tree-blossom season, and bee wranglers would ensure there were hives close to the blossoms.

Bees typically foraged two miles from their hive, and even though some were thought to forage two to three times that distance, bee owners trucked hives in during blossom season to ensure the trees were properly pollinated.

Elias loved his bees and wintered some of his hives behind the house. It was Elias who had helped me design the glass-walled hive that took up a portion of my shop. Bees are important to the environment, and he'd been thrilled when I told him I wanted a safe way to give my customers a look inside a working hive.

He'd helped me build the hive on the exterior of my shop and introduced the queen bee and her court to the hive. It had become so successful that it was one of the biggest draws to my shop. The kids loved to come and watch the bees work, making honeycomb and depositing honey.

The rain stopped, and the sun came out as I walked up on the porch. I pulled my hood off, letting my curls spring out, and knocked on the door. "Elias? It's Wren." There wasn't an answer, but I wasn't worried. Elias was probably out in the back with the one or two hives he hadn't hired out. I moved off the porch and followed the sidewalk around the side of the house to the back. The house didn't have a garage or even a driveway. Instead, there was a two-track alley in the back where Elias would pull his truck in and out to move the hives.

I heard someone moving through the back bushes. "Elias? It's Wren." Rounding the corner of the house, I came upon a horrifying scene. There were three hives tilted over, the roofs pushed off and the bees swarming, angry and confused. I caught the sound of car doors slamming and saw a blue car speed away down the alley.

"Elias! The bees!" Instinct had me stepping back to keep the side of the house between me and the angry bees. "Elias!" I called and peered around the house. Whoever did this must have taken off in the car. I didn't want to get stung, so I stayed on the side of the house and dialed Elias's cell phone.

I could hear ringing coming from the backyard. "Elias?" The only sound was the phone ringing, and it went quiet as I was dumped into voice mail. If Elias was in the backyard, he might be hurt or, worse, attacked by the confused bees. The only safe vantage point to find out for sure would be from inside the house. I hurried around to the front of the house.

The door was unlocked, and I walked into the small living room. "Elias? It's Wren. Are you okay?" I made my way quickly through the tidy kitchen to the bedroom in the back. No one was there. The bedroom was a mess of scattered papers and files on top of the made bed. I hurried to the back door that led out to a tiny screened porch.

Elias lay on the ground, unmoving, while the bees swarmed around him. "Elias! Don't move. I'll get help."

I knew better than to rush into a swarm of angry and confused bees. I dialed 9-1-1.

"Nine-one-one. What is your emergency?"

I recognized Josie Pickler's voice. "Josie, it's Wren Johnson. I'm at Elias Bentwood's house. He's lying on the ground in his backyard and not moving. I think he's hurt."

"Okay, Wren, I've got an ambulance and police on their way. Can you check for a pulse?"

"No," I said. "Someone has disturbed Elias's bees. They're swarming the entire backyard. We'll need bee wranglers with protective gear."

"I'll call animal control," Josie said. "Or should I call an exterminator?"

"Don't call an exterminator! I don't want the bees hurt."

"I'll advise the ambulance that bees are swarming," Josie said.

"Have them park out front," I said. "I know another beekeeper. I'll hang up and call him."

"Okay," Josie said. "Stay safe."

I hung up and scrolled through my contacts to find Klaus Vanderbuen's number. Klaus was a friend of Elias, and although he lived twenty miles from town, he was the only person I could think of to call.

"Hello?" Klaus's voice was deep and comforting.

"Oh, thank goodness you answered," I said. "It's Wren Johnson. I own the bee-themed shop near Main in Oceanview. I'm a friend of Elias Bentwood."

"What's going on, Wren? You sound out of breath."

"I'm at Elias Bentwood's place. Elias is on the ground and not moving. I called emergency services, but some-

one has vandalized his hives. Bees are swarming everywhere. I don't think we can get to Elias to help him."

Klaus muttered something dark. "I'm on my way," he
said. "Don't let anyone do anything stupid to the bees."

"I'll do my best," I said. "Please hurry. I don't know
how badly Elias is hurt."

Klaus hung up the phone, and I walked back through
the house to the front porch to wait for emergency services to arrive. I had some practice working with beehives, but they had always been docile. As angry as these
bees were, there was no way I could reach Elias without
help.

I heard sirens in the distance and ran off the porch to
the street to wave them over. It was a police car. Officer
Jim Hampton parked the car. Riding with him was
another officer I didn't know.

"What's going on?" Jim asked when he opened his car
door.

"It's Elias," I said. "He's on the ground in the back, but
someone has attacked the bees, and they are too angry for
me to get to Elias."

The second officer got out of the car. "I can't help," he
said, his dark gaze flat. "I'm allergic to bee stings. Got an
EpiPen in the glove box."

"Show me where Elias is," Jim said. He was six feet
tall, had blue eyes in a tan face, and looked a bit like the
actor Paul Newman. "Ashton, check out the house."

"It's open," I said. "I found the door unlocked and
went inside to get a better look at the backyard."

Jim frowned at me. "Elias is in the backyard, and you
went into the house?"

"Yes," I said. "It was the only way to safely see the entire backyard. It's how I found Elias." We took off down

the sidewalk as I continued to explain. "I called Klaus Vanderbuen. He's the closest bee wrangler. But he's about fifteen minutes out."

Jim followed behind me. I stopped at the corner and peered around the side of the house. Jim stepped around me and then ducked back beside me. "Those are some angry bees. Any thoughts on how to handle them? Should we smoke them?"

"Smoke them?" I asked.

"You know smoke tends to calm bees."

"I think that only works if you are gently moving parts of the hive," I said. "You need protective gear and maybe a bee box to capture them."

"I'll call it in," he grabbed his radio. As he spoke into it, I crouched down, wondering if I could somehow crawl slowly toward Elias. But the bees swarmed the entire backyard.

"Ashton," I heard Jim say into the radio when I moved back beside him.

"Yeah, boss," the radio crackled.

"Can you see anything from inside the house?" Jim asked.

"I'm looking out the bedroom window. Bees are swarming the back porch as well as the yard. Looks like we have one man down and three hives demolished. I don't see how whoever did this got away without being stung multiple times."

"I'll put a call into the ER to watch for bee attacks," Jim said. "Can you tell if Elias is moving?"

"I'm not seeing any motion," Officer Ashton said. "Looks like maybe blood pooling near his head. Also the back bedroom looks tossed."

"I can hear the ambulance," I said and hurried back to

the front of the house. The ambulance arrived, and I rushed to the driver's side. EMT Sarah Ritter stepped out. She was five foot nine with short brown hair and serious eyes.

"What do we have?" she asked as she headed to the back of her rig to get out her equipment.

"Bees," I said. "Are you allergic?"

"Nope," she replied and opened the back door. I saw Jim go into the house as the second EMT came around and parked behind the ambulance.

It was Rick Fender. He was my height, and rail thin with bleached blond hair and a surfer look. He grinned at me. "Maybe you can lure them out with that honey candy you make."

"There are three hives of angry bees," I said. "I don't think my candy is going to soothe them. I hope you're not allergic."

"I'm not," he said and grabbed the end of a stretcher.

"Where's the victim?" Ritter asked.

"He's in the backyard, but the bees are there, too, and they're swarming. Listen, I called a bee wrangler." I glanced at my phone. "He should be here in about ten minutes."

"The victim could be dead by then," Ritter said and pulled the stretcher and her kit toward the side of the house.

"I don't think you understand," I said. "The bees are bad."

"I'm not afraid of a few stings," Ritter said and moved quickly down the side of the house.

"Fine," I said and threw up my hands. "Don't say I didn't warn you."

They rounded the back of the house, and I counted to myself. "Five, four, three—" Both EMTs came scrambling back to the side of the building without the stretcher.

Ritter waved a bee from in front of her face and stopped next to me. "That's more than a few angry bees. You run the honey shop. Do you have a bee suit?"

"No, I only wrangled for a season and used one of Elias's suits," I said.

"How far out is the bee wrangler?" Jim asked as he and Officer Ashton stepped off the porch.

I glanced at my phone, "Maybe ten minutes? Is there anything we can do in the meantime? Elias could be dying."

"I hate to break it to you," Jim said. "But until we get those bees under control, there's no getting to Elias."

"I can try a hazmat suit," Sarah said. "We have a couple back at the station. Don't know if they will be protective enough against that many bees. But it's worth a try."

"Go get it," Jim said. "Ashton and I will stay here and monitor the situation."

"Dispatch wanted to call animal control," I said. "But even if they have a bee suit, Klaus will get here before they can dig it out."

"What if Elias moves?" Jim asked. "Will the bees attack him?"

"There's a chance they will," I said.

"Then we'd better hope he keeps his head down," Jim said. "Fender, monitor the victim from a safe distance. Ritter, go get the hazmat suit."

"And me?" I asked.

"Stay out of the way."

Honey Peanut Butter Cookies

Ingredients:
½ cup butter
½ cup peanut butter
½ cup honey
½ cup white sugar
1 egg
1 teaspoon vanilla
1½ cup all-purpose flour
¾ teaspoon baking soda
½ teaspoon baking powder
¼ teaspoon salt
¼ cup of sugar for topping

Directions:

For a soft cookie, preheat oven to 325°F. In a medium bowl, cream the butter, peanut butter, honey, and sugar. Add the egg and vanilla, stirring until combined. Add the flour, baking soda, baking powder, and salt. Beat until well combined. Line a cookie sheet with parchment paper. Roll dough into 1-inch balls and place on cookie sheet, leaving 2 inches between. Place a fork, tines flat, in the sugar and then make cross hatch marks on each cookie, dipping the fork in sugar before each cross so the dough doesn't stick to it. Bake for 15–18 minutes. Look for a golden-brown cookie that is crisp on the outside and chewy on the inside. Remove from the cookie sheet and let cool. Makes 30 cookies. Enjoy!

Chapter 2

"That's a mess," Klaus said as he eyed the backyard. He wore a full bee suit with gloves and carried a helmet in his hands.

"Is there anything you can do to calm them?" I asked.

"Not really," he said. "Elias hasn't moved?"

"Not an inch," I replied.

"It could mean he's hiding from the bees," Klaus said.

"Except for the pool of blood we can see around his head," EMT Ritter said. "What's the plan?"

"Well, to start, that hazmat suit might help, but chances are, if you go into that swarm, you will be stung, no matter how well you're protected," Klaus said.

"I'll take that chance," Ritter said.

"Then we'll go in slow. The number-one rule is to act calm. We will walk slowly along the edge of the porch.

When we are directly in front of Elias, then we will walk slowly and calmly to him. Chances are that's when we'll be stung the most, as we will be approaching the hives."

"And you can't just smoke them?" Jim asked.

"Smoking the bees is a diversion. It makes them feel as if the hive is under attack, and they digest as much honey as possible to save it. These bees are beyond that. I would love to get in there and recover the queens and reset the hives, but that will take a lot of time," Klaus said.

"Time we don't have," Ritter said. "Let's go in."

"Wait, how are you going to remove Elias?" I asked.

"We are going to slowly and calmly two-man-lift him," Ritter said. "No sudden jerking movements."

"When we bring him out, there will be bees that follow us, so I recommend that everyone stay back and away from the ambulance," Klaus said, his pale blue gaze serious. "Anyone who has a bee allergy needs to move at least a block away."

"That's me," Officer Ashton said.

"Ashton, call the ER. Let them know there will be live bees on the victim," Officer Hampton said.

"Got it," Ashton pulled out his radio and walked quickly away from the house and the emergency vehicles.

Somewhere in the mix, the fire truck had shown up, but I cautioned them from hosing the bee swarm. Bees could be badly hurt from that kind of water pressure, and it wouldn't help Elias.

The firemen hung out on the side of the road. We all watched as the bee wrangler and EMT calmly and carefully walked the same path along the back of the house. Bees swarmed the screened porch and the two people.

They stopped and counted to ten before they moved away from the porch and toward Elias.

Unable to take off their gloves to feel for a pulse or check for neck injuries, they both squatted and slowly lifted Elias to sitting. His head lolled, and the bees buzzed louder. I listened as the EMT and the bee wrangler stopped until things settled. Next, they slowly put Elias's arms around their necks. Then lifted him to his feet by holding his wrists. It was clear Elias was not conscious. His head lolled to the side, and his skin was a funny blue color. Bees swarmed around their heads. I hated to think how badly Elias was getting stung. If he survived the fall, he might not survive the stings.

The two slowly and calmly retraced their steps, dragging Elias between them. We scattered as they rounded the corner of the house, bringing bees with them. Retreating to the safety of the car, I watched as the two loaded Elias into the ambulance and shut the door.

Sirens blaring, the ambulance took off down the street. Calmly, Klaus retreated to the back of his pickup and sat on the tailgate, waiting for the bees to settle.

The firetruck left with the ambulance, but Jim Hampton sat in his squad car and waited, as I did, for things to calm down. Twenty minutes went by, and Klaus got up and walked toward the squad car. He took off his helmet and motioned for Jim to roll down his window.

Jim opened the door instead and got out. I got out as well. Bees still hovered around Klaus, but were more calm.

"How long until we can get the swarms under control?" Jim asked.

"If we do nothing, it could be days or weeks, depending on what the queens decide," Klaus said. "If I have your permission, I'd like to call in a few friends and see if we can't save the hives."

Jim's mouth set in a straight line. "I was radioed that Elias was pronounced DOA when he got to the ER," Jim said. "That means this is a crime scene. If you bring in a bunch of people, they can ruin any evidence we may be able to collect."

"Look, those bees could swarm so long all the evidence would be lost and the bees could be lost," Klaus said. "Let's see if we can't get your crime scene under control."

"We already lost Elias," I said. "Let's save his bees."

"I'll make a call," Jim said and got back into his squad car, closing the door to keep us out.

I put my hand on Klaus's shoulder and walked toward my car. "I have some bottled water," I said. "Let's get you something to drink."

"Thanks."

I knew from experience that bee suits were hot, and if he got the permission he needed to save the bees, he'd be wearing his for hours. I opened my car door and grabbed a bottle from the back seat. "I keep water in the back, as a rule," I said. "You never know when you might need it." I handed him the water. "How badly are you stung?"

"I've been worse," he said and twisted the cap off the bottle. "Did you find Elias?"

"Yes," I said. "I wanted to talk with him about branching out on my locally sourced honey supplies."

"Did you see who did this?"

"No, just a car speeding away," I said and frowned. "What's going to happen to the bees?"

"I've put in a call to the Tillamook chapter of the Beekeepers Association. Several members have stepped up to help me save the hives. We need to get in there and see how the queens are doing. They might have already left the hives; if so, it's a dead deal."

"And if you can save them? Where will they go?" I asked.

"Not sure," Klaus said and rubbed his bearded chin. "Depends on whether Elias had a will or not. Do you know?"

"We were good friends, but not that close," I said.

Just then, a small purple pickup truck screeched to a halt in front of Elias's house. Millie Brown rushed out, slamming the door behind her. "I got a call for beekeepers. Is Elias all right?" Millie was in her mid-forties, bone thin, with gray hair pulled back in a long braid. She wore a waffled, long-sleeved tee under a plaid shirt with the sleeves rolled up, exposing the tee sleeves, jeans, and thick hiking boots.

"Brace yourself," Klaus said and put his hand on her shoulder. "Elias's dead."

"What? No!" She pushed past us to the house. "Elias?" She went inside before Officer Hampton could stop her. I could hear her tearing through the place, with Jim calling her name as we approached the porch.

Officer Hampton brought her outside and sat her down on the small front-porch stoop. "I'm sorry, Millie," he said softly.

"But we had a date tonight," she said. Her eyes were wide, and her mouth trembled. She glanced at me. "You found him?"

I nodded.

"Millie," Jim said, "you and Elias were dating?"

"We're engaged," she said and held out her left hand to show off a ring that had two bees sleeping together in a flower. "We were meeting tonight to talk about wedding venues."

"Do you have any idea who might want to hurt him?" Jim asked.

"No," she shook her head. "He was a great guy, loving and considerate." Her gaze washed over us. "Why would anyone do this?"

"Maybe he caught them sabotaging his hives," Jim suggested.

"No," Klaus and I said at once.

"They had to have vandalized the hives to cover what they did to Elias," Klaus went on. "There's no way they could have stayed in the yard to hurt him with the bees swarming."

"Did they hurt the bees?" Millie asked.

"The hives have been vandalized," Klaus said. "It's why I put out the call. We need to get to them and see if we can find and save the queens."

"I've got my gear," Millie said and stood.

"Are you sure you're up to this?" Klaus said. "You've just had a shock."

"Those bees might be all I have left of Elias," she said, her expression grim. "Let's get started."

I watched as she strode to her pickup and grabbed beekeeping gear out of the passenger seat.

"Millie has grit," Jim said. "Did you know they were dating?"

"No," I said. "I've been busy and hadn't talked to Elias in a couple of months." A stab of guilt went through me. "We were friends for years, and I didn't really know him."

"It happens," Jim said.

"It doesn't happen to me," I whispered.

More patrol cars pulled up, and cops got out. Then Alison McGovern parked her SUV, grabbed her kit, and got out. I stepped aside as Jim pointed them inside the house. Alison was a no-nonsense CSU. There was no point in doing anything but sending her a small wave of acknowledgment. Within minutes, two more beekeepers arrived, and soon there were five people working on the swarming hives.

My cell phone rang. "Oh, Porsche," I said. "I'm sorry. I got hung up."

"I heard," Porsche said. "Three people have come into the store looking for you. They heard about Elias and the bee swarm. Did the bees kill him?"

"Not unless they could bash him in the head with a blunt object," I said. "When they pulled him out, I saw blood on his face. A lot of blood."

"Wow," Porsche said.

"Hey, did you know Elias and Millie Brown were engaged?"

"Millie and Elias? No," Porsche said.

"She had a cute ring with two bees sleeping in a flower," I said.

"Oh, poor Millie," Porsche said. "I didn't know. Not that I know her or Elias that well, but I am pretty attuned to the rumor mill. If anyone knew anything about an engagement, someone would have told me."

"I do count on you to keep me up to date with things going on in town," I said, wryly.

"Listen, the kids are out of school in fifteen minutes, and Jason is stuck in a meeting. May I call your aunt to come mind the store?"

"Wren!" I turned to see Aunt Eloise pushing through the crowd with a bee suit in her hands. "Brought you a suit when I heard about the swarm."

"Porsche," I said and pointed at my phone. "She needs to go pick up her kids from school. Jason's stuck in a meeting."

Aunt Eloise handed me the gear. "Tell her I'll be right there."

"Thanks," I said to my aunt.

"I heard," Porsche said through my phone. "Good luck bee wrangling."

"Thanks." I hung up and pulled the bee suit on. I might have had only a year of bee wrangling behind me, but it didn't mean I couldn't help. Suited up, I walked around to the backyard. The bees were still angry, but the wranglers had gotten two of the hives put back together.

"Wren, go get the smokers out of the back of my pickup," Millie said. "We've got two of the queens."

"Got it," I said and hurried back to the pickup. I grabbed the smokers and lighted them, carefully putting the lids on so that we could concentrate the smoke where we wanted it. I glanced over to see that barriers had been put up at the end of the block to keep the lookie-loos safely away from the bees.

I brought the smokers, and we were able to calm down the bees with queens. But the third hive was lost. I could see the tears in Millie's eyes.

"I don't think the queen is dead," I said. "They will move on, and we will find them."

She nodded, and as I reached out to pat her shoulder, her knees crumpled. I put my arm around her and walked her away from the backyard crime scene to her pickup.

We took off our bee hoods, and I opened her front door so she could sit down on the seat. "I'm sorry."

"Oh, no, you are doing so well. Thank you for helping with the bees."

"Oh, Elias, what happened?" She put her head down into her hands.

"You don't know anyone who might have done this?" I asked.

"No, Elias was well liked." She looked at me. "You found him?"

"I did," I said. "I didn't see it happen, but I did see a blue sedan race away down the alley. Do you know if Elias knew anyone with a car like that?"

"No," she said. "I don't think so. I . . . I can't think."

"It's okay," I said. "It's a shock. Do you need someone to drive you home?"

"I'd like to talk to her first," Officer Hampton said from behind me.

"Oh, okay," I said. "I should get back to my shop anyway." The sun was setting, and things had calmed down as much as they could.

"Good idea," Jim said as I moved away from him. "I'll call you later."

I took one last look at Elias's home, got into my car, and left. It seemed like a lifetime since I had been on my way to make a quick stop at a friend's house to discuss new suppliers.

Parking around the back of the shop, I went in by the back door. The shop itself was bright after the darkness that was falling outside. "Aunt Eloise?"

"In the front," she called back. I walked through the small hallway, where I had coat hooks on the wall and a place to leave rain gear. Luckily, tonight there was no rain, an unusual occurrence for May in Oregon.

The honey store was warm and bright. It smelled like candles and hand cream. I preferred to stick to essential oils when I made my products. It kept things natural and brought out the beauty of the products.

"There she is," Aunt Eloise said as I stepped into view. "Wren, I'd like you meet—"

"Travis Hutton," I said and stopped cold.

"Hello, Wren," he said. "It's been a while."

It had been five years, seven months, and eight days, but I wasn't going to let him know I'd been keeping track.

Chapter 3

Honey has been used as a salve on burns for centuries. It has been proven to prevent infections and reduce the time required for burns to heal.

Travis Hutton was six foot two inches of brawn, brains, and blue eyes that could melt my heart a block away. His dark hair was long and pulled up into a man bun. It didn't matter if the style was old; he made everything look hot. Lucky for me, I was dressed in full beekeeping gear. That way, he couldn't see the flush that went over most of my body. I couldn't hide the blush in my cheeks unless I put the hood back on, and I wasn't going to be that person. "Oh, you two know each other," Aunt Eloise said with a smile and a wave of her hand. "Wonderful, then there's no reason why we can't all sit down for dinner tonight. I'll cook, of course."

Everett sat on top of the cashier's counter and peered at Travis with interested eyes. Knowing my cat, he could tell how excited I was to see Travis. I swallowed hard and tried to remain calm.

"Someone has to watch the store," I said. "You two go ahead." I waved my gloved hands toward the door.

"Eloise told me her niece had opened a honey store in Oceanview," Travis said. "She didn't tell me you were her niece. I think we can hold dinner until after you close." He made a show at looking at the hours of operation in the window. "Nine p.m., is it? I don't mind a late dinner."

I had to work hard not to give him the stink eye.

"Of course we can eat late," Aunt Eloise said. She was in full-on flirt mode now, and I didn't blame her one bit. Travis was the type of guy women young and old want to be around. "Wren, if you don't mind, I'm going to run to the store and pick up the ingredients for my magic lasagna." She put her hand on Travis's arm. "You're going to love it."

"I'm sure I will," he said.

We watched my aunt grab her jacket from the hooks and wave to us as she left through the back door. There was a stillness in the shop. The faint sound of music played around us. I struggled for something to say.

He stuck his hands in his pocket. "I didn't know you were Eloise's niece."

I turned and moved behind the counter. "I didn't know you knew my aunt. How do you know my aunt? Aren't you supposed to be in Tokyo?"

"Has it really been that long?" His voice was velvet to my ears. I pulled off the gloves I was wearing, set them on the counter, and looked him in the eye. "Right, well, I've been out of Tokyo for three years," he said. "I went from Tokyo to London to Seattle. I'm living in Seattle now." He took a step toward the counter, and I took a step back.

"That's a two-hour drive from here," I pointed out.

"I like driving," he said.

"Why are you here?" I blurted out, trying to figure out what to do with my hands.

"I met Eloise at the Portland Night Market. She was working a booth for the Havana Brown cat-rescue group. We got to talking about cats, and she invited me to Oceanview to pick out a new pet."

Everett had taken a shine to Travis. He paced in front of him, rubbing up against the black wool coat that stretched across Travis's wide chest. Travis reached out and ran his hand along Everett's fur. My cat purred up a storm.

"Oh, that's right," I said and sent him a smile. "You love cats."

"It's how we met," he said. "You were walking Everett on campus. I was sitting on a bench doing my homework."

"Everett was less than a year old," I said.

My cat meowed at the sound of his name. He kept pacing the countertop in front of Travis to get pets.

"Such a clever cat," Travis said. "He's the reason I met your aunt. I remembered this girl I'd fallen for once having a Havana Brown, and I wanted one."

"That was a long time ago," I said and swallowed hard.

"When I met your aunt? No, that was just last week."

"When you knew that girl," I said. "Before you chose your career over her and broke her heart."

He lifted his hand and stepped back from the counter. "I don't remember it that way." He sent me a small smile. "But then I was young and not ready to settle down."

The door to the shop opened, and Officer Hampton

strode inside. The bells jangled as the door closed behind him.

"Hey," I said. "Are you finished with the crime scene already?"

"Crime scene?" Travis asked.

"There wasn't much left to process once the bees were contained," Jim said. He glanced at Travis and back at me. "Do you have time for a few questions?"

"Sure," I said.

"Are you a customer?" Jim asked.

"Oh, Officer Jim Hampton, this is Travis Hutton," I said. "We went to college together. He's here to adopt a cat through my aunt's rescue program."

The two men shook hands. They sized each other up for a moment, and then Travis turned toward me. "I'll leave you to your questions. I'm looking forward to dinner later, Wren." He nodded and left the shop.

Jim watched him go and then turned to me. "Old flame?"

"Is it that obvious?"

"I'm a trained observer," he said. "I see you're still wearing the beekeeper's suit." He pointed toward my outfit.

"I haven't had time to change." I pushed my bangs back out of my eyes. "Do you know what killed Elias?"

"The autopsy will be done tomorrow or the next day," Jim said. "Do you have time to go over what happened today?"

"Sure," I said and unzipped the suit. "I stopped by Elias's place to talk about local suppliers. He didn't answer the door, so I went around the back to see if he was outside working with the bees. That's when I saw the swarms, and a blue sedan drive off in a hurry. I checked to see if Elias was inside and if he'd seen what the vandals did, but he wasn't inside. So I looked out the bedroom window and saw him on the ground."

"Did you get a license plate number on the car?" he asked.

I closed my eyes and thought back. "No, I wasn't at a good angle to see it. The sedan was older though, I think maybe American, like Ford or GM. Sorry, I'm not the most knowledgeable when it comes to cars."

"Whoever did this more than likely got stung more than once," Jim said. "I've got word out at the local hospitals and clinics in case they get a walk-in."

"Any idea who would want to hurt Elias?" I asked.

"No," he said. "Everyone I've talked to, from his neighbors to his girlfriend, Millie, tells me he's a nice guy. He wasn't into drugs or anything illegal."

"I've known Elias for three years," I said. "I studied bee wrangling under him. He is . . . er, was the past president of the Tillamook chapter of the Beekeepers Association of America."

"Are there any rivalries in the association?" Jim asked.

"What do you mean?"

"These kinds of associations are pretty political. Could someone from the association want Elias dead?" Jim studied me.

"No," I said. "No, it couldn't have been anyone from the association."

"Why not?"

"Because we all see bees as an endangered species. Not a single one of us would ever harm a hive or risk destroying a colony like these killers did."

"So you think I can scratch off the beekeepers association members from my list of folks to investigate," he said.

"Oh, I think you'll look into whatever you think you should look into, but you're not going to find a killer there. Besides, wasn't Elias's bedroom searched? Maybe this has nothing to do with bees at all."

"What would it be about then?" he asked. "What else was Elias involved in?"

I leaned back against the back shelves. "That's the question of the day, isn't it? I wish I knew."

"All right, if you think of anything else, let me know," he said. "You have my number."

"I do," I said. "And I will."

He studied me for a moment. "Try to keep out of the investigation this time. Okay?"

"I'm a store owner, not a private detective," I said.

"That's the right answer," he said. "Thanks, Wren."

I watched him leave my store and glanced at the clock on the wall. It was eight o'clock. One hour left before dinner with Travis at Aunt Eloise's home. What the heck was I going to wear?

"You had dinner with Travis Hutton?" Porsche said the moment she walked into the back door of the shop the next morning. "*The* Travis Hutton? The man who ran off to Tokyo with a cute coed and left you with a broken heart?"

It was Tuesday, and the shop wouldn't open for another thirty minutes. I brewed coffee for the coffee bar, where we offered people a chance to try different honeys in their beverage.

"Yes," I said and took the tall carafe off the brewer and placed the pump top on it.

"Okay, spill, what happened? Is he still drop-dead gorgeous? Did he come crawling back to beg forgiveness? Did you slap his face? Did he give you a toe-curling kiss and beg you to take him back?"

"No," I said and added some pretty spring candles to the candle display.

"What happened?"

"Nothing, I said.

She grabbed me by the forearms. "I don't believe that. I happen to know you still have feelings for him."

"It's been five years," I said with a long breath. "People change."

"Then what did you talk about?"

"Cats," I said and went to the cash register to count out the money for the day. "He's adopting one of Aunt Eloise's rescue cats."

"Okay . . . and?"

"And he's living in Seattle now, still working for an international company in sales management," I said as I closed the register, ensuring everything was ready for opening.

"Only two hours away? Wonderful," Porsche said. "So, are you going to see him again?"

"He didn't ask," I said and studied her. Porsche was a lovely blend of both of her parents, Korean American and German American. Today, she wore a flowered top over skinny jeans and knee-high riding boots. She'd hung up her jacket on one of the hooks near the back door.

"Oh, come on, the man who broke your heart suddenly shows up at your aunt's door and only adopts a cat? I think there's more going on here."

I flipped over the OPEN sign and unlocked the door. "He was as surprised to see me as I was to see him. Trust me, he's not looking to bring me back into his life."

"I don't believe it," she said. "And even if it's true, now that you know he's in Seattle, are you going to ask him out?"

"I was in love with him years ago. We're different people now. Besides, I have a second-anniversary celebration to get ready for and Elias's murder to investigate."

"Ah, I wondered when we'd get to that," Porsche said as she grabbed a feather duster and started to dust the shelves. "How are you doing after yesterday?"

"I'm okay," I said and straightened the display in front of the register. "I still can't believe that Elias was engaged to Millie Brown. He never mentioned it. Why wouldn't he mention it?"

Porsche shrugged. "Maybe he thought you already knew, but then I'm not as much in the know when it comes to the beekeepers association as you are. I would say good for them both, but knowing that Elias is dead, it's kind of a moot point."

"He was murdered," I corrected her, "and the fiends who killed him also damaged three beehives. We were able to save two, but the third lost its queen. I don't understand why this would happen. Why Elias?"

"Do you need some time off today? Jason's working from home. I can call him and free you up for the day."

"I don't think I need that," I said.

The door opened, the bells jangling with the effort. "Oh, good, you're here." It was Millie Brown. "I think I know who killed Elias."

My heart rate sped up, and I pulled her over to the counter. "Shouldn't you call the police?"

"I can't," she said. "I don't have any proof. But I heard you helped when Agnes Snow was murdered."

"I was involved, yes," I said. "But I had to be. I was a suspect."

"I want you to help me now, please," Millie said.

"Do what exactly?" I asked.

"Help me find who did this to Elias and bring them to justice," Millie said, her brown eyes filled with tears. "You have to help me. You were Elias's friend, right?"

"And apprentice," I said. "I studied beekeeping under him for a year."

"So you'll help me?" she asked.

"I don't know how . . ."

Millie grabbed my arm and looked at Porsche as if worried she would overhear something. Porsche turned her back on us, pretending to dust. "Elias was looking into something."

"What do you mean?" I asked, confused.

"There have been a number of hives vandalized in the last six months. Members of the Tillamook association have reported them, but bees aren't exactly on the police list of major crimes."

"So Elias was looking into the problem?" Porsche asked.

Startled by the intrusion, Millie looked from Porsche to me and back. "It may be what got him killed." She swallowed back tears, pulled a large manila envelope out of her purse, and turned to me. "The last time we had dinner, he gave me this to keep for you." Millie handed it to me. The envelope was marked with my name. "He wouldn't tell me why or even when to give it to you. He said I would know when the time was right. I put it in a drawer. I thought he was talking about our wedding presents. I mean, I had mentioned it would be fun to register with your shop . . ."

"But now you think he meant if anything happened to him," I said. I didn't know what to do. Should I open the envelop now? What if it really was a wedding registration list?

The bells jangled, and two middle-aged women entered. They wore jackets over sweatshirts, jeans, and boots. The sun was shining, and the air was still crisp from the ocean breeze.

"Welcome," Porsche said and went over to talk to the women.

I tugged Millie behind the counter. "Do you want me to open this now?" I asked. "What if it's just a list of things he wanted for your wedding?"

She swallowed and dashed the tears off her cheeks. "I have to know. Whatever it is. I have to know if bringing it to you was the right thing."

"Okay," I opened the envelope and took out three sheets of paper. Elias's scrawling handwriting ran across the first sheet. "If you're reading this, then something bad has happened to me." I read the letter aloud and glanced at Millie, who hugged her waist. "Please tell Millie that I love her and I'm sorry." Tears rolled down Millie's cheeks, and I hugged her, then went back to reading the letter. "I've been investigating beehive vandals. If anything has happened to me, it's because I have gotten too close to discovering the vandals. The only thing I can tell you is to follow the bees."

"That's it?" Porsche said as she approached us. "It's so cryptic."

"I agree, there's no way we can go to the police with this," I said. "Why didn't Elias give more specifics?"

"I don't know," Millie said. "Maybe he didn't know who it was when he wrote that and didn't want to lead us in the wrong direction."

"Any direction is better than no direction," Porsche said.

"What do you know about the hive vandals?" I asked Millie.

"Actually, not that much," Millie said. "Every time I brought it up, Elias would change the subject." She sniffed, and I grabbed her a tissue off the counter and handed it to her. She blew her nose. "We had a fight over it last week. I wanted him to tell me exactly what he knew, and he said he wanted to keep me out of it." She sobbed. "For my own good."

"Maybe he went to the police already," I suggested. "I can ask Officer Hampton."

"I don't think Elias went to the police. If anyone from the beekeepers association was involved, he'd want to keep it internal," Millie said.

"I can't believe anyone who is a member would harm hives. It has to be someone who doesn't understand the importance of bees," I said.

"When did the vandalism begin?" Porsche asked. "Is this a new thing?"

"I think it started with a few tipped-over hives at the Wrights' farm last fall," Millie said. "Since the Wrights live close to the road, we all wrote it off as kids messing around. Alfred Wright was angry, but mostly they simply knocked the tops off the hives. It was an easy repair."

"And then?" I asked.

"Then things started to escalate. In January, four hives were opened and the racks pulled out and tossed about at the Hanson farm. Two weeks later, three more hives were attacked at the Remingtons' place. Then in March, two more hives were completely destroyed. It's as if they took an axe to them."

"Surely they would have gotten stung doing that," I said.

"We had an emergency meeting of the association board," Millie said. "We put out a notice to members to put cameras on their hives and to check on the bees."

"Did that stop the vandals?" Porsche asked.

"No," Millie said. "They started to attack the hives with power washers. They stood just outside the camera's line of sight and soaked six of Elias's hives that were prepped to be moved to the orchards. Then they knocked out the camera. That's when he got serious about figuring out who was doing it and why."

"Why isn't this making the news? Or at least been mentioned to beekeepers?" I asked. "I'm a member of the association, and I don't remember hearing about this."

"I'm guessing you got a notice about protecting your hive, but because yours is in the store, you didn't think twice about it," Millie said. "You don't own any other hives, do you?"

"No, I only own this hive right now," I said. "You're right. I may have ignored it because I didn't think about vandals in my store." I grabbed my phone and scrolled through my emails. "Yes, here it is, the email notice from the association. I'm sorry I didn't pay closer attention to this."

"I've called a meeting of the board," Millie said. "I'd like you to be there, Wren. You understand investigations. I think you could help us."

"She'll be there," Porsche said.

The door bells jangled. "She'll be where?" Aunt Eloise

asked, walking into the store. Everett ran to meet her and get picked up. Aunt Eloise obliged.

"At the emergency meeting of the beekeepers association board," Porsche said. "We may have a lead into why Elias was murdered."

"Now, wait, I haven't said I would help." I held up my hand. "Officer Hampton made it clear that I'm to stay out of this one."

"But you have experience," Millie said. "And you are Elias's friend."

"Plus you found his body," Aunt Eloise said. "That means you are meant to investigate."

"The only thing it means is that I was at the wrong place at the wrong time," I said.

"Please, Wren, Elias needs you, and I need you," Millie said.

"Fine," I said with a sigh. "I'll go to the board meeting and see what I can do, but I will go straight to Officer Hampton with anything I find. Is that clear?"

"Perfect," Millie said and gave me a big hug. "Thank you! Okay, the meeting is at six tonight in the Methodist church basement on Pine Street. See you then." She walked out, and I looked at my aunt, who was petting Everett.

"What did I just agree to?" I muttered.

"You agreed to help a friend," Aunt Eloise said.

"And solve a murder," Porsche said, with a glint in her eye.

"Before I do any of that," I said, "let's talk about the events surrounding the anniversary sale."

"And when we're going to the UFO festival," Aunt Eloise said. "Don't forget, you promised you'd go."

It seemed I'd done a lot of promising lately. I hoped I wouldn't regret it.

Honey and Blueberry Muffins

Ingredients:

2 cups all-purpose flour

½ cup sugar

1 tablespoon baking powder

½ teaspoon salt

1 cup blueberries, fresh or frozen; if frozen, let thaw and pat dry before use.

1 large egg

1 cup milk

¼ cup butter, melted

¼ cup honey

Directions:

Preheat oven to 400°F. In a large bowl, combine ingredients until just moist. Fill paper-lined muffin cups ¾ full. Bake for 15–8 minutes until a toothpick comes out clean. (Beware: If you hit a blueberry it will come out juicy, so try a toothpick again in a new spot.) When done, remove from oven. Cool for 5 minutes and remove from pan. Eat warm or freeze for later. Makes 12 muffins. Enjoy!

Chapter 4

I spent the next three hours researching all the notices of beehive vandals in the last twelve months. Between customers, of course. Which meant I was only covering the surface of what had happened to the bees.

"Anything interesting?" Porsche asked.

"I found two other incidents that Millie didn't tell us about," I said. "Why would anyone harm beehives? It's not like they are targeting one keeper, so it has to be about the bees, not the keepers."

"Is it only in our area of Oregon?" Porsche asked as she glanced at my phone screen.

"I just looked at news in Oregon," I said. "It seems to have happened up the coast and in the orchards and vine-yards around Mount Hood."

"Well, that's good, isn't it?" she asked.

"Yes, it means the vandals are relatively local," I said.

"You should call the news station," Porsche suggested. "Maybe you could, you know, put some pressure on them by going public."

"There's not much of a story here," I mused. "Let me go to the meeting and see what the board has to say." I glanced at the time. "Speaking of the board, they meet in ten minutes. Are you okay with watching the store?"

"I'm good to be here until nine p.m. The boys have a scouts meeting, and Jason is taking them," Porsche said.

"Great." I grabbed my jacket from the hooks near the back door. "This should only take an hour, but if I'm not back by six, can you feed Everett? There's a can of wet food in the cupboard above the coffee maker."

"Sure can," Porsche said and stroked Everett's back. Knowing my cat and store were in good hands, I stepped out into the cool, wet air. I could smell the ocean, as I was only a few blocks from the beach and fog had rolled in.

The church meeting room was only a few blocks away. I saw no reason to drive there, and I needed the exercise. I waved at Mrs. Anderson as I crossed the street. She waved back from her front window and let the curtains fall. The best part about a small town was that there were always people watching. It was also the worst part of a small town.

I crossed Third Street and Pine and had the strange feeling I was being followed. I stopped and looked around, but the streets were quiet. Shrugging off the feeling as leftover anxiety about Elias and the bee vandals, I hurried up the side stairs at the church and entered. There was a short foyer and then stairs that lead to the basement and the well-lit meeting rooms. I unzipped my coat and followed the sound of voices to the conference room on the right.

The room was well lit and painted a cheery yellow. There were four tables set up in a square, with chairs surrounding them so that everyone sat facing each other. Along the walls were whiteboards and bulletin boards stuffed with papers and flyers for various church events.

"Ah, here's Wren," Millie said and stood. She waved me over to the empty seat beside her. "Wren, do you want coffee or water?"

"I'm fine, thanks," I said and slipped off my damp jacket, draped it on the back of the chair, and sat down. There were five people in the room, and I made it six.

"Wren, do you know Bill Chechup? Bill's the current president of our chapter and owns Chechup's Bee Service."

"Hello, nice to meet you," I said.

"Then there's Rachel Grimsby, past president," Millie continued. "Paul Shoemaker, treasurer, and Sarah Luce, secretary."

I nodded toward them as she said their names.

"Everyone, this is Wren Johnson. She owns Let It Bee and is a beekeeper herself."

"Let's cut to the chase," Bill said. He was a bear of a man, about five foot ten with a big bald head, green eyes, and a gray beard. He wore a plaid shirt over a dark navy T-shirt. "We understand you were the one who found Elias dead."

"I was," I said. "I'm not sure if I can give you all the details without hurting the police investigation."

"That's fine," Bill said, making a chopping motion with his hand to cut that idea short. "We heard the killers vandalized Elias's beehives. How, exactly?"

"Well, the tops were removed, and it looked as if they had been bashed with a blunt object, like an axe," I said.

"I called Klaus, and he called in a few others. We were able to save two of the hives, but we lost the queen from the third hive, and those bees scattered. We righted the hive, and since it has honey and comb and some larvae, we hope the bees will return and create a new queen."

"But there's no guarantee," Rachel said. "Did the vandals use dust or water with dish soap?"

"It looked like they simply smashed the hives," I said. "It took us a while to calm the bees and repair the hives."

Bill nodded. "That fits the pattern. What did Millie tell you?"

"She told me that Elias was investigating a series of vandalized hives. I did my own research and saw the reports. They weren't hard to find."

"We didn't want to make them hard to find, but they're not exactly breaking news, either," Sarah said. "But with Elias's death, it feels like the vandals are escalating."

"Right now, there's no link between the vandals and Elias's murder," I said. "Klaus and I think the murderer damaged the hives in order to destroy evidence and to distract the police from discovering them."

"I have to say that I strongly believe these incidents are connected," Millie argued. "Elias was well loved. The only thing he was doing was looking into the vandals. They have to be the people who killed him."

"I can tell you that, from my experience with Agnes Snow's murder investigation, you have to go to the police with proof before they will look deeply into a connection," I said. "Do you have proof?"

"We don't," Bill said. "The last two vandalisms included water and dish soap. The vandals didn't use that this time."

"So we might be jumping to conclusions to think there

is a connection," Rachel said. Rachel was in her fifties, with short brown hair and blue cat-eye glasses. She wore a pale blue blouse with rolled-up sleeves.

Sarah was a redhead with her long hair pulled up into a messy bun and a bright red lip color. She wore a Haystack Rock sweatshirt that included a picture of the puffins that inhabited the rock part of the year.

"Does anyone know who Elias was investigating? Did he have a primary subject?" I asked.

"He was to bring his report to the meeting on Friday," Bill said.

"Millie," I said, turning to her, "do you know where the report is? Can I see it?"

"I didn't find it," Millie said. "When the police released Elias's home after the crime-scene guys had finished, I went into his bedroom to see if he'd printed out a report. But there was no paper there. Even Elias's journals were gone."

"Do you think the killer took them?" I asked.

"I think so," Millie said with a frown.

"What about his computer?" I asked. "Is there anything on it?"

"I don't know," Millie said. "The police took it into evidence. Can you ask Officer Hampton?"

"No," I said. "He'll tell me to stay out of it."

"Which we should," Rachel said, her blue glasses glinting in the florescent light. "This is something for the cops."

"But they aren't going to look at the vandals," Millie said. "They have no proof there's a connection. We have to look into this."

"Let me talk to Officer Hampton," I said. "I can tell him what's going on. Then they will look into it."

"But they won't have the advantage we have of understanding the community," Bill said. He narrowed his eyes. "When they look into this, they're going to need us."

"Let me call him now and bring him here," I said. "We can all talk to him."

"That's probably a good idea," Sarah said.

"I'll call him right now," I said and grabbed my phone. I walked out into the hallway and hit the button in CONTACTS under "Jim."

"This is Hampton," he answered his phone.

"Hi, Jim," I said.

"Wren? Did you think of something else?"

"Well, Millie did," I said. "Listen, we're in a meeting room in the Methodist church basement. Can you come and hear us out?"

"Who's us?" he asked.

"The board of the Tillamook chapter of Beekeepers Association of America," I said. "Millie has a theory."

"I'm on Main Street, so I'll be right over," he said and hung up his phone.

"He's just down the street and will be here in a moment," I said as I walked back into the meeting room.

Millie stood and hugged her waist. "Will he listen to us?"

"If he doesn't, I will do what I can to help," I said and put my hand on her shoulder. "Elias was my friend. I'm not going to let his murder go unsolved."

"We also need to get these vandals shut down. We have enough problems with colony collapse. We don't need help from people ruining our hives," Bill said.

"You know I love my bees," I said. "It's why I started Let It Bee. I want people to understand the importance of bees and the good that bee products can do. If I can help with either Elias's murder or the bee vandals, I will."

"You will what?" Jim entered the room. He was dressed in uniform and held his hat in his hand. Rain glistened on his coat.

"Help," I said and lifted my chin.

"Officer Hampton," Millie stepped toward him. "I think that Elias was murdered because he was looking into whoever is vandalizing beehives up and down the coast."

Jim glanced at me and then at the rest of the people. "All right," he said and took out his notebook. "Why?"

"Please have a seat," Bill said with a wave of his hand. He introduced the board to Jim. "We asked Elias to look into the vandals. He told us he was getting close to uncovering the fiends and was planning to report back to the chapter next week on the outcome of his investigation."

"Were these vandalisms reported to the police?" Jim asked.

"Yes," Rachel said. "We have the police report numbers here." She handed him a piece of paper with the numbers on them. "But we keep being told that it's a minor violation and not important enough for police to pursue. So Elias took matters into his own hands."

"And now he's dead," Millie said with a soft sob.

"His journals are missing," I said. "We think the vandals took them. Perhaps they were inside his home and Elias surprised them. They dragged him outside, killed him, and then covered up the act by tearing up Elias's hives."

"I see," Jim said. "Any idea who they are?"

"None," Bill said and clasped his hands together on

the table. "Elias was tight-lipped about the matter. He told us that he would bring forth his conclusions, and then we would know what was going on."

"But his journals are missing," Millie said. "And you have his computer in evidence. So any information he dug up on the vandals is missing."

"Okay," Jim said and sat back, closing up his notebook. "You think that Elias discovered who was behind the vandalism of local hives and that before he could tell anyone, that person killed him."

"Yes," Rachel said, with a nod of her head. "The information must be on his computer. So you can send it off to evidence, and they can open it up and just look, right?"

"The computer is at the county lab to be processed," Jim said. "If there is information on the vandalism, I'll know about it."

"Good," Bill said and slapped the top of the table. "Then our work here is done." He stood. "Oh, and Officer Hampton, when you catch the killer, let him know it's a crime to harm beehives. "

"I will," Jim said.

I walked him out. "So what do you think? Is this a lead?"

"You did the right thing asking me to come down and hear them out. If it's a lead, I'll follow it. If it's nothing, then we'll worry about the hive vandals another time."

"I agree that Elias comes first," I said. "But Millie feels there's a strong connection. She initially asked me to look into it."

He stopped and studied me with his flat cop gaze.

"I know," I said to his silence. "That's why I talked them into letting me call you. If there's information that the bee vandals killed Elias, then you need to know. The last thing I want to do is to slow down the investigation."

"I appreciate that," he said. "You have to understand that I can't share anything about the investigation with you. Right?"

"So I have to share everything I know, but you don't?"

"That's the way it works," he said. "I'm the professional."

"Who made me a person of interest in Agnes Snow's murder when I was clearly innocent."

"I thought that was behind us, Wren." His tone had turned soft and low. It made me feel embarrassed that I still harbored feelings about it.

"It is," I said. "I was just pointing out that mistakes can be made. You are human, after all."

"That's why we have police procedures," he said. "To minimize mistakes. I need you to trust me, Wren. Thanks for calling me with this information and not going out on your own this time."

"Just check Elias's computer," I said. "If this was the bee vandals, there might be a clue there."

"Have a good night, Wren," he said and touched the bill of his police cap before crossing the street and climbing into his squad car.

I waved as he passed and walked back to the store. My thoughts whirled around who would be vandalizing beehives and why. Why hadn't Elias told me about this? I bit my bottom lip. Maybe he had told me, and I just hadn't been listening. I mean, I got the emails from the association. I'd simply not had time to read them.

No-Bake Chocolate Peanut-Butter Honey Bits

Ingredients:
$1\frac{1}{2}$ cups oats, to be divided
$\frac{1}{3}$ cup flax seed
$\frac{1}{2}$ cup all-purpose flour or almond flour
3 tablespoons unsweetened cocoa
2 tablespoons peanut-butter powder
$\frac{1}{2}$ cup peanut butter
$\frac{1}{3}$ cup plus 1 tablespoon honey
2 tablespoons milk
$\frac{2}{3}$ cup mini chocolate chips, to be divided
1 cup finely chopped peanuts

Directions:
Line a cookie sheet with parchment paper. In a large food processor, combine 1 cup of oats, flax seed, flour, cocoa, and peanut butter powder. Pulse into a course meal texture. Add peanut butter, honey, and milk. Process until the meal forms a ball. Transfer into a large bowl, and use your hands to mix in the remaining oats and chocolate chips. Roll into 1-inch balls. Dip into finely chopped peanuts and place on cookie sheet. Chill until set, then keep in an airtight container. Makes 30 balls; serving size is 2 balls. Enjoy!

Chapter 5

"Are you sure you aren't going to wear a costume with us at the UFO festival?" Aunt Eloise asked as she removed a papier-mâché alien head from her head. It was Wednesday afternoon at the shop. "I made two of these. You can use the other one, if you're having a problem coming up with a costume."

Her alien head was spray-painted green and had two large eyeholes covered in black mesh that she was able to see through. The nose was long and thin, and the mouth tiny and closed.

"Your costume is so cool," I said, and truly meant it. "It looks like something straight out of a Hollywood production. I'm sure you're going to get a lot of compliments, but my heart just isn't in it this year."

"Your heart doesn't have to be in it," she said. "Just your head. Oh, and don't forget, I've got a great silver cat

suit with metallic silver booties and metallic silver gloves."
She pulled the costume out of the bag.

I rolled my eyes. Everett jumped up on the cashier
counter to delicately sniff at the costume. "I don't have a
choice on this, do I?"

"Of course you do," my aunt said innocently. Her dangling earrings jangled as she shook her head. "But you
promised you'd go, and since you are going . . . and I
have a costume . . . then there's no reason not to wear it.
Besides, no one will know it's you if you are worried
about your reputation."

"I'm not worried about my reputation," I said and blew
out a long breath. "Fine, give me the bag. I'll wear it."

"That's my girl," Aunt Eloise said and stuffed the costume back into the bag and handed it to me, along with
the head. "Now, tell me what's going on with Elias's murder case. I heard you met with the board of the Tillamook
beekeepers association yesterday. They had a lead for
you?"

"They think whoever has been vandalizing beehives
up and down the coast might have killed Elias," I said. "I
called Officer Hampton, and he came to the meeting. We
filled him in on everything, and he's going to look into it."

"Oh." Her shoulders slumped. "So you're not going to
do any sleuthing?"

"I've got a lot of product to make for our second-
anniversary sale," I said. "Porsche is working overtime in
the store this week so that I can set everything up for the
sale, which starts Friday. You're helping by working Saturday and Sunday, remember?"

"Of course I remember," she said. "I just thought you
might do some sleuthing. Elias was your friend."

Now, why did that sound accusatory? "I helped by telling Jim everything," I pointed out.

"And I'm sure he's looking into it, but that doesn't mean you can't as well."

Luckily for me, Porsche came in through the back to start her shift. "Good afternoon, ladies," she said cheerfully and left her damp jacket on the hook in the back. "How's the store? Been busy?"

"No," I said with a slight frown. "It's been unusually quiet."

"Maybe everyone is waiting for the big sale," Porsche said. "You have advertised it everywhere. Why pay full price now when they can buy two and get one free in just two days?"

"Why, indeed," I muttered. "Which reminds me, I have to go up and make more candles. I don't want to run out when the crowds come through."

"Oh, just one thing," Porsche said, as I gathered up the bag with the alien costume and took the big papier-mâché head from my aunt.

"What?" I asked.

"I heard through the grapevine that they made an arrest in Elias's murder case," Porsche said.

"They did?" Aunt Eloise asked.

Everett meowed as if to echo her question.

"Yes, and you won't believe who they took into the station," Porsche said.

"Who?" Aunt Eloise and I said at the same time.

"Klaus Vanderbuen," Porsche said.

"Klaus? Why? He loved Elias. They were best friends. He wouldn't hurt him," I protested.

"It seems the police have evidence that Elias was

going to name Klaus as the man behind a series of bee-hive vandalisms. They think that Elias called Klaus out on it and Klaus killed him." Porsche crossed her arms and studied my reaction.

"That's ridiculous," I said.

Porsche shrugged. "I heard that someone told the police about the hive vandalism and that lead them to Klaus."

Aunt Eloise looked at me. "Wren, what have you done?"

"I didn't do anything," I said, with my hands out. "I'm going to call Klaus." I headed upstairs as I dialed Klaus's number. I lived above the shop. The stairs to my place were near the back door. My apartment had a main living area, with a small kitchen at one end, a bathroom, and two bedrooms. One bedroom was small enough that it should have been called a walk-in closet instead. I used it as a den. That's where I had my desk and work computer.

I opened my door, entered my place, and put the costume down as I was sent to Klaus's voice mail. "Hey, Klaus, it's Wren Johnson. I heard a bad rumor that you are a person of interest in Elias's murder case. Please call me back. There must be some mistake."

I hung up my phone and put on an apron. My thoughts went around and around as I put a large pot of beeswax on the stove to melt. Beeswax candles burned completely and evenly. As I melted the wax, I added essential oils and blended them for signature scents, such as tea tree and lavender and sage and lilac. Then I set up various molds. I had long taper molds and short column molds. I also had mason jars that I filled. They were very popular candles.

I was glad Everett was a social cat. He stayed down-stairs in the store while I worked upstairs in my sunny yellow kitchen. I didn't like to work with hot wax while he was nearby. The chance of an accident was too high.

My kitchen window was open slightly, held in place by a block of wood. I had views of the nearby rooftops and could hear the sound of the waves coming up on the beach, interspersed with the softly falling rain. The apartment smelled wonderful, of beeswax and essential oils.

My phone rang, and I wiped my hands on my apron and picked it up. The caller ID said it was June, Klaus's life partner. "Hello?"

"Oh, Wren," June said. "We need your help." Her voice was filled with tears.

"I heard about Klaus," I said and sat down at the small dining table. "Where is he? Is he okay? What happened?"

"He's at the police station. I called Henry Frankfurt from Portland to be his lawyer. Do you know Henry?"

"No," I said. "But calling a lawyer is a good thing. Do you know why they think Klaus did this?"

"They think he's the vandal, but he would never hurt a beehive. You know this."

"I do know this," I said. "I'm so sorry this is happening. What can I do?"

"Can you talk to Officer Hampton? Be a character witness for Klaus?"

"Yes, I can do that," I said.

Her fear was palpable in her voice. "I don't know what I'd do if Klaus went to jail. He didn't do this. I . . . I don't know how to care for the bees. We're going into flower season. I just, I don't know what to do."

"Where are you?" I asked.

"I'm at work," she sniffed. "I work for Pendleton as an office manager. I can't take time off. I'm calling you on my break time."

"I understand," I said. "I'll call Officer Hampton and see what I can find out. I'll get back to you."

"Thank you, Wren," she said. "I didn't know who else to turn to, and I know you helped with the Agnes Snow murder. You are a good friend."

I hung up the phone feeling like not so good a friend. Not if it was my tip about the vandals that got Klaus in trouble. I dialed Jim's personal cell phone. What was he thinking?

"This is Hampton, leave a message," his voice mail said.

"Jim, it's Wren. I just heard about Klaus. It's ridiculous to think he would hurt Elias or bees. Call me back." I hung up and paced. Then I dialed his number again.

"This is Hampton, leave a message."

"It's Wren," I said. "Call me back. Also, I'm coming down there." I hung up my phone, poured the last of my candles, grabbed my car keys, and headed down my back stairs. "Porsche, I'll be back in a few minutes."

"Gotcha!" Porsche called back.

I pulled my jacket off the hook near the door and went out back. The building backed onto a small parking area and a gravel alley. My car was parked there. I got in and headed straight for the police station.

Oceanview was a relatively small tourist town, and I could walk almost anywhere, including the police station. But it was raining and damp, and I wanted to get to Klaus as soon as possible. I didn't know what I could do, but I had to try to help.

I pulled into the parking area, got out of my car, slammed the door shut, and hit the LOCK button on my key chain. The car beeped, and I strode quickly into the police station, a one-story building with a tin roof and yellow siding. Inside was a small waiting room and a front desk, where a young man sat in a blue uniform like the one Jim wore.

"How can I help you?" he asked.

I noted that his name tag said Hinze. "Hi, I'm Wren Johnson. I need to speak to Officer Jim Hampton."

"He's busy right now," Officer Hinze said.

"I'll wait," I said and pulled off my wet jacket. "Can you tell him I'm here?"

"Okay." The young man had blond hair cut close to his head in a military-style cut. "I'll let him know."

"Thank you," I said, and hung my coat on the back of a blue plastic chair in the waiting area. The police waiting area was not like a doctor's. There were no comfy chairs, no magazines, and definitely no TV or piped-in music. It consisted of a hallway about nine feet long filled with four plastic chairs pushed up against the wall.

Twenty minutes later, Jim opened the door to the back offices. "Wren, what can I do for you?"

I stood. "We need to talk."

"All right, since you're here. Why don't you come back to my office?" He opened the door and waved me through.

The station's office space was limited. In fact, Jim's office was actually one of many desks amid clusters of file cabinets. It was noisy and smelled of stale coffee and old printers. His desk was in the back corner, and he borrowed a nearby chair and wheeled it over. "Have a seat."

I sat down and held my purse. "I can't believe you brought Klaus in for questioning," I said. "The man helped us get to Elias's body."

"Many times the killer will insert themself into the investigation," he said as he sat down. "I expected you to call. Why did you come in?"

"I wanted you to tell me to my face why you're doing this ridiculous thing. A killer is out there on the loose, and you're wasting time grilling Klaus."

"Klaus's name was found in a file on Elias's computer," he said.

"That's ridiculous.

He shifted in his seat and leaned toward me. "Klaus was in direct competition with every single one of the beekeepers who have been vandalized. And, before you repeat that it's ridiculous, Klaus's business has tripled since the vandalisms started. Elias made a map of all the registered beekeepers and their business territories. It clearly shows Klaus as a winner in the beekeeping war."

"Klaus wouldn't hurt bees," I said. "I've known him for two years. He is reliable and kind."

"Klaus is a felon," Jim said and leaned back. "He has a rap sheet that goes back to his childhood." He pulled up a file on his computer screen. "Assault, robbery, assault with a weapon, battery, DUI . . . do I need to go on?"

My heart sunk. "I don't understand. That's not the Klaus I know."

"Criminals are good at hiding in plain sight," Jim said. "Klaus owes a lot of money to some very bad people. He has motive and means, and he has history."

I sat back confused. "Can I speak to him?"

"No," Jim said. "He's being questioned, and unless you are a lawyer, you need to wait until he gets out."

I tilted my head. "So you haven't arrested him yet?"

Jim blinked.

"If you arrested him, he'd have to have a hearing . . . right? For bail or not?"

Jim didn't answer.

"So you haven't officially arrested him," I said and stood. "You don't have a solid case yet, do you?"

"I can't talk to you about what we have or don't have," Jim said. "Sit down."

"Oh, no, I don't need to sit," I said. "June said she called Klaus a lawyer. Has he arrived?"

"Not yet," Jim said.

"Then I'm going to call Klaus a lawyer." I grabbed my phone out of my purse and dialed Matt Hanson, the lawyer who helped me when I was wrongly arrested. I walked out of Jim's office, through the door of the station, and out into the parking lot.

"Hanson law offices, this is Sherry. How can I help you?"

"Hi, Sherry, it's Wren, Wren Johnson. I need to speak to Matt, please."

"I'm sorry, he's not in the office at this time. May I take a message or put you through to his voice mail?"

"I'll take his voice mail, thanks," I said and was immediately put through to a recording of Matt's voice asking me to leave a message. I asked him to call me, saying it was urgent. Then I hung up and looked at the courthouse across the street. As I've said, Oceanview is a small town, and it was convenient to put the police station across from the courthouse. I took the chance that Matt would be in court and walked over to the courthouse.

I had to put my purse and jacket on the X-ray belt and walk through a metal detector before I could go up the flight of stairs to a landing area for four courtrooms. The floors were made of marble tile, and the high ceilings echoed a bit. I peered into two courtrooms before I found the one Matt was in. There weren't a lot of people in the room, so I slipped inside and sat in the back.

It was a DUI case, and the defendant had pled guilty. Matt and the assistant DA were arguing sentencing. I half-listened as I pulled out my cell phone and turned the ringer to vibrate. It wouldn't do to interrupt the court and make a scene.

Matt finished his argument, and the judge made his decision. The defendant was Albert Hines, who was sentenced to thirty days of rehab and to pay five thousand dollars restitution to the city for hitting a light pole.

I waited for Matt to move to pack up his things and leave the courtroom. He spotted me as he reached my row of chairs. "Wren! What brings you here?"

We walked out of the room together. "I need your help," I said.

"In what way?" he asked.

"I don't know if you have time, but a friend of mine is being questioned by the police in connection with Elias Bentwood's murder. I don't think he did it, and I don't think he should be alone in an interview room."

"You know I don't really argue murder cases," he said. "Who's your friend?"

"Klaus Vanderbuen," I said. "Officer Hampton says he has a long record, but I know that Klaus wouldn't hurt Elias. They were friends. Klaus came to the scene and helped us to remove the bees so that Elias's body could be cared for and the scene secured."

Matt stopped in his tracks, his mouth set in a thin line. "I know Klaus. He does have a record."

"He needs your help. I know in my gut he didn't do this," I said. "Jim didn't arrest him. He's only holding him for now. That means they don't have enough evidence yet. Can you help?"

"I don't know . . ."

"If you can't, can you recommend someone who can help?" I asked.

"Why are you so invested in helping this guy?" he asked.

"I've known Klaus for over two years, and he's been nothing but helpful and kind," I explained.

"And?"

"And I feel as if it's my fault because I told the police that we think Elias's death is connected to recent beehive vandalism, and Jim said Klaus has the most to gain from the beehives being vandalized."

"Does he?" Matt asked.

"Jim thinks so, but I'm sure it's not Klaus. I need to get him a lawyer so he can get out of jail and I can talk to him about all this."

"Okay, listen," Matt said. "I'm not sure you should be worrying about this guy."

"But—" I started to reply.

He raised his hand to stop me from talking. "But you're going to do it anyway. I like you, Wren. You have a good heart." He opened the leather-bound notepad he was holding. "Here's the card of a friend, Nathan Wolfbane. He's a new lawyer, he lives here in town, and he's hungry for business."

I took the card. "Thanks, I appreciate it."

"No problem," Matt said. "We should get drinks sometime."

"I would like that," I said with a short smile. "Excuse me while I call this guy. Thanks again!"

"Any time I can help," Matt said and walked down the stairs. I hurried to a quiet corner and called the number on the card.

"Hello?" The man's voice sounded young.

"Hi, um, I'm looking for Nathan Wolfbane . . . the lawyer?"

"Oh, that's me. I mean, this is Nathan Wolfbane, the lawyer. Criminal law is my specialty. How can I help you?"

"Great," I said. "Matt Hanson gave me your card. My name is Wren Johnson, and I have a friend who's being questioned by the police right now for the Elias Bentwood murder. My friend Klaus needs a lawyer. Do you have time to take the case?"

"Oh, great! I mean, yes, yes, I do," he said. "Does your friend not have a public defender?"

"I'm not sure he's even asked for a lawyer yet," I said. "But if he can't pay, I'd like to help. Can you meet me at the police station?"

"Yes, I can be down there in fifteen minutes."

"Great, see you then," I said and hung up. I hurried out of the courthouse and across the street to the police station. Once inside, I made a beeline for the reception desk. "You have to tell Officer Hampton to stop questioning Klaus."

"Excuse me a minute," Officer Hinze said into his phone. He put the caller on hold and then looked at me. "What did you say?"

"You have to tell Officer Hampton to stop questioning Klaus right now. His lawyer is on the way." I felt breath-

less. I knew what it was like to be the subject of an interrogation, and it wasn't fun.

Officer Hinze stood and looked around me at the
empty waiting area. "I don't see a lawyer, unless you
are." He raised his right eyebrow skeptically.

"I'm not, but one is coming."

"Did Klaus ask for a lawyer?" He put his hands on his
gun belt.

"I don't know. I haven't been allowed to talk to Klaus,
but he does have a lawyer. Nathan Wolfbane's on his way,
and Klaus needs to be informed."

"I'm sorry, Ms. Johnson, is it?" He studied me with a
flat expression. "But until a lawyer actually shows up,
and signs in, there's nothing I can do."

"But Klaus needs to know I've hired a lawyer for
him," I said. "Send someone back to tell him."

Just then the front door opened, and a young man
stepped into the foyer. He pulled a dark gray hoodie off
his head, revealing thick black hair, copper skin, and in-
telligent brown eyes. He wore blue jeans and hiking
boots and carried a briefcase. "Wren Johnson?"

"That's me," I said. "Are you Nathan Wolfbane?"

"Yes," he said.

"Great!" I rushed over, grabbed his arm, and dragged
him to the front desk. "Here's Klaus's lawyer. You have
to tell Officer Hampton to stop questioning Klaus until
his lawyer is present."

The desk officer narrowed his eyes at the young man.
"You're a lawyer?"

"Passed the bar last fall," Nathan said and got out a
business card and gave it to the desk guy. "Please let my
client know I'm here."

"You have to sign in," Officer Hinze said and pulled out a clipboard with a sign-in sheet attached. "I'll call Hampton and let him know you're here."

I blew out a long breath of relief as Nathan signed the sheet. He turned to me. "Sorry to be so informally dressed, but you sounded like you were in a hurry."

"I was," I said. "I'll pay your fee. My friend Klaus needs help."

"Can you tell me what is going on?" he asked. "How is Klaus connected to the Elias Bentwood murder?"

"He isn't," I said. "At least, I don't believe that he is. You see, Klaus is a beekeeper. We belong to the same association."

"So, you're a beekeeper?"

"In a way, yes," I said. "I have a hive. I'm the owner of Let It Bee. I'm also the person who found Elias's body. He had three hives vandalized, and the bees were angry, so I called in Klaus to help us wrangle the bees so that emergency crews could get to Elias."

"So Klaus was at the murder scene."

"Yes, but because I called him," I said, wringing my hands. "Now they're saying Klaus is a person of interest, but I'm certain there's no way he would do this."

"Okay," he said and patted my shoulder. "I'll see what I can do."

"You can go on back," Officer Hinze said.

I started walking with Nathan when the officer cleared his throat. "Not you, Ms. Johnson. Just the lawyer."

"Okay," I said and watched as Nathan disappeared back into the offices. I was pacing when my phone vibrated. I pulled it out. It was a text from Aunt Eloise.

You've been gone a while. Are you okay?

I texted back. *I'm fine. I got Klaus a lawyer. Jim thinks*

he is a good suspect, but they don't have enough evidence yet to charge him. I'll let you know when I find out more.

OK, she texted back. *Porsche and I are filling the shelves and extra bins you requested for the sale. Can you pick up the signs from the printer? Also the newspaper called. They emailed a proof of tomorrow's advert in the paper. Can you take a look at it and send an approval?*

Will do. I texted back. Taking a deep breath, I sat down and opened my email on my phone. I found the proof of the advertisement we were running about the anniversary sale. It was a bee coming out of a beehive graphic, and 50% OFF was written over the top of the hive. SECOND ANNIVERSARY SALE appeared at the top of the half-page ad. The name of my store was scrawled across the bottom in the proper font, along with my website address. I checked it carefully and then emailed off the approval form. I saw an email from the printer letting me know that I could pick up the small shelf signs I'd ordered for the sale anytime until five p.m. A quick glance at the time told me I had thirty minutes. I stood and chewed on my lower lip.

Then I made a quick decision. Striding across the floor to the reception desk, I leaned toward Officer Hinze. "Excuse me, do you think they'll be long in interrogation?"

"Depends," the young officer said.

"On what?" I asked.

"It will depend on whether he wants to talk or not," the officer said.

I chewed on my lower lip and glanced at the time. I now had twenty minutes. "I'll be right back. If they come out, can you tell them I want them to wait for me?"

"I'm not your secretary," the officer said.

"Right." I turned on my heel and texted both Nathan and Klaus that I was going to the printer and to wait for me if they got out before I got back. Now all I had to do was hope they would be here when I came back. I opened the door and stepped out into the misty gray day. I pulled my hood over my hair and strode off to my car. If I hurried, I'd just make the printer in time.

Chapter 6

Make a honey hair mask that makes your hair
shiny and manageable. Mix 1 egg yolk, 1 tablespoon of honey, and 2 tablespoons of coconut
oil in a bowl. Apply this mixture to your hair.
Cover with a shower cap and leave it on for
30 minutes. Shampoo with cool water. Take
care not to use hot water or the egg yolk will
cook and your look will be scrambled.

"Hey, Wren," Stephen Boyd said as I walked into
the print shop. "You got here with just a few minutes to spare. Let me go get your order." The print shop
had a small front filled with racks of cards, paper, en-
velopes, and other sundries. The cashier area was domi-
nated by a smooth wooden table; the register sat next to a
tabletop display rack with brochures listing all the services they offered.

The shop smelled of toner and paper. There was a door
to the back through which you could see a large color
copier, an old, single-color printing press, racks of paper,

and a table with a cutter and a binder on it. The floor was covered in old linoleum and stained with ink from forty years of printing.

"Here you go," Stephen said as he came through the doorway and placed a box on the counter. "Let me know what you think."

I opened the box and admired the printed shelf talkers, small signs that gave product details, and midsize signs advertising our sale. They were printed with black and gold ink on cream card stock. "These are perfect. Thanks!"

"I can't believe you are celebrating your second anniversary already. It seems to me we were just printing your grand-opening signs." He rang up my total, and I swiped my credit card.

"Time flies when you're having fun," I spit out the old cliché as I typed in my four-digit code and watched the transaction go through.

"Say, word is that you were the one who found Elias dead. Is that true?" Stephen asked.

"Yes," I said, with a shake of my head. "It was horrible. Did you know Elias well?"

"For over fifty years," Stephen said. "I printed his honey-jar labels and any signage he needed when he went to farmers' markets. He had some of the sweetest honey around."

"Elias knew where to place his hives to get the best pollen. I think his marionberry honey was my favorite."

"Yes, and his buckwheat honey," Stephen said and bagged up my box. "Don't know who would hurt that man. He would give anyone the shirt off his back if he thought they needed it. Heck, even if he thought they didn't need it, but they asked for it. He had a good heart, and it's a great loss to the community."

I took my bag filled with printed materials. "I agree," I said. "He will be missed."

"Are you going to solve his murder?" Stephen asked.

"Why would you ask me that?"

"Because you solved Agnes Snow's murder," Stephen said. "Also, you were close to Elias."

"Well, Officer Hampton said to let him do his job and solve this, so I think that's what I should do." Then I stopped and studied him. "But you wouldn't happen to know who might have wanted Elias dead, would you?"

Stephen leaned against the counter. "Well, I did hear that he got into an argument with old man McGregor a few days ago. Missy Sandstrom was walking by his place on her way into town when she saw them arguing in front of Elias's house."

"Really? What was the argument about?" I asked and leaned in to narrow the gap between us and create a cozy bubble for talking.

"Well, see, Missy wasn't quite sure. She heard old man McGregor shouting something about Elias having too many hives in town. Said he'd gotten stung and was allergic. Said all those bees were a health hazard."

"Wow," I said. "That sounds bad. Bees really won't sting you unless they feel you are a threat."

"Well, old man McGregor is a threat to everyone," Stephen chuckled. "Can't wait until I'm a grumpy old retired man. I'll finally get some threat cred."

I laughed. "Thanks for the great job on the printing." I held up my bag and waved goodbye. I made a mental note to talk to Missy, and maybe, if I were truly brave, I would go see Mr. McGregor. I wasn't about to tell Jim anything further. Not if he was going to use the information against my friends.

The trip back to the police station was short. I found a parking spot in front, and as I got out of my car, I caught Nathan and Klaus walking out. "Klaus!" I called and went over to him. "Are you all right?"

"I'm fine," he said, but his face was stern, his eyebrows drawn together in concern, his blue eyes angry.

"Obviously, they didn't arrest you," I said. "That's good."

"I didn't do this, Wren," Klaus said.

"I know," I said and patted his forearm. "That's why, when I heard they were questioning you as a person of interest, I came right down here and gave Officer Hampton a piece of my mind."

"You did that?" Klaus tilted his head and looked confused. "Why?"

"Because I know you didn't do this, and I know what it's like to be wrongly viewed as a murder suspect. That's why I hired Nathan to come down and help."

"You didn't have to do that," Klaus said. "June tried to hire someone, too. I can help myself, you know."

"It's misty and cold and dark out here," I said. "Can I buy you both a coffee? We need to talk."

"I'm not sure we should go out in public," Nathan said. "It's a small town, and people will want to know what we're talking about."

"Oh, yes," I said with a nod. "Why don't you two come over to my shop? We can make coffee or tea and talk about our strategy."

"Our strategy?" Klaus said.

"Yes. Oh, we can call June and involve her, too," I said. "After all, I feel like I got you into this, and I'm going to help get you out."

Klaus narrowed his eyes. "What did you do?"

"I'm the one who told Jim about the possible connection between the bee vandals and Elias," I said. "He took it and pointed the finger at you. But I know you would never hurt Elias or bees."

Klaus ran his hand over his damp hair and pulled up his hoodie. "I think I need to go home right now."

"But we need to figure out how to clear your name," I said.

He studied me. "I'm innocent. That's enough for me. You have a good night." He walked off, and I opened and closed my mouth like a fish out of water for a whole moment before turning to Nathan. June pulled up in her pickup, and Klaus got in and they sped away.

"Okay," I said, blowing out a breath. "Can I buy you a coffee? Or would you prefer to come to the shop. I have tea, too, if you prefer it."

"Let's go to the shop," he said. "Do you have your car?"

"Yes."

"I'll meet you over there." He stepped off the sidewalk and got into a Honda SUV. I got into my car and hurried back to the shop. Parking in the back, I walked in to find Porsche and Aunt Eloise finishing up the touches necessary for the sale.

"I have the signs," I said as I walked in and undid my damp coat. I pushed back the hood, and Everett came running to rub against my leg. "Hi, buddy," I said. "Sorry I'm late."

"Wren," Porsche called out. "What happened?"

"I got Klaus a lawyer, and they let him leave without charging him," I said and picked up Everett and gave my kitty a hug. "I also picked up the signs for the sale." I lifted the bag.

"Great job," Aunt Eloise said and came and took the bag from me so I could cuddle Everett.

"But don't put those out until Thursday," I said as they pulled them out of the box to ooh and ahh over them. "Stephen did a great job."

"They always do," Aunt Eloise said.

The bells on the door jangled, and Nathan walked in. His coat was damp from the mist, and he shook off excess water before he stepped into the store. "Ladies," he said as he headed toward us.

"Who's this?" Aunt Eloise asked, her eyebrows lifted up high.

"This is Nathan," I said and put Everett down on the cashier counter. "He's the new lawyer Matt told me about. I hired him to represent Klaus."

"Hello," Porsche said and stepped up to shake his hand.

"Nathan, this is my friend and store manager, Porsche," I said. "And this is my Aunt Eloise."

"Hello, Nathan." Aunt Eloise shook his hand. "So nice to meet you. Are you here to help Wren solve this murder?"

"Aunt Eloise!"

She shrugged. "It seems to me that the police have the wrong suspect, and that means you all need Wren to help solve this case. Where's Klaus? Is he doing okay?"

"Klaus isn't coming," Nathan said.

"June picked him up. He wanted to go home. It seems he needs time to wrap his head around what's happening to him," I said and nodded toward Nathan.

"Well, Wren would understand that," Aunt Eloise said. "She went through the same thing last fall. Horrible."

"Why don't you come up for some coffee," I said. "Porsche's closing tonight. Ladies, feel free to come up and join us."

"Sounds good," Nathan said. He followed me through the back of the shop to the stairs along the back wall that led up to my apartment. Everett raced up the stairs ahead of me and waited at the top. I unlocked my door and let him in, turning on the light.

"Come in," I said and put my purse down on the table beside the door. Everett ran into the kitchen, so I put the kettle on for French press coffee and poured some kibble in his dish. He jumped up on the counter and ate his dinner.

"Nice place," Nathan said as he took off his jacket. "How long have you lived here?"

"I've been here two years. The store is celebrating its two-year anniversary on Friday."

"Have you always lived in Oceanview?" He sat down on my couch, and Everett jumped up for attention. Nathan absently stroked my cat's fur.

"You must not be from here if you had to ask that question," I said with a laugh. "It's a small town, so most people know who has lived here their whole lives and who is new." The kettle whistled, and I poured the hot water over ground coffee in the press, stirred it for a few seconds, put the top on, wrapped the carafe with a towel, and placed it on a tray with two cups and a tiny pitcher of cream and a sugar bowl, two spoons, and a couple of napkins. Picking up the tray, I walked to the couch and set it down on the coffee table.

"You got me," he said and sat back. "I moved to Oceanview out of Stanford Law."

"You're a California boy," I said and pressed the top of the coffee pot, pushing the grounds down, leaving a lovely dark coffee on top.

"My dad was military," he said, "so we moved every four years or so."

"Me, too!" I sent him a smile. Military kids had a comradery that most people didn't understand. But when you moved a lot growing up, you had equal parts an ability to make friends fast and an ability to be comfortable on your own. "My dad was Air Force. What about yours?"

"He was a marine," Nathan said as I poured the coffee and handed him a cup. "Retired now. My folks live in Brewster, near the Colville Reservation, in Washington State. Are your parents nearby?"

I grabbed a cup, added cream to my coffee, and sat back in an armchair. "My dad died in Afghanistan when I was in high school. Mom moved us here to be close to my Aunt Eloise."

"The woman downstairs," he said.

"Yes," I agreed. "But Mom didn't live much longer than my dad. I think she died of a broken heart. So I moved in with Aunt Eloise. Went to college at Oregon State. Spent a year bee wrangling around Mount Hood and then opened my store. What brings a Stanford lawyer to Oceanview?"

He shrugged. "I always liked the Oregon coast and small towns. The county doesn't have a lot of criminal lawyers, so I set up my practice here. Not that it's much of a practice yet. I bought a small house near the beach and work out of my living room. Klaus is my second client. Thanks for calling me."

"Thank Matt Hanson; he recommended you," I said

and sipped my coffee. "Just out of curiosity, who was your first?"

"Mrs. Tennhey," he said. "She was in over her head with parking tickets . . . and a Facebook friend of my mom. They're in the same online crochet group."

"Were you successful?" I asked with a smile on my face at the idea of Nathan representing an elderly woman with unpaid parking tickets.

"She didn't think so," he said and sipped coffee as he continued to pet Everett. "But I managed to talk the judge down to community service and no fine if she sold her car."

"She didn't have to pay the tickets?"

He shook his head. "She's on Social Security, and the tickets were close to five thousand dollars plus interest. She didn't have the money, and her argument was she no longer drove the car. When I told her that she could get a nice tax write-off if she donated the car, she was pretty happy to get rid of it."

"What was her community service?" I asked.

He flashed me a sideways grin. "She had the choice to pick up trash or work with the meter maid on parking issues."

My eyes grew big. "What did she choose?"

"She said she was a parking ticket expert and went to work with Susan Pritchet."

"Can she do that?" I asked.

"Write a ticket? No," he said, "but she can help with marking tires and searching out violators. Now she wants to train to be an official meter maid."

"Isn't she retired? I mean, you said she doesn't drive."

"Oceanview is so small, she can walk most of her

usual route, especially near the beach, or ride a bike," he said. "I think she might be rehabilitated."

"It's a happy ending," I said and saluted him with my coffee cup. There was a quick knock on my door, and Aunt Eloise came inside.

"Hi, kids," she said and went to the cupboard to grab a mug and a tea bag. "So, Nathan, what is the deal with the police bringing Klaus in for questioning?" She poured the hot kettle water in her cup and eyed us over the top of her reading glasses.

"I've got a meeting time set up to talk to Officer Hampton and see what he wants from my client," Nathan said and sat back.

"He told me that Klaus has a record," I said. "I was shocked to hear that. Klaus has never been anything but kind and helpful."

"I can't talk about Klaus's record," Nathan said. "But he told me that they think he's involved in the bee vandalism because his business has picked up since the competitors lost their bees to the vandals."

"I swear he would never harm a bee," I said.

"No, the Klaus we know would never harm a bee," Aunt Eloise said.

Nathan nodded. "He told me he was simply moving in more hives to help out the farmers. In fact, he's sharing the proceeds with the people who lost the bees until they can get their hives back up and running."

"So, he's innocent," I said and sat back with a smile. Aunt Eloise took a seat on the other armchair across from the couch. Everett left Nathan for Aunt Eloise's lap.

"Well," Nathan said and tipped his head back and forth, as if to say maybe. "It seems there might be something on Elias's computer that points to Klaus as a person with motive."

"What?" I asked.

"They have to share it with me," he said. "But not until they charge him with the crime. So I've got to get Klaus to tell me the whole story. He wasn't up for that tonight."

"This is all my fault," I said. "I'm the one who told Jim to check the computer."

"Oh, now, Wren," Aunt Eloise said. "You didn't put anything on that computer. If there is something on Elias's computer that led to Klaus, then they would have found it anyway."

I shook my head and frowned. "We don't know that. I need to figure out who really did this, not just for myself as Elias's friend, but for Klaus."

"Okay," Nathan said and stood. "I'm going to go before I hear any more."

"Why?" I asked and stood with him. Everett jumped into Aunt Eloise's lap.

"I'm Klaus's attorney, and if you are going to mess with the case, I can't know about it." He put his coffee cup on the kitchen counter and grabbed his jacket from the coat tree near the door.

"Wait, but what about attorney–client privilege?" I asked.

"That's between myself and Klaus," he said.

"But I hired you," I said, confused.

"To represent Klaus. Until Klaus asks you to be a part of his team, I can't know what you're doing. That said, if you come across anything that helps Klaus, call me. I'll meet with Klaus and see if he wants you to be part of the team."

"Oh," I said as I watched him put on his jacket. "Okay. Well, can you at least let me know if the police arrest Klaus and why?"

He studied me with his dark eyes. "I'll let you know, and you'll let me know when we need each other. Okay?"

"Sounds good," I said. "Let me walk you out."

I walked him down the stairs and through the store to the door. "Thanks for taking Klaus's case," I said.

"Thank you for trusting me with your friend," he said and nodded toward Porsche. "Have a good night."

I watched him leave, and Porsche came to stand beside me. "He's cute."

"I hired him to help Klaus."

"That's a good thing, right?" she asked me.

I studied the door that Nathan had exited through. "He doesn't want to know when I investigate."

"What? Doesn't he want to help?"

"He said I hired him for Klaus, and so he can't be a part of my investigation," I said and turned on my heel. "Is he afraid I'll do more harm than good when it comes to Klaus?"

"I don't think he knows how good you are at this," she said and put a hand on my shoulder. "And he's doing his job, which is protecting Klaus."

"I guess that's for the best," I said, then glanced at the clock. "Have we had any customers this evening?"

"No," Porsche said. "I bet they're all waiting for Friday's sale."

"Let's close a little early, then," I said and went to the door and turned the sign. I locked the door, and Porsche headed over to close the cash register. "Is there any product I need to make for the sale? I think I stocked up on everything."

"Everything looks great," Porsche said as she counted money and evened the register. I always keep one hundred dollars in the register. We put the rest in the bank at night. Then we count it again in the morning before we open to make sure we have enough. Porsche put the extra in a pouch and zipped it closed. I swept up, and we turned off the lights."

"Want to come up for coffee?" I asked. "Aunt Eloise is still here."

"Sure," Porsche said. "I told Jason I'd be home around nine-thirty. So we have some time."

We took the stairs to the apartment and entered to find Aunt Eloise had made a quick hot fudge chocolate pudding cake.

"It smells yummy in here," Porsche said as we walked in.

Everett greeted me by rubbing against my leg. "Dessert!" I said with a smile.

"I thought we could use some as we start to figure out who killed Elias and why," Aunt Eloise said. "Too bad that nice lawyer boy wouldn't be a part of our group."

"He's pretty by the book," I said and pulled out bowls for the cake. Aunt Eloise dished out three pieces and added the extra hot-chocolate sauce on top of the chocolate biscuit dough. Then sprayed each serving with a mound of whipped cream. I handed her and Porsche their bowls, grabbed my own, and went to sit in the living area.

"So, what do we know?" Porsche asked as she curled up on the couch with her bowl.

"Someone is setting up Klaus for Elias's murder," I said and took a bite of warm chocolate pudding cake. "Wow, this is good, Aunt Eloise."

"Thanks, it's a go-to recipe," she said. "I use honey in your honor, of course."

"Only the best from Aunt Eloise," I said. "Now, oh, so I'm not sure if you know what happened, Porsche, but Millie was certain that the string of bee vandalisms was tied to Elias's death."

"Yes, I do know," she said. "You went to that meeting with the board of the local chapter of the beekeepers association, and they told you to go to the police."

"Which I did, because Elias's journals were missing and the police needed to know to check his computer for clues."

"And that's why they hauled Klaus in today," Porsche said. "But why on earth does Officer Hampton think Klaus killed Elias?"

I explained about Klaus's record and the fact that he was gaining business by replacing the vandalized bee-keepers. "But Klaus said he was giving a significant portion of the money he made back to the original beekeepers, so the police's case is all washed up."

"Unless it's not," Porsche said.

"Exactly," I said. "Remember how they fixated on me last fall? I need to find this killer to keep them from sending an innocent man to jail."

"So what do we do?" Aunt Eloise asked.

"Do we make a murder board?" Porsche asked, her eyes alight with excitement.

"I'm not sure we have anything . . . wait!" I went into my small second bedroom and grabbed the whiteboard on the easel and hauled it out to my living room. "Okay, we have Elias, who was murdered." I drew a stick figure with a large head to represent Elias. I put crosses on his eyes, like a dead cartoon character. "Now, we know that Elias was investigating hive vandalisms. This led the police to Klaus." I drew a stick figure with a big head and a beard. "But we also know Klaus didn't do it. So maybe it had nothing to do with the hive vandals. I heard that Elias and old man McGregor got into a fight the day before Elias was killed." I drew a stick figure bent over with a cane on the other side of Elias from Klaus. "I think we should investigate that. I mean the police are looking in this direction and not seeing this other direction." I drew arrows toward Klaus and then from Elias toward old man McGregor. "Someone needs to talk to old man McGregor."

"Finley won't talk to anyone," Aunt Eloise said and put her bowl down on the coffee table. "He's notorious for not leaving his house and not answering the door if people knock on it."

"Why?" I asked.

"Maybe he's a hermit," Porsche said and licked her spoon.

"If he were a hermit, he wouldn't live in town next to Elias," I pointed out.

"And he probably wouldn't have come out to yell at Elias, either," Aunt Eloise stated.

"Do you think he'd talk to me about why he fought with Elias?" I asked.

"There's no telling," Aunt Eloise said.

"Well, rumor has it that they fought over Elias's bees. Do you think if I told him that the police were probably going to question him, he'd tell me more?"

"He's not going to talk to you," Aunt Eloise said.

"How did you hear about Mr. McGregor?" Porsche asked.

"Stephen at the print shop mentioned that Missy Sandstrom told him about it," I said.

"You can start by questioning her," Porsche said.

"But that's hearsay, isn't it?" I asked. "Don't we need definitive proof?"

"It's proof if she's a witness," Porsche said. "I say try her first. What do you think, Eloise?"

"I think it can't hurt," she said. "Listen, girls, I need to get home to my cats. Porsche, next week is the UFO festival. We're all going and bringing the cats. Want to come?"

Porsche glanced at me. I shook my head in warning until Aunt Eloise glanced at me, then I stopped and smiled at her.

"I'd love to come," Porsche said. "Are you dressing up?"

"We are," Aunt Eloise said.

"Great," Porsche said. "I'll bring the boys. They love those alien movies. But who will run the shop?"

I was about to say I could when Aunt Eloise interrupted me. "I already talked to Anna Wilkins. She said she would love to watch the store for a few hours on Friday of next week. Anna Wilkins was my backup cashier and usually only worked during holidays or if one of us couldn't mind the store.

"I don't know about asking Anna to work while we all go play," I said and stood.

"Nonsense," Aunt Eloise said and put her bowl in the sink. "Anna needs the money, and you know she does a good job. She was a great help over Christmas."

Porsche took her bowl into the kitchen and put it on the counter. "She did a great job when Jason and I took a week to take the boys to Disneyland. I'm sure it will be fine."

"Fine," I said. "I'll call Anna in the morning. If she's going to work next week, I want her to come in for a few hours beforehand so I can refresh her on procedures and such."

"Great!" Aunt Eloise said and kissed my cheek. "I'm so looking forward to the festival." She put her arm through Porsche's, and they walked out of the apartment and down the stairs together. "If you need any help with costumes, you just let me know," she shouted up the stairs. "I've got some great ideas."

"Lock the door on your way out," I called to them as they grabbed their coats and headed out.

"Good night," Porsche called, and they left. I stood in the small landing in front of my apartment door until I heard the clang of the dead bolt locking mechanism. Then I turned to find Everett suspiciously close to the dessert bowls, so I closed and locked my apartment door, set the alarm system, and hurried to the kitchen to do the dishes.

A glance at the murder board had me wondering. If Mr. McGregor didn't leave the house, how could he kill Elias, ruin the beehives, and race off in a blue car? If he hadn't left his house, maybe he'd hired someone who did.

Chapter 7

Thursday morning, I had the early shift at the store. The clouds had departed, and the sun shone through the windows, highlighting the dirt and salt the rain had left on them the night before. I got out my squeegee and spray bottle to wash the outside.

The air was crisp and clean off the beach. It was too dark to take Everett for an early-morning walk along the beach. Still, it was so nice right now I knew I had to take him out soon. Maybe when Porsche came at one for the afternoon shift.

I used a spray bottle of water and vinegar to spray my windows and then squeegee them off until they shone. The store was off Main Street, and a Thursday in May wasn't exactly a bustling tourist time for me. I saw a few people walking down Main, but only the postman came by the shop. "Hi, Fred," I said as he walked up in his blue and gray uniform.

"Wren," he said. "Sorry to hear about Elias. I understand you found him?"

"Yes," I said. "It was terrible. Whoever hurt him bashed his hives to get away. I got there in time to see a car speed off. I don't know if the bees hadn't swarmed if we could have saved him or not. The police aren't giving away the exact time of death."

"Hmm, when did you get there?" Fred asked.

"Around three p.m.," I said. "Why?"

"My route takes me by there around two p.m."

That gave me pause. "Did you see anything?"

"What do you mean?"

"Like, did you see Elias? Or a blue sedan in the alley?" I hugged myself, trying to contain my excitement.

"Come to think of it, Elias did come out to get his mail. We didn't talk," Fred said. "I waved, and he waved, and he turned back to go inside. I think he left his door open. I remember hearing the slam of the screen door on his back porch."

"So he went inside at two p.m.," I said. "Did you see anyone unusual hanging around? Maybe in the alley?"

"I don't usually look down the alley, Wren," he said and handed me my mail. "But I did see a blue sedan." He drew his eyebrows together and pursed his lips in thought. "I think I remember it moving slowly up the street. I thought it was a bit out of place at the time. I assumed they were lost."

"Did you get a look at the driver?" I asked.

"Not really, no," he said with a shrug. "I was looking through my mail sort at the time the car caught my eye."

"But it was a strange car, right? Not, someone you know?"

"No, usually if it's someone I know, we wave," Fred said. "I didn't think much of it. They just seemed lost. You know? The car drove slowly. The driver wore a beanie, I think, and a black coat. I didn't see the face."

"Huh, okay," I said. "Thanks."

"Are you investigating the case?" he asked.

"No . . . not officially." I paused. "The police think Klaus is the killer."

"Bee Klaus?" He asked his expression showing that he was taken aback.

"Yes," I said. "But I don't believe it."

"Well, if the blue car was Klaus, I think I would have noticed," Fred said. "But don't hang a case on my words. I can't swear to anything other than seeing a blue car moving slowly."

"No, no worries. Did you ever see Elias argue with old man McGregor?"

He laughed. "Those two had a love-hate relationship. The old man loved to hate Elias."

"Do you think he might have done this?" I asked.

"Mr. McGregor? No way," Fred said. "That old guy loved to harass Elias. He wouldn't hurt Elias; otherwise, who'd be left to argue with?"

"Okay, thanks," I said.

"You have a good day," Fred said and walked into the shop next door to deliver the mail. I finished up my window quickly and went inside when a misty rain began to fall. So, old man McGregor fighting with Elias might not have been a good lead, but that didn't mean he didn't see something. After all, he lived behind Elias. I'd have to find a way to get him to talk to me. Maybe if I brought him something from the store, like a box of honey chocolates.

"What do you think, Everett?" I asked my cat, who followed me around the shop. "Do you think Mr. McGregor will talk to me if I bring him a box of chocolates?"

Meow.

"You're right," I said and tapped my chin. "It might not hurt to sweeten the deal. Maybe a gift basket with some pillar candles and a nice hand lotion. Nothing too scented, of course."

Meow.

When it came to figuring out what to get people, Everett was always right.

I loaded the small gift basket, wrapped with cellophane and a manly bow, into my car. It was after lunch, and Porsche was taking care of the store. I had a few customers today, but most told me they were looking to see what they would pick up during the anniversary sale. Tonight we would put the signs out, and hopefully I'd have a nice line of people waiting to get in when I opened in the morning. In the meantime, I was off to pay Mr. McGregor a visit.

The McGregor home was a cottage with white clapboard siding and green shutters. The tiny patch of front lawn was filled with wild, overgrown bushes and vines. It had to be years since anyone had done any landscaping. A small driveway ran along the side of the house. I parked in front, so he would be sure to see me coming, and got out with the gift basket in hand.

The roof was low, and the small porch was big enough for one or two people to stand under an eave while they waited to be let in. I rang the doorbell and waited. Rang it again. No answer. I knew he was in there. He didn't go anywhere. I think I saw the front curtain jiggle a bit, so I knocked. "Mr. McGregor?" I waited for four heartbeats and pounded even louder, in case he couldn't hear me. "Mr. McGregor? I have a gift basket for you."

"Who are you? Go away," a raspy voice said through the door.

I leaned in against the door. "Mr. McGregor, I'm Wren Johnson. Eloise Johnson is my aunt."

"Go away!"

"Look, I know you are missing Elias," I said.

"Who?"

"Elias, your neighbor," I shouted through the door.

"Go away." This time it was a little less harsh.

I didn't know if I was losing him or if he was giving in, so I stood my ground. "Mr. McGregor, I thought you might be missing Elias, so I brought you a gift basket."

"Don't want it. Don't want you. Go away!"

I thought I heard him walk away, and I sort of panicked. I pounded loudly. "Mr. McGregor, I'm not going away until you open this door!"

The door swung open sharply. "Fine." He grabbed the gift basket and slammed the door in my face.

I stood there a moment in shock and then sighed. I turned and sat on the small stoop and put my elbows on my knees, resting my chin in my hands. The rain made a small pattering sound against my jacket and his roof. I could hear the ocean in the distance. The air smelled of spring flowers and sea salt.

Contemplating what I could possibly do next to help Elias and Klaus, I studied the wet sidewalk that ran up to the door from the street. That cement must have been nearly one hundred years old. It was punctuated with cracks and upheavals, and grass poked out.

"Are you going to sit out there all day?"

I turned toward the sound of Mr. McGregor's voice and saw that the door was open. He was walking into the living room, so I got up and went inside. I wiped my feet on the front mat and closed the door behind me. The inside of his house reminded me of my grandma's when I was a tiny girl. It was neat and tidy and smelled of beeswax and muscle rub.

He sat down in an old easy chair and put his feet up. There was another chair in the room, but it was made of hardwood and was more in line with a kitchen chair than living room seating. I wasn't going to complain. I was inside.

The room was plain—a wood floor, with a threadbare rug in the center. The bare walls were faded from what might have been cream to a faint yellow. His chair faced an old TV in the corner next to a fireplace. A fire roared in the fireplace, adding heat and light. There was a wooden side table beside his chair covered in newspapers. A floor lamp hung over his shoulder. The curtains were as faded and dusty as the walls and closed, leaving only a thin slit of sheer to let in light.

I waited for him to speak. He seemed to do the same. It was that kind of uncomfortable, awkward silence that made you squirm. I noticed that my basket sat beside the door on the floor.

"You a beekeeper?" he asked, finally staring at the turned off television. "I don't like beekeepers."

"I'm Wren Johnson," I said, not sure if he had heard me.

"I know who you are," he grumbled. "That's not what I asked."

"I have bees," I said. "I own Let It Bee."

"You're not from here." It was a statement, not a question.

"No, my dad was in the military, so we moved around until he died." My voice cracked on that statement. Why, after all these years, did I suddenly feel pain at his loss? Maybe it was this strange old man.

Mr. McGregor wasn't very tall. He was thin and stooped. His head was bald, and his jaw had a shadow of grizzled beard. His blue eyes and jutted chin betrayed a belligerent attitude. It softened for a brief moment. "I served, too, in Vietnam."

"Thank you for your service." The words were a knee-jerk reaction. The silence echoed around us. I waited to a count of thirty. "I don't know if anyone told my dad that."

"Feels weird to hear it," he said. "Makes me not want to say I served. I didn't have a choice like your father did."

"Yes, he chose the life," I said softly, then cleared my throat. "Anyway, I came to say I'm sorry for your loss."

"What loss?" he grumped.

"I know Elias was a big part of your life."

He turned his blue eyes on me and narrowed them. "Who says?"

I tried to hold back my smile, but I don't think I was successful. "I heard from more than one person that you regularly talked to Elias, and he lived right behind you."

"He was a nuisance."

"Did you see what happened that day?" I asked softly.

"Are you implying that I stare out my kitchen window all day long, like some kind of stalker?" He crossed his arms over his chest.

"No," I said quickly. "I'm implying that you care about what happens on your property, including your alley. I saw a blue car speed away that day."

"Are you the one who found him?"

"I am," I said. "The killer bashed his beehives so badly we couldn't get to the body until we took care of the bees."

"Somebody should have bashed those hives," Fred grumbled. "Nuisance bees."

"Bees were named the most important being on the planet," I pointed out. "Without them, we wouldn't have much food at all."

He gave me a sideways look. "Have you been in Oregon in the spring? The place is a virtual storm of pollen. We don't need bees to spread it."

I tilted my head. "Are you allergic to bees, Mr. McGregor?"

"No," he said and stared ahead. "Got stung a few times. Don't care to ever get stung again."

"Did you see the swarms?"

"Had a whole bunch of them up under my eaves; was thinking I would have to get an exterminator. I was going to send Elias the bill, but heard he was dead, so no use in that."

I had to assume the missing bees had swarmed around their queen in his eaves before they moved off to find a new home. I was hopeful they didn't just die. Maybe it was time to talk about something other than bees.

"Did you see the blue car in the alley that day? The one I saw speeding off?"

"I might have," he said. "They aren't supposed to be in the alley. That's there for the garbage man and for emergencies only. I told them that the first time I saw them."

"You saw them more than once?" My heartbeat picked up, and I leaned in toward him.

"Yes, they were parked there the day before. Don't know what they thought they were doing, but they were blocking the alley."

"Did you go talk to them?"

"I sure did," he said. "I told them to get going or I'd call the cops on them."

"So you got a good look at them?"

He scowled at me. "Of course I did. They rolled down their window, and I gave them a piece of my mind."

My heart was racing with excitement. I tried to keep a calm head. "How many people were in the car?"

"Two, one driver and one in the passenger seat," he said. "The back seat was empty, as far as I could tell. I asked them what they were doing and told them to move along. They were blocking the alley."

"Did they?"

"They moved, but only after I threatened to call the cops," he said.

"Do you remember what they looked like?"

"Of course I do," he said and glared at me. "I'm old, not senile."

"That's great! Did you know them?"

"No, I did not know them," he sounded sarcastic. "They were young punks. Why would I know young punks?"

I shrugged. "Oceanview is a small town. There's a good chance you know everyone."

"I don't like people," he grumped.

"That might be so, but it doesn't mean you don't know people." I folded my hands in my lap. "So these punks. How old would you guess they were?"

"Don't know," he shrugged. "Get to be my age and everyone looks young."

"Younger than me or older than me, would you guess?"

"Well, you look like you're fresh out of high school," he said. "There's a whole lot of people older than you."

"So, like Klaus?"

He scowled at me. "No, younger than Klaus. Maybe thirty or so."

"Men?"

"Yeah."

"What were they wearing?"

"What am I, the fashion police?" He harrumphed and pushed back into the headrest of his chair. I waited in silence. I started counting silently to see how long it would be before he answered. It was a trick I used to stop uncomfortable things from feeling like they took forever. I had counted to eighty when he cracked. "Black hooded sweatshirts. Isn't that what everyone wears nowadays?"

"Sometimes people wear plaid," I said, with a hint of sarcasm. "Did you see their faces?"

"Got a good look at the driver. The passenger, not so much."

Now we were getting somewhere. "Could you describe them for a sketch artist?"

"Why would I want to do that?" he asked.

I blew out a long breath and decided to change the subject. "Do you like cats?"

"What does that have to do with anything? Don't you want to know who the driver is?"

"I do," I said. "Do you know who it is?"

"I told you I didn't, but I could describe him."

"Wonderful. Can I tell Officer Hampton so he can bring a sketch artist to see you?"

"Why would I let a police officer and some fancy artist in my home?" he asked. "No, I'll tell you, and you can go figure out who they are. That's what you do, isn't it?"

"What do you mean?"

"I know you solved Agnes Snow's murder. I know you're trying to solve this. So I'll tell you."

"But the police—"

"I won't talk to anyone but you," he said, digging in his heels. "I barely let you in."

"Okay," I said and took out my phone.

"What are you doing with that?"

"I'm going to record what you say."

He narrowed his eyes. "Why?"

"So that I have it . . . to help me figure out who the driver was and who the killer was, and so that people will stop bothering you with questions."

"Fine."

I opened the recording app on my phone and set it down on my knee so he could see it. "What did the driver of the blue car look like?"

"He was white and had some ridiculous beard like those guys in Portland."

"Hipsters?" I asked.

"Yeah, whatever." He pushed back in his chair as if to distance himself from me and my questions.

"What color was his beard?"

"It was red, but I think his hair was more brown. It can happen, you know. Brown-haired guys growing red beards. Anyway, his nose was thin and narrow at the end. His face was triangular if you didn't include the beard."

"What shape were his eyes?" I asked.

"I don't know, eye-shaped."

I leaned in toward him. "Were they round? Oval? Almond-shaped? Were they wide-set? Close together? Beady? Hooded?"

"What are you, a thesaurus?"

"Mr. McGregor, do you know what they looked like?" I asked, trying to remain as calm as possible.

"They were dark," he said. "The guy had thick eyebrows. I don't know, almond or oval maybe. Not beady, I don't think I've ever seen a person with beady eyes."

"Okay," I said. "Me, neither. Was he thin?"

"Average," he said. "I don't know. There was a weird tattoo on his hand."

"What was weird about it?"

"I don't know, it was black and looked like a moth . . . or maybe a fly?"

"Could it have been a bee?"

"Don't bees have stripes on their backside?" he asked. I could tell he was thinking about the tattoo and not me and my recording device.

"Yes."

"I don't know. It could have had stripes, I guess, so it could have been a bee," he said, sounding frustrated. "That's it. That's all I know."

"That's a lot," I reassured him and stood as I turned off my app. "Next time I come, I'll bring Everett. You'll like him." I made my way to the door, picked up the gift basket, and put it on the chair I'd just vacated.

"I told you, I don't like people."

"He's a cat," I said and left, closing the door tightly behind me. I hurried to my car and checked to see if anyone had seen me. The last thing I wanted was to draw the attention of anyone who might want to hurt Mr. McGregor.

Getting into my car, I started it up and hit the windshield wipers to brush off the rain. I know the police usually canvass the area of a crime. Someone must have talked to Mr. McGregor. So the information I had was most likely not new. Which means I wasn't obligated to share it unless I had real information.

I checked the street. It was empty, so I pulled out and headed back to the shop. Now all I had to do was figure out where I was going to get a sketch artist.

Apple Honey Cake

Ingredients:
1½ cups flour
½ cup sugar
1 teaspoon baking powder
1 teaspoon baking soda
¼ teaspoon cinnamon
A pinch of cloves and a pinch of nutmeg
⅓ cup melted butter
2 eggs
½ cup honey
1 teaspoon dark beer (e.g., Guinness)
1½ Granny Smith apples, cored, grated, and drained

Directions:
Preheat oven to 350°F. Line a loaf pan with parchment paper. Combine the dry ingredients in a large bowl. Whisk the wet ingredients together—except the beer. Add ¾ of the wet ingredients to the flour mixture and mix. Add the remaining wet mixture and mix again. Add the beer and apples and stir to combine. Pour into the loaf pan and bake 30–40 minutes, until toothpick comes out clean. Makes 1 loaf. Enjoy!

Chapter 8

"My cousin Donny is an artist," Porsche said. "He draws caricatures at the farmers' market. He might be able to do a sketch for us." We stood around the register counter of Let It Bee. My phone was flat on the counter, and we'd just listened to the recording of Mr. McGregor's description.

"Let's say we get a drawing of the suspect," Aunt Eloise said. "Then what?"

"Well, we see if we know him," I said.

"And?" Aunt Eloise asked. She wore a pair of flowered harem pants, a cat T-shirt, and a long black sweater with a hood.

"Well, then we go talk to the guy," I said.

"Or just follow him and see what he does," Porsche said. Her long black hair was styled straight. She wore a black jumpsuit and high heels. On me, it would have looked too dressy. On Porsche it was sassy.

"Or we can tell the police," Aunt Eloise said.

I shook my head. "They will dismiss it. What we would need to do is investigate this a little more. Porsche, can your cousin come by today or tomorrow?"

Porsche looked at her smart watch. "It's after five, so tonight might be hit or miss, depending on his plans. Oh, and what does it pay?"

"I can make him dinner," I suggested.

"I'll call him," Porsche walked off with her phone.

Aunt Eloise stroked Everett's back. "Do you think that the police will convince Mr. McGregor to talk?"

I shrugged. "I don't know," I said. "But that's not my problem. Besides if I take this to Jim, he'll be offended that I think he and his guys aren't doing their job."

"Will you pay fifty bucks?" Porsche called from over by the door.

"Done," I called back. "Besides, we can't do much sleuthing in the next couple of days with the sale going on. It's been so quiet this week. All I can do is hope we're going to be swamped."

"You will be," Aunt Eloise said. "I've talked the sale up to everyone I know, and the half-page ad in the paper looked really good. You mention the sale on the website, too, right? People may have stuff in their cart waiting for the sale to start."

"The website sale goes live at midnight," I said. "I'm not sure many people use the website. I think we average a hundred or so visitors a day."

"That will grow," Aunt Eloise said. "You should post

on Etsy and Amazon. People who sell through them really get more visitors."

"As I'm the only one making product, I'd rather sell through the store," I said.

"You aren't thinking big enough," she said. "You should hire some part-time help to make product and really push online sales as well. People like to take home a reminder of the Oregon coast, and people really like to help bees. I saw a Facebook ad for a bee necklace, and the seller says they will donate a portion of their revenues to bee-preservation causes. You should think about doing something like that."

"I work with bee preservation," I said confused.

"I was talking about having a Facebook ad. Everything is digital these days," Aunt Eloise said.

"Oh," I replied.

"Okay," Porsche said as she returned to us. "We're in luck. Donny needed fifty bucks to make his rent this week. He'll be out here in about an hour."

"Great!" I picked up my phone and Everett. "I'm going upstairs to make the final batches of hand cream for tomorrow's sale."

"Is that the gift hand cream?" Porsche asked.

"Yes, I'm pouring it into pre-labeled little pots. I want everyone who makes a purchase to get a free hand cream. It's a new product, and I want people to try it. I think they'll love it."

"I know I do," Aunt Eloise said. "Listen, I have to run an errand, but I'll be back in time to see the sketch. Hopefully, it will be someone we recognize."

"I don't know if it will be or not," I said. "Mr. McGregor said he didn't know them, so I'm not sure they're from Oceanview."

"If they aren't from Oceanview, we might have a problem," Aunt Eloise said. "Oregon is a big state."

"Well, they have to be from the coast," I said. "That's where all the vandalism has happened."

"It's a long coast," Porsche pointed out.

"We'll cross that bridge when we come to it," I said and took my cat upstairs. Running a store with products you made yourself was hard, but sleuthing was even harder. As they say on cop shows, so far there was not a lot to go on.

Three hundred pots of hand cream (blended with essential oils and honey) later, there was a knock on the apartment door. Everett jumped down from his window perch and went to the door to see who it was. "I'll be right there," I shouted as I tightened the last lid, grabbed a towel, and wiped my hands dry.

I opened the door to find a young man with long blond hair, wearing a black hoodie and jeans. He held a sketch pad. "You must be Donny," I said.

"Yeah, Porsche said I could come on up." He stepped into the apartment and smelled faintly of weed. "Where should I sit?"

I pointed to the couch. My kitchen countertop was filled with pots of hand cream or I'd have sent him to a stool. "Can you sketch without a tabletop? I can get a tray or something if you need a hard surface."

"Naw, I can just draw on my lap. I'm used to just knocking it out." He took a seat. "Can I hear the description?"

Everett jumped up and sniffed him, then meowed and

sat down beside him. Donny scratched my cat's head and looked at me expectantly.

"Right." I grabbed my phone, placed it on the coffee table, and hit PLAY to start the recording. I watched intently as he sat and listened throughout the description without moving his pencil. "Are you going to draw?"

"I need to hear it a couple of times," he said. "Can you hit REPLAY?"

I did.

He listened to the whole description a second time and nodded. "Okay," he said and started drawing circles on the paper. "One more time."

I hit REPLAY and watched, fascinated, as a portrait of a young man emerged from the paper. It was a caricature, but done in such a way that I think you could recognize the person if you saw him on the street. He added touches like the black hoodie.

"What do you think?" he asked and turned the portrait toward me.

"That's amazing and fast!"

"Will this do?"

"I sure hope so," I said. "Let me get your money." I went into the den and pulled fifty in cash from my small fireproof vault. When I entered the living area, I found Donny looking at my pots of hand cream on the kitchen counter.

"Do you make this stuff yourself?" he asked.

"I do."

"Cool," he said and took the money from my hand. "I do like a maker." He sent me a quick boyish grin. "Nice cat, too. Let me know if you need any other sketches." He handed me the drawing, patted Everett on the head, and left.

Meow.

"I agree," I said to the cat. "He seems like a nice guy."

After putting the hand cream in a big box, I carried it and the portrait down to the shop. Porsche was bagging up some candles in a gift bag for a young woman who seemed to be in a hurry. Aunt Eloise had gone to get take-out for dinner.

"Thanks for stopping in," Porsche said to the young woman. "Good luck with your dinner."

"Thanks," the woman said and left.

"What was that all about?" I asked as I put the box on the floor behind the counter and began to arrange some of the pots in a display beside the cash register. Everett had followed me down and jumped up on the counter to watch.

"Ah, her boyfriend asked her to go to an impromptu dinner at his parents' house. She hasn't met them yet and wanted something for a hostess gift," Porsche said. "I advised the beeswax tapers and the cut-glass candle holders."

"Great choice," I said.

"I saw Donny leave," Porsche said. "How'd the sketch turn out?"

"See for yourself," I said and pulled it out of the box.

She took the picture and studied it. "I think I could recognize this person if I saw him on the street."

"I do too," I said. "Donny has a real knack for this."

"Are you going to run this by Mr. McGregor to see if it's close?"

I stopped and studied the paper. "That's a great idea. Maybe I'll bring Everett with me. Mr. McGregor seems like he could use a new friend."

The shop-door bells jangled as Aunt Eloise hurried in.

She shook the rain from her jacket and put a bag filled with Chinese takeout on the counter. "Well, ladies, the streets are empty, so I think the shoppers are all gone for the day. We could close up now and put up the signs for tomorrow's anniversary sale."

"Great," I said and pulled out the signs. "We have some work to do. Oh, and I have a sketch." I pointed to Porsche, who waved the paper at Aunt Eloise. My aunt first went to hang up her coat and then came back inside. She took the paper as Porsche started removing the takeout boxes from the bag.

"Oh, this is quite good," Aunt Eloise said. "It looks like an actual person."

"It does," I laughed. "Let's get the shop ready for the morning, shall we?"

On Friday morning, I was up at five a.m. and took Everett for a short walk down to the beach and back. Main Street was quiet. The roar of the ocean echoed through the buildings. The fog was damp and cold, but the spring flowers seemed to relish the rain. It was dawn, and they turned their bright faces to the streetlight and the water.

Everett was fearless, enjoying the walk on his leash, moving along the edge of the sidewalk, exploring dark crevices. I know cats love to roam, but I also know that a free-roaming cat has an average life expectancy of three years. So the only time I purposely let Everett out was when he was on a leash. We didn't walk the beach. I had too much to do, so we just did a quick turn down Main and back toward the shop.

On the way, I thought I heard steps behind me. I turned,

but it was hard to see anything in the fog. "Hello?" I called.

Meow? Everett mimicked me.

"Who's there?" I asked.

There was no answer. I shrugged and kept walking. I didn't hear the sound of steps again, but I couldn't shake the feeling I was being watched. I hurried Everett, and we turned down our street and through the alley into the back of the shop. I shook the rain and damp off my jacket and hung it up. Then I took Everett off his leash. He ran up the stairs to get his breakfast. I turned on the lights inside the shop and looked around. The place was quiet and empty. Nothing was out of place, and yet I still had the feeling of being watched.

I shook it off and went upstairs to feed Everett and prepare for the busy day of sales ahead.

Porsche showed up at eight thirty. "There's a line outside," she said excitedly.

"I know," I said as I counted the cash we had on hand, then put extra money in the register. Last year, I didn't have enough cash and had to make a bank run. "Amber Leightner was here at eight. I had to tell her we don't open until nine."

Porsche put on a bee-patterned apron and grabbed a duster for a final touch-up before we opened. "She's had her eye on the limited-edition bee candlesticks you had made."

"Oh, I love those," I said. "I got this wonderful woman on Etsy to make them for me. There are only fifty sets. She even marked the number and year on them."

"I hope you kept the number one set," Porsche said.

"I did."

We opened to a rush of the sales crowd, and time flew.

Aunt Eloise came in at ten to let Porsche take her morning break. I loved working a sale. It meant that we barely had time to breathe.

I managed to slip away at two p.m. for a small lunch and to read my email. The night before, I'd scanned the caricature, creating a digital photo, and shared it on my social media. The ruse was simple. The man with the bee tattoo had won a prize package from the store. If anyone knew him, they should let him know.

I was happy to see the photo was being shared by quite a few people. Most comments said they didn't know who he was, but would be on the lookout. One comment was from a woman named Cyndi2.0 who said the picture looked like her brother, Chris. I sent her a direct message asking her to call me and left my cell phone number. Then I ran downstairs. The crowd had swelled again.

More the half of the hand cream pots had been given away by the end of the day. The shelves looked emptier.

"Wow," Porsche said when our last customer left at nine-thirty p.m. "That was intense."

"It was," I said. "I've ordered pizza as a thank-you for working such a long day."

Aunt Eloise smiled at me. "It's going to be an even longer night for you. I have a suspicion you'll be making more hand cream."

I pulled more of the tiny jars out of the box and again stacked them up as a display on the counter. "Yes, and candles, too." I waved toward the nearly empty candle shelves.

"Everyone loves your essential oil beeswax candles," Porsche said. "And selling them buy two get one free means people are stocking up."

There was a knock at the door, and I went to answer it.

It was the pizza delivery guy standing there with two pizza boxes. I opened the door and let him in out of the damp night air. He pulled his hood off.

"I need you to sign here," he said.

I'd paid online, so the signature was nothing but my acknowledgment that I had received the pizza. I took the receipt and pen from him, but stopped when I noticed a tattoo on his hand. I looked up at his face. He looked familiar. "I'm sorry, but that's a cool tattoo," I said. "Is it a bee?"

"Yeah," he said with a shrug.

Aunt Eloise came swooping up. "He does look like the caricature," she said.

"Where did you get the tattoo?" I asked as I slowly signed the receipt.

"Tattoo parlor in Portland," he said and shrugged.

"Why a bee?" Porsche asked, and he took a step back because we were kind of surrounding him.

He shrugged again. "Bees are cool."

"We think so, too," I said and waved toward my hive.

"Cool." He handed me the boxes and put up his hood.

"Can I ask you another question?" I stopped him with my hand to his arm.

"I guess."

"Do you drive a blue car?"

"Yeah," he said. "It's my uncle's car."

"Who's your uncle?" Aunt Eloise asked.

"You wouldn't know him," the boy said. He pushed his way out the door, got into the car, and sped away.

We stood there staring out into the dark night.

"You don't think that's our killer, do you?" Aunt Eloise asked.

"He was just a kid," Porsche said.

"I think Mr. McGregor got things mixed up," I said with a sigh.

"Maybe," Aunt Eloise said thoughtfully and took the pizza boxes from me. "But what if he didn't?"

"I think we should talk to Officer Hampton," Porsche said.

I made a face. "He would say, 'You think Elias's killer is delivering pizzas in Oceanview?' And then I would feel like a fool."

"What if he is, though?" Porsche said.

"Is the killer?" I asked. "Did he look like someone who would kill Elias with a blunt-force object?"

"He could have been driving the getaway car," Aunt Eloise said.

"I think it's best if we talk to Mr. McGregor first," I said. "And I can't do that until we close on Sunday and the sale is over."

"You could sneak out at lunch tomorrow," Porsche said as she picked up a slice of pizza and took a bite.

"I think the talk with Mr. McGregor is going to take longer than a thirty-minute break," I said. "Come on now, ladies. We have shelves to restock, and I have hand cream to make."

"Don't forget you need to feed Everett," Aunt Eloise said and pointed to my cat, who watched over the pizza boxes like he was hoarding gold.

"How could I forget?" I laughed. "Come on, Everett. Let's go upstairs. There's some tuna waiting for you."

Meow.

Chapter 9

"Wren, I need to talk to you," Jim Hampton left a message on my phone. "Call me, please."

It was Saturday, and the store was swamped with shoppers for the sale. I'd managed to take a moment to read the transcript on my phone's voice mail service. Sometimes reading it was easier than listening to the voices, especially in a crowded shop. This was the second message Jim had left me since we'd opened this morning—to a longer line than yesterday.

"Excuse me, can I have one of these hand cream samples?" A young woman asked me.

"They're free with a purchase," I said and tucked my phone into my apron pocket. "We have some great lip balms and honey candy over there." I pointed to the area with all the least-expensive items, in case that was a concern.

"Thanks," she said and turned.

"Next," Porsche called as she worked the cash register. It was at times like these that I wished I had two registers. It didn't make sense to have two during most of the year, but during sale days, people got restless waiting in line.

I grabbed a tray of candy samples. "Thank you for your patience with the line," I said as I offered the candies to the people waiting. "Enjoy a free honey candy on us. We have chocolate fudge, honey taffy, and salted honey caramels."

Aunt Eloise was stationed near the door to welcome people, point out areas of interest, and discourage shoplifters. There weren't too many shoplifters in Oceanview, but large crowds tended to bring out the worst in people, so we had to be prepared. I'd read once that shops had to expect at least 10 percent of their store inventory to come up unaccounted for.

"Are those real bees?" a young boy asked me as he clutched his mom's jacket and pointed to my hive.

"Yes," I said. "You are safe on the other side of the glass if you want to watch them work. All I ask is that you don't pound on the glass. Okay?"

"Okay," he said and looked up at his mom. "Can I?"

"All right," she said, "But stay in sight of me."

The boy ran off, dodging shoppers to get closer to the beehive.

"You should bring him in on the second Tuesday of the month. We do a reading session in which we read books on bees for children."

"I'm from Portland," she said with a shrug and took a piece of fudge. "It's hard to get to the coast on a school night."

"Sign up for my email, and I'll send you times for the

summer," I said, then made my way down the line, answering questions about bees and our bee products.

"Wren!"

I turned to see Aunt Eloise waving me over. Jim Hampton stood near the door in full police uniform. I hurried over before people got nervous about a police officer being at the sale.

"The place is busy," he said.

"It's our second-anniversary sale," Aunt Eloise stated. "There's some really good buys if you need anything."

"I'll keep that in mind," he said and turned his blue gaze on me. "You didn't call me back."

I lifted my hands to show the tray with its dwindling number of treats. "I've had my hands full keeping the crowds happy."

"We need to talk."

"Now?" I asked and glanced around.

"Yes," he said. "It won't take too long."

"Fine," I handed Aunt Eloise the tray. "Let's go upstairs." I dodged customers as I walked through the shop. Some people stopped me with questions, and I answered them. But I was fully aware of the speculation in their gaze as a police officer shadowed me through the shop. Finally, we hit the back and took the stairs up to the apartment. I opened the door and waved him inside. "It's quieter here." I closed the door and the sounds of shoppers dimmed a bit.

Everett came out of his closet and jumped up on the counter to take a good look at Jim.

"Like I said," he said, his hat in his hand, "I don't think this will take long." He glanced over at my whiteboard and turned his gaze on me. "Another murder board?"

"Can I get you something to drink?" I ignored his

question and moved to the sink. I took down two glasses and filled mine with water.

"No, thanks," he said, his gaze briefly narrowing. "I heard you were looking for someone with a bee tattoo."

"Yes," I said. "I posted it on social media."

"Why?"

I leaned against the counter and petted Everett with my free hand. "I talked to Mr. McGregor. He said he'd seen a blue sedan in the alley and had gone to tell them to clear the area."

"He wasn't talking to us," Jim said and frowned. "Why did he talk to you?"

I shrugged. "I recorded his description of the driver." I pulled out my phone.

"Why didn't you bring this to me?"

"I figured you already knew," I said and hit my voice-recorder app. We listened to Mr. McGregor describe the driver.

"Can you send me that?" Jim asked, his expression solemn.

"Sure," I said. "But I'm not sure how helpful it will be."

"Why?"

"Well, because our pizza delivery guy last night had a bee tattoo on his hand and drove a blue sedan."

"Are you telling me you think you found the car driver?"

I shook my head. "No, I think that Mr. McGregor mis-remembered who he saw in the alley. I think it was just the guy delivering pizza."

"That's for me to find out," he said.

"I didn't want to bring you something that was nothing, again."

His mouth was a thin line. "You shouldn't be looking for things to bring me."

"But you're not listening to me. Klaus didn't do this. I don't care about his so-called criminal past or his so-called motive. Did you know he was sharing the profits with the beekeepers who lost their hives? Did you?"

"No."

"Well, he is, and you can ask them."

"I'll ask them," he said. "You need to let me do my job."

"So are you going to look into the driver Mr. McGregor saw?" I asked.

"Yes, of course," he said.

"Even if he's just remembering the pizza delivery guy?"

"Wren," Jim said my name like a warning. "Why don't you worry about your sale and stay out of my investigation. Okay? Are we on the same page?"

"Sure," I said, with my fingers crossed behind my back.

We headed out of the apartment, and he stopped me at the landing at the top of the stairs. "I want you to know that I understand how much you care about your friends. I am doing my best to find Elias's killer, wherever that leads me."

I sighed as I looked into his sincere gaze. My heart rate might have gone up just a tad. I might have leaned toward him. "I know," I whispered.

"Good," he said and took the top step, moving away from me, breaking the moment. "Enjoy your sale."

I watched him retreat down the stairs, put his hat on, and go out the back door. The sounds of the sale swirled up the staircase, and I wondered briefly what it would be like if Jim and I worked together and were not at odds.

I had a feeling it might be magic.

"Anniversary Sale day two is in the books!" Porsche did a little whoop as we stood around the cashier counter and studied the trashed store.

"My feet hurt," I said. "In a good way."

"My feet hurt, too," Porsche chimed in.

"Well, they wouldn't if you two wore good shoes," Aunt Eloise said and showed off her glittery pink sneakers. "You'll learn as you get older."

"Are we going to have enough inventory to finish the sale tomorrow?" Porsche asked.

I looked at the empty box of hand cream. "I'll be working tonight to make candles and hand cream and lip balm. Porsche, you should go home. Your family must miss you."

"Right," she said and leaned against the counter. "And leave you to clean up? I don't think so."

"Go on," I said. "I can do it, and Aunt Eloise will help me, won't you?"

"Of course," Aunt Eloise said. "Go on home, Porsche. Tomorrow is a shorter day."

"Okay, kids," Porsche said and straightened. "Oh, wait, I saw Officer Hampton come in, and you two went upstairs. What was that all about?"

"He saw my Facebook post on the caricature and wanted to scold me for investigating," I said.

"He loves to scold you," Porsche said and waggled her right eyebrow. "When are you two going to go out on a date?"

"I don't think that's ever going to happen," I said. "I drive him crazy."

"That's the best person to date," Aunt Eloise said. "Did you tell him about the pizza delivery guy?"

"I did," I said. "Turns out Mr. McGregor didn't tell the police about seeing the car in the alley before that day. Jim had me send him the recording."

"Uh-oh, I bet they went to visit Mr. McGregor today," Porsche said and waggled her finger. "He's going to be so mad at you. Now you're never going to get him to let you back into his house."

I made a face. "I still plan to take Everett over to see him after we close tomorrow."

"That is, if you don't fall asleep on your feet first," Aunt Eloise said, "what with everything you have left to do tonight."

"I can sleep on Monday," I said.

Porsche patted my arm. "Just don't burn yourself making candles."

"Yes, Mom," I said as she walked to the back with a wave. She grabbed her purse and her jacket and left.

Aunt Eloise was sweeping the floor, so I grabbed a clipboard and did a quick inventory as I straightened the shelves. I needed pillar candles, tapers, and votive candles. I also needed lip balm, hand cream, hand cream samples, and three kinds of honey candy. It was going to be a long night.

My alarm went off at eight a.m. on Sunday. I had not gotten to bed until nearly five, but all the inventory was made. I hit SNOOZE, but it wasn't meant to be because Everett was batting my face and meowing.

"I know you're hungry," I said. "Give me ten minutes." I closed my eyes, but he kept tapping me and finally sat on my head. "Fine." I sighed, got up, and turned my alarm off. Shuffling to the bathroom and then to the kitchen, I poured kibble into Everett's dish and made a cup of coffee.

The sun was up, and the fog was burning off, slowly revealing the city streets below. I poured my coffee and went through the window to the fire escape on the back of the building. From here, I could see the ocean on the horizon. It was peaceful, and for a brief moment, I forgot about the sale and the investigation into Elias's murder.

Millie had called and left me a message. The funeral was set for Tuesday, with visiting hours on Monday. The morgue had completed its job, and Elias's body had been moved to Brant's Funeral Home. I made a mental note to send food and flowers to Millie and the funeral home.

There was a sound underneath me that caught my eye, and I thought I saw someone walking away from the back of the building. "Hey," I called. "Hey!"

But they didn't stop. If anything, they went faster. I crawled back through the window and went downstairs and opened the back door. Behind me was an alley and two parking spaces. My car was parked there, and there was a place for one more car. "Hello?" I asked.

I didn't want to go far, because I was still in my pajamas. Everett stood beside me and meowed. But I didn't see anyone. As best I could tell, nothing was done to the back of the building. We went back inside, and I double-checked the locks. "Do you think it's just a coincidence?" I asked Everett.

Meow.

"Yeah, probably someone cutting through the alley," I

said. They were heading toward the beach, so most likely just someone cutting through.

I went upstairs, showered, and got dressed. The rain clouds and fog had left, revealing a cool blue sky. Opening was at eleven on Sunday, and it was now after nine-thirty. I thought it would be a good time to go back and visit Mr. McGregor. I put Everett's halter and leash on him and took him to the car.

"We only have a short bit of time," I said to the cat as we parked outside Mr. McGregor's house. "So charm this guy quickly."

Meow.

We got out, and I put Everett down in front of the porch stairs. I hurried up the stairs, blew out a breath, and looked at Everett. "Okay, buddy, here we go." I knocked on the door. There was no answer. I rang the doorbell and knocked again. "Mr. McGregor?" I shouted. "It's Wren Johnson." I snooped in the window. "I brought Everett."

The house looked empty from the window, which made me frown. Mr. McGregor wasn't the kind of person to leave his home. "Mr. McGregor?" I moved around the house to the back porch. The door was slightly open, and Everett went right in. "Everett, wait!"

I grabbed the door and followed my cat into the old kitchen. "Mr. McGregor!" I called. "It's Wren. Your back door was left open." I followed Everett's leash as he raced down a hallway off the kitchen. "Everett! Mr. McGregor, it's Wren. I'm sorry to barge in, but my cat is being a—" I stopped short at the bedroom door.

Mr. McGregor was facedown on the floor of the bedroom. He wore a checkered bathrobe, pajama pants, and a T-shirt, and his feet were bare. Everett sat on the bed above him.

Meow.

"Mr. McGregor!" I called his name and remembered my training in first aid. I went to him and shook his shoulder. "Mr. McGregor, are you all right?"

I heard him moan, and my heart beat faster. He was alive! I pulled out my phone and dialed 9-1-1.

"Nine-one-one. What is your emergency?" It was Josie on the line.

"Hi, I'm at Mr. McGregor's home, and he's unconscious on his bedroom floor. Please send help."

"Yes, ma'am. Wait, is this Wren?" she asked.

"Yes . . . Josie?"

"Yes," she said. "Oh, dear, is he dead? Is this another dead body?"

"No, Josie," I put my fingers on the indentation between his neck and his collarbone. "I can feel a pulse, but it's weak."

"Do you see any obvious wounds?" Josie asked.

"No," I said. "He's on his stomach, with his head turned to the side. So maybe he's lying on his wounds." I winced. "I don't think I should turn him."

"Okay, are you safe? Is anyone else in the house?"

I glanced around, as the question made me wonder if I was alone. "I don't think anyone else is here; besides, I don't want to check, because I don't think I should leave him."

"Okay, well, stay on the phone with me. The police and first responders are on the way."

"Have them come around to the back," I said. "The front door may still be locked."

"Okay, I'll send them a note right now."

"Should I get a blanket and cover him? He might be in shock."

"You probably shouldn't touch anything," Josie said. "He's unconscious, right?"

"Yes."

"But his heart is beating."

"Yes," I said. "Is there anything I can do?"

"Did you check if he is breathing?"

I put my hand near his mouth. "It feels like he's breathing."

"Is it hard? Is it slow? Is he struggling to breathe?"

I leaned down and listened. "He seems to be making a kind of gurgling sound."

"Okay," Josie said. "The ambulance should be in there in about two minutes. I know it's going to feel like an hour. He's probably got something going on with his lungs. Let me contact the EMTs and see what they want you to do. Hold on."

She put me on hold, and I reached up and gently wiped the hair away from Mr. McGregor's forehead.

Meow.

I glanced over at Everett, who was sitting tall on the bed. It was made, so it wasn't like Mr. McGregor tripped or fell out of bed. Plus, the back door was open. Something bad had happened here.

"Okay, Wren?" Josie said

"Yes," I said into my phone. "I'm here."

"They said as long as he continues to breathe, it's best if you don't move him. You should start to hear the sirens."

Meow!

"Everett hears them," I said.

"Everett?" Josie asked.

"My cat," I said. "I brought my cat to visit with Mr. McGregor, and then we found the back door open, and he ran right into Mr. McGregor's bedroom, where I found him." I found myself flustered. At least Mr. McGregor was still alive.

The sirens grew closer, and I looked out the bedroom window to see the ambulance pull into the driveway. Two EMTs rushed through the front door.

"We're in the bedroom on the right," I called.

It was my friends Sarah Ritter and Rick Fender. They came in with kits and a backboard. I got out of their way and picked up Everett. Somewhere along the way, I hung up on Josie. It was all a blur of nerves and worry. Jim Hampton showed up next, along with Officer Ashton. Jim didn't say much, but he put his arm around my shoulder and walked me and Everett out to the kitchen, where he pulled out a chair from the small kitchen table.

"What happened?" Jim asked.

I told him everything, from my deciding to visit Mr. McGregor this morning to the moment the EMTs arrived. His gaze studied me solemnly throughout my short story.

"Did you see anyone?" he asked.

"No," I said and shook my head.

"And the door was open?"

"Yes," I said.

"Did you touch anything?" He glanced around the kitchen. It was pretty spare, with only the tiny table and two chairs. There were no rugs, no pictures, nothing but dingy curtains and a brown hand towel draped over the oven handle. To be fair, the place was spotless. Empty and undecorated, but spotless.

"No, I didn't touch anything, except Mr. McGregor to see if he was alive. I didn't see if he was hurt anywhere, but his breathing sounded gurgled."

"He was attacked," Officer Ashton said as he walked into the kitchen with his hat in his hands. "The EMTs said he had a knife in his chest. Seems he was attacked and stumbled into the bedroom and went facedown."

"Falling facedown saved his life," Sarah Ritter said as they pulled Mr. McGregor into the kitchen on the stretcher. They had an IV in his arm and a blanket wrapped over him. His face was pale. "He might have bled out if he hadn't fallen on the wound." She looked at me. "It was a good thing you didn't turn him."

We watched them take him out through the open front door and put him in the ambulance. The house grew quiet, and then more police cars showed up, along with the crime-scene van.

"You called in reinforcements," I said to Jim.

"The front room is tossed. It looks like whoever attacked him was looking for something. Do you know what that is?"

"I have no idea," I said and hugged Everett, who sat in my lap.

"Really?" Jim tilted his head.

"Really," I said. "I just stopped by this morning to check on him and introduce him to Everett."

"Okay," he said, his mouth a thin line. "Ashton, escort Wren back to her home."

"I don't need that, I have my car," I protested.

"See she gets back home in one piece."

"Yes, sir," Officer Ashton said and waved toward the door. I got up and carried Everett out.

"Well, buddy," I said to my cat as we walked out, "this wasn't the morning I thought we were going to have."

"Is that your car?" Officer Ashton asked and pointed

toward my car, parked in front of the house. Cop cars had me cut off.

"Yes," I said.

"I'll get them to let you out, but you need to wait until I can follow you. Okay?"

"Fine," I said, "but you don't have to do that."

"Yes, I do," he said. "Don't try to lose me."

"I won't. Why would I?"

"Just doing my job, ma'am."

Chapter 10

Never trim your cuticles. Instead moisturize
them with this honey recipe. Mix 1 teaspoon of
apple cider vinegar together with 1 teaspoon of
coconut oil and 1 teaspoon of honey. Massage
into cuticles. Relax for 10 minutes and wash
with warm water.

Porsche's car was parked in the back behind the shop.
She waited near the door.

"Where were you?" she asked when I opened my door.
The cop car that pulled up first must have tipped her off
that things weren't normal.

"We went to visit Mr. McGregor, and things didn't go
well," I said.

Meow.

"I'll tell you more when we get inside," I said and
opened the back door and waved to the officer that he
could move on. I closed the door behind me and took
Everett off his leash. "I really boosted the inventory. We
need to stock the shelves in a hurry, because I slept a couple of hours."

"Well, of course you slept. Are there any boxes upstairs yet that you need me to bring down?" she asked. Today Porsche was dressed in black flowing pants and a silky black turtleneck. She wore a statement necklace that was the same color blue as her eyes.

"I brought it all down last night," I said. "We just need to stock the shelves."

She glanced at her watch. "We only have thirty minutes to open."

"We can do it," I said and checked my phone. "Aunt Eloise just texted that she'll be in at one, which will be about the time for you to take a break. It's great that we're only open until six today."

"It's been a crazy sale weekend," Porsche said. "It's exciting."

"Yes, it is," I said with a smile. "I was up packing up the online orders as well. There's a huge bunch in the back closet ready to go to the shipping company."

"Are you going to take them today?"

"Yes, when Aunt Eloise gets here and you get back from your lunch break." I put candles on the display shelves.

"So, you said you were going to tell me what happened today," Porsche said as she added lip balm and hand cream to the displays on the shelves.

"Oh, I thought I'd take Everett to meet Mr. McGregor," I said. I proceeded to tell her what happened when we got there.

"And someone stabbed him?"

"That's what the EMT said," I said. "He was lucky he fell on the knife, actually. It kept him from bleeding out. I think he was trying to get to the phone in his bedroom."

"Oh, man, that's terrible," Porsche said. "Do you have any idea who might have done that?"

"No," I said and shook my head. "He doesn't talk to anyone. I can't imagine him letting anyone in his house."

"Was it broken into?"

I frowned and tried to remember. I'd been so worried about Everett surprising Mr. McGregor that I'd run after him. "You know, I didn't notice any damage. The back door popped open when I knocked, and Everett ran inside."

"So it was someone he knew," she surmised.

"He was a recluse."

"But he'd lived here his whole life," Porsche said. "We need to ask Aunt Eloise if he's always been a recluse."

"That's a good idea," I said.

"Why did the police officer escort you home?"

"I think they were being overly cautious," I said with a shrug. "Or maybe they just wanted to make sure I didn't do more sleuthing."

Porsche laughed. "As if that would deter you."

"I know, right?" I chuckled as I counted out the cash to open the register. Today we went back to the same amount of money that we normally used. With shorter hours, I was pretty sure we wouldn't need extra money. "I hope to get a second register for next year," I said absently. "Then we can have two of us checking people out."

"Gee, I can't wait," Porsche said. She went to the front and glanced out the window. "There's a line again today. I would have figured everyone who wanted to shop the sale would have been here already."

"I put out some social media advertising," I said.

"Maybe that's what's bringing them in. I targeted Portland and Lincoln City."

"Well, I think it paid off," Porsche said. "Ready?"

"Ready." I picked up a tray of candy samples, and Porsche opened the door to a crowd of people looking for a sale.

When Aunt Eloise arrived, the place was humming. The lines waiting for the cashier were huge, and again I wished I had two registers. Instead, I placated the buyers with honey candy and tea while they waited.

"Wow, this is great!" Aunt Eloise said when she tied on her apron. It was white, with bees in the right bottom corner. My aunt wore flowy black slacks and a white T-shirt.

"I know," I said. "Can you take over for Porsche and give her a break?"

"Sure will," she said. "But first, I heard you were involved in an incident this morning."

"It wasn't me," I said. "Someone hurt Mr. McGregor. We need to talk about that later, though." I shooed her toward the register, where Porsche was doing a bit of a dance. She looked relieved when Aunt Eloise took over. I waved her toward the back when the front-door bells jangled. I turned on my heels to see Travis walk in. My heart rate sped up just a little.

"Wren," he said, and his face lit up.

"Travis," I said and let him envelop me in a quick warm hug that miraculously avoided the candy tray in my hands. "What brings you back? How's your kitten? Is everything all right?"

"Hi, Travis," Aunt Eloise waved over the head of a customer.

He waved back. "I'm here for the sale," he said and rubbed his hands together. "I love a good bargain."

"You came all the way from Seattle for my sale?" I tried not to sound too amazed or confused, but I didn't have a good poker face.

"I like bees," he said, "and I knew you would be here. It was great seeing you the other day, and I was thinking I needed to see you again. You close early today, right?"

"Yes, we close at six," I said and passed the tray of candy toward two women who had just walked in. They took candy samples and moved around us.

"Great, I'd love to take you to dinner," Travis said. "Are you free?"

I blinked a moment. "Sure, that would be nice."

His smile grew. "Perfect. Now, I'm going to do some shopping." He picked up a hand-held shopping basket and moved toward the honey and food part of the store. I stared at his back for a moment.

"Oh, hot date!" Porsche said behind me. I turned toward her and felt heat rise in my cheeks. "Is that Travis?"

"Yes."

"I thought he lived in Seattle," she said.

"He does."

"Oooh, a really hot date then, if he came all the way down here to see you," Porsche said.

"I'm surprised he didn't call," I said.

"Did you give him your phone number?" Porsche asked.

"No."

"Well, there you have it. The problem with cell phones is no one uses a phone book anymore," Porsche said. "Okay, I'm off to get some lunch."

"Good. When you get back, I'm going to go see Mr. McGregor at the hospital."

"I hope he's okay and they figure out who did this to him," Porsche said.

"Me too," I said.

An hour later, Travis had left with a bag full of goodies and a promise to stop by at six thirty to take me to dinner. Porsche returned, and the crowds started to thin. So I grabbed my jacket and my purse and went to the hospital.

"I'm here to visit Mr. McGregor," I said to the lady at the info desk. "He came in this morning."

"He got out of surgery about an hour ago and will be moved to a room soon," she said.

"Are you a relative?"

"A friend," I said. "I found him."

"Well, he had to go through some pretty extensive surgery," she said. "He didn't have any family to contact, so we called his doctor and got all his insurance information. As best we can tell, he doesn't have an advance directive or anyone in charge of his care, should he be incapacitated."

"Maybe he put something in his will?"

She gave me a small smile. "We wouldn't know that."

"Right. Well, is he awake?"

"Like I said, he's still recovering," she repeated. "The waiting room is to the left. Someone will come get you when you can go see him."

Thirty minutes later, a nurse stuck her head into the small waiting room. "Is someone here waiting to see Finley McGregor?"

"That's me," I said and stood.

"He can see you now. He's on the third floor, down the

hall on the right, in room three nineteen. The elevators are to the left."

"Thanks," I said. I'd brought a small gift basket with me filled with honey samples, lip balm, and hand cream, as well as pillar candles. I would have brought Everett with me, but I knew from past experience that he wasn't allowed in the hospital. Oceanview Memorial wasn't progressive in their policies. Unless I could get Everett certified as an official comfort animal and get the hospital to allow comfort animals, I wouldn't be able to bring him.

The door to his room was cracked open, so I knocked and stepped inside. There was a nurse and a police officer. "Hello," I said.

Mr. McGregor opened his eyes and frowned at me. The nurse checked his IV and stepped out. The officer stood when I entered.

"I'm Wren Johnson," I said and extended my hand to the officer, whose name tag said Petree.

"Howard Petree," he said. "You're the one who found Mr. McGregor."

"Yes," I said and put my basket on the window shelf. "How are you doing, Mr. McGregor?"

"How do you think?" he groused. "I was beaten and stabbed, darn near died, and was in surgery for hours. You sound like one of these nurses who come in here every five minutes. No, I'm not good. It hurts!"

"Are they giving you pain medication?" I asked.

"I don't like the way that stuff makes me feel," he grumbled. "Besides, I don't want to sleep. What's keeping those scoundrels from coming in here and finishing me off?"

"Well, sir, that's why I'm here," Officer Petree said.

"Right, like that's going to work," he said. "There's so many people coming and going; how are you going to keep me safe?"

"You're going to need to sleep," I said, "if you want to recover."

"We can bring in a second officer," Howard said. "One in your room and one at the door. I'll go make that call right now."

I waited until he left, then turned to Mr. McGregor. "What happened? It didn't look like they broke in. Do you know who did this?"

"Punks," he grumbled.

"Someone you know? You let them in?"

"There was a knock at the back door," he said. "Nobody comes to the back door, so I went back there to give them what for."

"And they attacked you when you opened the door," I said.

He winced. "I don't remember too much. I remember the knock and getting out of my chair and thinking what the heck? I opened the door, and next thing I remember is waking up after surgery."

"You lost a lot of blood," I said and patted his hand. "Trauma gets the brain mixed up."

"Cops have been in and out, trying to get me to remember," his eyes teared up. "I don't."

"Well, stop trying, because the harder you try, the harder it will be," I said. "I found you in your bedroom. It looked like you were going for your phone. The EMTs tell me you were lucky to land on the knife. It kept you from bleeding out."

"How'd you find me?" he asked.

"I brought my cat, Everett, by to see you, and when

you didn't answer the front door, I went around to the back," I said. "When I knocked on your back door, it was open, and Everett ran inside. He found you before I did. I was glad you were alive."

"Saved by a cat," he said. "I need to meet this cat."

"I'll bring him by when you get home," I said. "Do you know why someone would do this to you?"

"No idea," he said. "But I'm going to start keeping my shotgun by the door."

"I don't think that's a good idea," I said. "They could grab it and shoot you."

"Stabbing isn't any better," he grumbled, then moved and winced.

"Do you think this is my fault?" I asked. "I mean, I was talking to you about Elias's murder. I'm afraid they tried to kill you because you know who killed Elias."

"I sure wish I could remember who did this," he said. "But I can't, and that means I can't connect it to you or Elias's murder."

"Is there anyone else who would want to hurt you?"

He shook his head. "I don't know. I mean, I can be a bit of a pill sometimes. But nobody ever killed a man for complaining about them."

"Maybe not," I said. "Maybe they didn't mean to kill you."

"Well, they made a good attempt," he said and started coughing.

The nurse came into the room. "You need to leave now. He needs his rest."

"Okay," I said. "Try to sleep."

"Wren?" he asked.

"Yes?" I turned to look at him.

"Thank you."

"You're welcome." I left, and the nurse closed the door behind me. Officer Petree stood just outside the door. "Are you bringing in a second officer?"

"I called the chief, but there isn't anyone available. He thinks we'll be okay with just one officer if I sit outside the room."

"What if you have to use the facilities?" I asked.

"Then we'll have a known nurse stay with him," Officer Petree said.

"He's not going to sleep," I warned. "I don't think only having one officer is enough. Is there something I can do?"

"There's nothing," he said with a shake of his head. "I have my orders. Also, we believe these were just kids getting back at the old man. Things just went a little too far."

"You don't think it has anything to do with the fact that he might have seen Elias's killer?"

Officer Petree glanced around to see if anyone was listening. "No one knows what the old man saw or didn't see."

"Except Mr. McGregor and me," I said.

"I wouldn't tell anyone you know anything, if I were you," he said softly, "until the killer is caught. I'd hate to see you get hurt."

I blinked slowly and left the hospital. A quick glance at my watch told me it was four p.m. In two hours, the shop would be closed, the sale would be over, and I would be having dinner with Trevor. That is, if I could get over my unease that Mr. McGregor's attack was due to what he saw the day Elias died.

Chapter 11

"Thanks for coming to dinner with me," Travis said as he scooted his chair up to the table. "This barbeque place is great!"

"I thought you would like it," I said. "They offer local microbrews." I ordered a hard cider, and he ordered a custom IPA. "They have great pulled-pork sandwiches."

"Done!" he said, and we gave the waiter our orders. "So, your sale looked like it was a huge success."

"It was," I said. "Another year in the books."

"So the shop is doing well."

"It is," I said. "Thanks for coming all this way. How's the new kitty?"

"She's great," he said. "I'm actually going to pick up a second. I think cats benefit from having more than one in the house. I travel a bit, and having two cats will keep her from being lonely."

"You have a pet sitter, right?"

He smiled, and my heart tripped. "My next-door neighbor loves cats, so she helps out when I'm out of town."

"That's so great."

He took my hand in his and ran his thumb along the top of my hand. "I heard you found your friend dead. That must have been terrible."

"Elias let me apprentice with him as a beekeeper for a year. He also supplied me with things for the store. We've known each other for three years."

"Elias was a beekeeper?"

"He came from six generations of beekeepers," I said. They were some of the first beekeepers in Oregon. Losing those hives is devastating, but losing Elias is even more so."

"And you found him. Were you alone when you found him?"

"Yes," I said. "The killers had beaten him and left him for dead in the middle of his backyard."

"Did you see them?"

I paused and looked into his eyes. "I wish I had," I said and pulled my hand away. "If I had, the police would have arrested them, and my friend Klaus would not be under suspicion. But I know Klaus didn't do it. He wouldn't."

The waiter came with our meal, and I changed the subject. We ate and talked about our memories of the past and our thoughts of the future. He paid the bill and walked me home. "Thank you for tonight," I said.

"You're most welcome," he said. "I have some business to attend to over the next few days. Can I call you?"

"That would be nice," I said, and he waited for me to unlock my door before he kissed me.

It was a rich, deep kiss that tasted as smoky as bar-beque and salty male. I wanted to put my hands on his chest and pull him toward me, but it was too soon for that. "Good night," I said and stepped inside my door.

"Good night."

I locked the door behind me and entered the dark back of the shop. Aunt Eloise and Porsche were both gone. I hurried up the stairs and unlocked the apartment door. Everett met me at the door, and I picked him up and swung him around until he protested. Then I carried him to the cupboard, where I poured him some kibble, set it on the floor, and looked out the window. There was a thick fog outside. You could see it mist around the lights from the streetlamps and the buildings.

The day had been a success. Mr. McGregor was alive and relatively safe. The sale had gone swimmingly, and I had had a date with a lovely man who loved cats. I slipped into PJs, sat on my couch, and opened my laptop. There was an email from Paul Reich, a beekeeper I bought supplies from.

"Wren, can you stop by the house tomorrow morning? I have your wax supply, and I have some notebooks from Elias you might be able to use."

I emailed a quick reply that I would be there by nine. Then Everett and I went to bed.

The next morning, Everett went with me to Paul's farm. He had a honey stand along the road in front of his acres, but it was closed until summer. So I drove up the long, two-track driveway to the farmhouse. The house was small, with two stories. There was a large barn in the back, and about a half an acre behind that was the group-

ing of beehives. Everett loved walks, so I put him on his
leash and walked him out of the car to the back of the
house.

"Hey, Wren," Paul's wife, Sylvia, waved at us as we
came around the car.

"Hi, Sylvia. Is Paul around?" I asked.

"He should be back with the bees," she said as she
hung clothes out to dry. I knew that hanging clothes on
the line was considered old-fashioned, but the outside
scent and the antibiotic properties of sunlight, along with
the sustainability of solar power, meant that many people
still dried their clothes on a line. "Wait, is this Everett?"
She hurried over, the clothespins in her apron pocket rat-
tling.

"Yes," I said. "Everett, this is Sylvia."

Sylvia was in her mid-thirties, with thick red hair
pulled into a messy bun. She wore a sundress, and her
pale skin was covered in freckles. Her blue eyes twinkled
with delight as she ran her hand along Everett's back.
"He's so soft."

Meow.

"And he likes to talk!" She smiled up at me.

Meow.

Sylvia straightened. She was thin and my height.
"Have you heard from Millie lately?"

"No," I said. "The funeral is tomorrow. Are you going?"

"We plan on it. Elias was a friend."

"To many, many people," I said. "Such a terrible loss."

"I know. Say, your aunt tells me that you all are going
to the UFO festival parade this week. That should help
get your mind off this terrible tragedy."

"We are," I said. "Aunt Eloise has costumes for almost everyone."

"Almost?"

"I like to keep my costume wearing to Halloween," I said. "But Everett is up to wearing a silver jacket."

"He's so cute," she said. "Well, I'm going to be a part of the Oceanview float. We would love to have you be a part of that."

"I wish I had time this year," I said. "But with all the sales at our anniversary event, I have to make a lot of replacement inventory. I just don't see how I can fit it in."

"Well, when you get to where you can hire more help, then give us a call. I think you'd be a great addition to the float committee," she said. "We'll see you there on Wednesday."

"Thanks, Sylvia," I said. "Paul sent an email that he had some beeswax ready for me."

"Like I said, he's working in the back with the bees. Just give him a holler, and he'll step out to get you what you need."

"Thanks!" I waved goodbye, and she went back to her clothesline. Everett and I made our way around the large barn. The Reichs had a small herd of dairy cattle, and besides keeping bees, they ran an artisanal dairy. Their kefir and cottage cheese were to die for. Across from the side track was a large open pasture where the cattle fed on fresh spring grass. It was a cool day, and I had on warm boots and a thick sweater under my rain slicker. Everett was fine in just his leash and halter. We picked our way to the back acres, where I could see Paul working away in his bee suit. When I was a few yards out, I called his name and waved my hand. He turned and sent me a short wave. I then turned to let Sylvia know I'd found him.

Suddenly a shot rang out. I froze, not sure of what was happening. A second shot, and I turned to see Paul on the ground. I started running toward him when a third shot had me crouching behind an old wagon. Everett was in my hands. I must have scooped him up and held him like a protected football against my tummy.

I turned to hear Sylvia screaming. "Paul!"

"Get down!" I shouted.

She didn't hear me and kept coming, screaming Paul's name. A fourth shot rang out. I put Everett down beside the wagon and rushed low to grab Sylvia by the knees and tackle her. I flung myself on top of her. We both lost our breath for a moment. All I could hear was my heartbeat pounding in my ears. Our breath came in and out fast. We waited for the next shot, but it didn't come.

"Are you hurt?" I asked her, not moving. I was afraid if I got off of her, she'd jump back up and race toward Paul.

"No," she said. "But there's a hole in your raincoat."

She pointed to the top of my shoulder. I reached out and felt the hole that was torn in my slicker and through my sweater; luckily, it seemed to have missed my flesh. "Oh."

"Are you shot?" she asked. "Is Paul shot? Who was shooting? Where's Everett?"

I swallowed my fear. "I don't know about Paul, but I don't think it touched me," I said. "Do you have your cell phone?"

"No," she said and tried to sit up. "I was hanging out the wash."

"I know, I know," I said and pressed her down. "Don't get up. I counted four shots." I reached into my coat pocket and withdrew my phone. My hands shook as I struggled to dial 9-1-1.

It was oddly quiet as shock shook us both.

"Let me up," she said. "I won't run."

"Nine-one-one," Josie's voice came over my phone. "What is your emergency?"

"I'm at the Reichs' place," I said. "Someone is shooting. I think they hit Paul Reich. Come quickly."

"Oh no," she said. "I've got police and first responders on the way. Wren, why does this happen to you? Where are you? Are you in the house?"

"We're in the back four acres, behind the barn," Sylvia said and grabbed the phone from me. "We're on the ground. Paul is with the beehives."

"I think he's hit," I said. "I can't tell."

"Get here, quick!" Sylvia said. "Wren might be hurt, too. "

"Was it an accidental shooting?" Josie asked.

"I don't know," I said.

"We don't know," Sylvia said. "We're about a hundred yards from Paul. Should we try to get to him?"

I slowly rolled off of Sylvia. She seemed more calm talking to dispatch. I stayed on my belly and started inching my way to the wagon. Everett sat near the wheel, licking his paw. My instinct was to get him. So I started a belly crawl toward him, but I didn't get far before Sylvia grabbed my ankle.

"Oh, no, you don't," she said. "If I can't move, then neither can you."

"But Everett," I said.

"And Paul," she said. "We don't know if the shooter is still out there."

I swallowed and nodded and stayed put. There were no more shots, and in what felt like an hour but was only five minutes or so, we heard sirens in the distance. Police cars rolled up, and officers opened the doors. I could see the guns pointing our way, and they wore tactical body armor and sought cover. No bullets were fired, and I wondered if the shooter was gone.

"Hopefully, they're gone," I said to Sylvia. "The shooter."

Her face was hard as stone. "I hope they are right where the police can get them."

The police crunched down and ran from cover to cover until they got to us. Two policemen dragged us back, while four more moved forward. You could tell they were concentrating on the downed figure in the bee suit.

We got into the cover of the barn as the ambulance pulled up. I felt light-headed. "How badly are you hurt?" the policeman beside me asked as I crumbled to the ground. "I think I'm okay. It's Paul. I think the shooter shot him twice."

"We've got guys bringing him in now," the officer said. I saw that he was about forty years old with blond hair and blue eyes. His name badge said Morgan.

The ambulance bay doors opened, and the EMTs jumped out, with kits and a stretcher. They ran out of sight behind the barn. A second ambulance arrived, and Rick Fender hurried toward me with his kit to take care of my wounds.

"Is Paul okay?" Sylvia asked.

"Please, ma'am," the policeman with her said, as he moved her toward the back stairs of the house. "Stay with me. Let me put this blanket over your shoulders. You have to trust that we are doing all we can to help right now."

"How badly are you hurt?" Rick asked me.

"I think the bullet just went through my coat," I said.

"Let's get this off you and take a look," he said and

helped me pull off my rain jacket. "I'm going to cut this sweater so I can have a better look," he said and got out shears. I didn't protest. The thick, woolly sweater was old, so it didn't matter.

By the time Rick got my clothes away from my shoulder, the first two EMTs were returning with Paul on the stretcher. I watched as Sylvia raced to his side, taking his limp hand. "Is he going to be all right?"

"I'm sure they're doing everything they can," EMT Sarah Ritter said as they passed by me.

Rick frowned at my shoulder. A bruise bloomed under my skin. "Looks like it just missed you. What happened, anyway?"

"Paul waved to me," I said. "And I turned to Sylvia to let her know I saw him when I heard a shot ring out. It didn't really register, but then I heard a second shot, and when I turned back toward Paul, he was on the ground."

Rick glanced over at the ambulance as they tucked the stretcher inside. "I'm sure they'll take good care of him."

I shook my head. "This is nuts. Three attacks in less than a week."

"There have been other shootings?" Rick asked. He held an ice pack on my shoulder. "I think if there'd been other shootings, I would have heard about it."

"Not shootings," I said. "Attacks."

"Wren," Jim came striding toward me. "What happened? Did you see the shooter?"

"No," I said. "The shots seemed to come out of the woods."

"We need to get her to the hospital," Rick said. "She is in shock. You can interview her after she gets care." He waved over the driver, and they got me up into the ambulance.

"I'll meet you there," Jim said.

It took two hours before Sylvia and I were released. Aunt Eloise rushed toward me. "Are you okay? They said you were in shock but wouldn't let me back to see you."

"A bullet went through my raincoat is all," I said. "It didn't do anything more than bruise me, but they kept me for shock."

"Porsche would have come, but we didn't want to close the store," Aunt Eloise said.

"Really, I'm going to be fine."

"But you're in a wheelchair." She wrung her hands.

"It's just policy," the nurse said. "Can you bring your car around?"

"Sure thing," Aunt Eloise said. She stooped down and gave me a hug. "Okay, I'll get the car," she said.

I noticed Sylvia in the waiting area. "Sylvia," I said and waved at her. "How's Paul?"

"He's still in surgery," she said. Her face was tear-stained. She stepped over to me by the door. "How are you?"

"I'm going to be fine," I said. "Do you want us to stay with you?"

"Oh, gosh, no," she said. "We've both had a shock. You should go home and get some rest."

"But you shouldn't be alone."

"Oh, I won't be. My mom and Paul's mom are on their way here."

I squeezed her hands. "Call me when he gets out of surgery."

"I'll do my best to remember to do that," she said. Her eyes looked tired.

"Your ride's here," the nurse said as she unlocked my

wheelchair and wheeled me out to the car. Aunt Eloise came around and opened the door. I climbed into the front seat, and we took off.

"What happened out there?" she asked as we turned out of the hospital drive and onto the road. "I heard there was a shooter."

"I went to see Paul to pick up some beeswax," I said. "Everett—wait, where's Everett?"

"Jim Hampton brought Everett by the store," Aunt Eloise said. "He said to tell you that he would be by later this evening to get your statement."

"Hopefully, that means they found the shooter," I said.

"I don't know. We've been listening to the radio, but the news hasn't said anything."

I shifted in my seat as we pulled into the alley behind the store.

"Does it hurt?" Aunt Eloise said.

"My bruise? I'm fine," I said. "I feel tired from the shock is all. I'm sorry I missed the day at the shop."

"Porsche is glad to help. Besides, the overtime is great," Aunt Eloise sent me a smile.

"And I'm sure you still want to go to the UFO festival on Wednesday," I said and sighed. "Has Anna said she can cover those hours for us? I really don't want to close."

"Oh, no, she backed out. Her mom is sick, and she needs to be with her. You could shorten your open time," Aunt Eloise said. "Close at three p.m. on Wednesday, Thursday, and Friday."

"We could do Wednesday and Thursday, but Friday is not the day to close early," I said as she parked beside my car.

"Don't make any choices right now," she said as she got out of the car, closed her door, and came around to help me out. "You've had a shock."

We walked inside, and Everett came running to meet us. I picked up my kitty. "Hey, sweet boy," I murmured as I scratched him behind the ears. "Are you okay?"

"He's been worried about you," Porsche said as she finished closing up the register. "We had some foot traffic in today, but mostly people coming in to see how you were doing and looking for a bit of gossip."

"Thanks for covering the store," I said to Porsche.

"Of course," she said. "I heard you got shot, and I wanted to come down to the hospital, but I knew you'd want someone to watch the store. Then Aunt Eloise called to let me know that you were fine."

"It just bruised my shoulder," I said. "It took so long because they wanted to make sure I wasn't still in shock."

"She has a bruise is all and will most likely be stiff in the morning," Aunt Eloise said and took my elbow. "Let's get you upstairs."

"I ordered pizza delivery," Porsche said. "It'll be here soon."

"That was sweet of you," I said as I started up the stairs.

"Not really," Porsche said with a laugh. "I'm taking half of it home for Jason and my boys."

"Killing two birds with one stone—brilliant," Aunt Eloise said.

I winced. "Let's not talk about killing, okay?"

"Of course," Porsche said. "You two go on up. I'll wait here for the pizza guy and be right up."

"Are you sure?" I said, but it came out sounding exhausted.

"Positive," Porsche said and shooed us up the stairs.

Twenty minutes later, Porsche came up to my apartment with four large pizza boxes in hand. I sat on the couch with Everett in my lap and covered by my favorite black-and-white throw blanket.

"Pizza party," Porsche said as she put the boxes on the counter.

Aunt Eloise grabbed plates from the cupboards and doled out slices.

"Say, was that the same pizza guy from last time?" I asked as Porsche sat down in a side chair and grabbed a bite of pepperoni pizza.

Aunt Eloise gave me a plate of Veggie Lovers pizza and then sat in the second armchair across from me to dig into her dinner.

"No," Porsche said. "Different guy this time. So, spill. What the heck happened this morning? You said you were going to pick up supplies and be right back."

"That's what I thought," I said and chewed a piece. Then I pinched off a piece and fed it to Everett. "When I got there, Sylvia was out hanging up wash, and Paul was in the back with the bees. Next thing I knew, someone was shooting at him and then us." I told them everything that I could recall.

"Yikes," Porsche said.

"Do you think it was a hunter?" Aunt Eloise asked.

"What can you hunt in May?" I asked.

"Nothing, as far as I know," Aunt Eloise said.

"They might have been poachers," Porsche said.

"I don't think this was an accident," I said. "In his email yesterday, Paul said he has some of Elias's notebooks. I went out to pick up some beeswax, but also to find out what Paul knew and see the notebooks."

"But he was shot before you could," Aunt Eloise said.

"Yes," I said and took another bite of pizza. "I don't think any of this is a coincidence."

"Whoever is hurting people must somehow know who you are going to see," Porsche said.

"Or who I have seen," I said and frowned. "I think someone's been following me."

"I don't know," Aunt Eloise said. "Even if they followed you to Paul's house, it would have had to take planning to hike out as far as they did to shoot from the woods."

"So how did they know you were going to talk to Paul?" Porsche asked.

"I don't know," I said. "I didn't tell anyone, and I doubt they have access to my texts. Maybe Paul confided in the wrong person."

"Or Sylvia told someone," Porsche said. "Unknowingly, of course."

"Oh, don't tell her that," I said. "She would never forgive herself."

"This has to all be connected to the bees," Aunt Eloise said. "Were the bees hurt during the shooting? Did they target the hives again?"

"I don't know," I said. "I had my head down most of the time, but I don't think so."

"Beekeeping has gotten pretty competitive," Porsche said with a shake of her head. "Elias and Paul knew each other, right?"

"Of course," I said. "We all were part of the local beekeeping chapter."

"Can you think of anyone who didn't like Paul and Elias?" Aunt Eloise asked. She got up and got herself a second piece of pizza. "Maybe we can triangulate the connection between all three of the attacks."

"So you think they were all the same person?" Porsche asked.

"There has to be a connection," Aunt Eloise said.

"We'll figure this out," I said and fed the last of my pizza to Everett. My eyes were half lowered. "Did Jim say he was stopping by?"

"He'd better hurry if he is, because you look half asleep," Aunt Eloise said.

"I'll text him and let him know it can wait until morning," Porsche said and grabbed her phone. "Then, if you two lovely ladies don't mind, I'm going to take the extra pizzas home to my hungry crew."

"Thanks for everything," I said as Porsche put out a quick text, scooped up the boxes, and headed toward the door.

"It's the least I could do," Porsche said. "See you tomorrow."

I gave Everett a squeeze until he squeaked. "We have to figure out who is doing this," I whispered in his ear. "Before we lose more friends."

Meow.

Chapter 12

Lighten your hair naturally. Use ¼ cup of raw creamed honey, ½ cup of water, 1 tablespoon of cinnamon, and 1 tablespoon of olive oil. Mix the ingredients together, and let set for 1 hour. Brush out your dampened hair, section it, and add the honey mixture evenly throughout hair. Pile your hair on top of your head, put on a shower cap, and leave it on for 2 hours or while you sleep. Wash and style as usual. The more times you do this, the lighter your hair will get. You can also use the same ingredients, minus the water, on your face as a mask that lightens acne scars and age spots. Plus, you will smell great!

Tuesday morning dawned clear. I swallowed aspirin with my coffee. My shoulder ached every time I moved. I opened a can of wet cat food, spooned it into Everett's dish, and set it on the floor. Outside, the day was cold and gray. Misty fog slinked around the buildings, and the scent of fireplace smoke layered with ocean salt permeated the room.

I usually loved this weather, but today I was not in the mood to enjoy anything. I sipped my coffee. "I feel just a bit salty," I muttered to Everett. "Nobody better cross me."

Elias's funeral was today. I wasn't sure I had the energy to go, but I would feel horrible if I didn't. It was eight a.m., and a text notification chimed in. I grabbed my phone and saw it was from Porsche. Her youngest was sick with a stomach bug. I texted her back to stay home. She deserved the day off. That also meant my funeral-going was canceled—probably for the best.

The next text was from Jim. He messaged that he was heading my way now. I sighed, took another sip of coffee, and hurried to the bathroom to wash and get dressed. Dressing was a struggle. My arm was sore and throbbed, and I could barely lift it over my head. I must have wrenched it somehow during the shooting. I dressed in an easy midi dress with short sleeves.

I brushed my hair, added small makeup touches, and grabbed a knitted shawl. The doorbell rang as I took a last swallow of cold coffee and put my mug in the sink. Everett was out the door and down the steps the moment I opened it.

The doorbell rang again as I carefully moved down the steps. My shoulder throbbed every time I took a step. "I'm almost there," I called down the stairs. Everett meowed at the bottom. This told me he knew who was on the other side of the door.

I hit the bottom step, slightly out of breath, and opened the door. It was Jim, and he was dressed in official uniform, so I figured this wasn't a friendly call. "Hey, come on in."

"Good morning, Wren," he said and stepped in, wiping his feet on the rug. The mist from outside hung on his shoulders. "How are you feeling?"

"I'm okay, just stiff and sore," I said. "Can I get you some coffee? I'll make it down here."

"Sure," he said. Everett rubbed up against Jim's legs and talked to him. Jim reached down and gave him a scratch behind the ears.

"I assume you're here to interview me about yesterday," I said as I made coffee in the pot that sat on the counter.

"You assume correctly," he said and leaned against the wall. "Are you sure you want to do it down here?"

"Well, it hurts too much to use the stairs, so yes, we can do it here. Have you heard from Mr. McGregor?"

"He's recovering well," Jim said and took out a notebook. "Okay if I take a few notes?"

"Sure." I poured us both coffee and offered him cream and sugar.

"Why did you go to the Reich house yesterday morning?" he asked.

"They supply me with honey and beeswax. I got an email yesterday from Paul letting me know they had my supply of beeswax ready, so I packed up Everett and went out to the farm."

I went over what happened from the time I left my car at the Reich house until I was taken to the hospital.

"You didn't see the shooter?" he asked.

"No," I said. "I think we were all shocked by the bullets. My first thought was someone was hunting nearby, but there isn't anything in season. Do you think it was a poacher?"

"I can't speculate yet," he said.

"Would a poacher come forward once they hear about Paul?"

"Depends on the poacher," he said. "I understand there's some speculation that this is all connected to Elias's death."

"It could be," I said and shrugged, then winced at the searing pain that caused. "It feels like it's connected, since I was present at all three attacks, or at least discovered the first two attacks."

"How would the shooter know you were going out to the Reichs' farm?" he asked and took a healthy swallow of the cooled coffee.

"I don't know," I said. "I told Porsche where I was going that morning so she could open the store. Heck, I didn't even know I was going until the night before when I got the email. Do you think someone has hacked my email?"

"That might be a little extreme," he said. "But Elias and Paul are tied to the beekeepers association, so I'm looking at that."

"Don't tell me you're still thinking Klaus had something to do with this?" I said. "He's innocent."

"All I know for sure is that Klaus didn't hurt Mr. Mc-Gregor," Jim said. "The old man says he was hurt by two guys. Said the one guy was the driver in the blue car."

"The one I had a sketch made up for?" I said. "I knew it!"

"It doesn't mean it's connected to Elias, and it doesn't clear Klaus," he said. His face was solemn. "It could be two punks, like Mr. McGregor said. They could have come back because they were mad that he ran them off the night before Elias was murdered. Besides, you don't know that that blue sedan has anything to do with Elias's murder. All you saw was it speed away from the scene."

"So you're telling me you think the kids make a habit of hanging out in the alley and just happened to be there a moment before I got there and sped away without helping Elias?"

"We're still looking into who owns that car," he said. "But, right now, we can't say it's connected."

I scowled at him. "Klaus didn't do it."

"I don't think that's for you to determine," he said. His expression was so cop-like.

I put my hands on my hips, my arms akimbo. "Have you talked to Klaus? I bet he has an alibi for yesterday."

"I'm going to see him this morning," he said and put his mug on the counter by the coffee maker. "But his lawyer has him not talking, no thanks to you."

"Everyone deserves fair representation. Will you let me know if you do anything drastic?" I asked.

"I won't promise anything," he said. "Have you spoken to Klaus? Last I heard, he didn't want anything to do with you or your meddling."

"Okay, who am I now? Scooby Doo? Am I meddling kids?"

"Stop," he said and turned off the recording app on his phone. "Don't be ridiculous."

"I'm not being ridiculous. I need to know if that's how you see me? As nothing more than a meddling kid?"

"You really want to know how I see you?" he asked, leaning toward me.

"Yes." I raised my chin in defiance.

He leaned closer and kissed me. The warmth of his

lips surprised me. The urgency behind the kiss melted my heart a little. Then he stepped back, and I felt a strange loss. It took me a moment to open my eyes. He touched my face gently. "I want you safe and unharmed."

All thoughts left my brain, and I just stared at him. His gorgeous eyes, his Paul Newman looks.

"All right," he said and stepped away, taking his phone with him. "I'm heading over to the Reichs' to get your car. Do you have the keys?"

I swallowed and blinked before his question registered in my addled brain. "Right. Um. They are in my purse, which is upstairs."

"If you tell me where, I'll go get it," he said.

"On the small table beside the door," I said.

He frowned. "You shouldn't leave your purse that close to a door. If there was a break-in, they could take it and be gone too easily." With that, he took the stairs two at a time. Everett followed him up, and I was left to stare at the empty stairs.

I touched my lips, which still tingled, and wondered why, if he felt attracted to me, he did not ask me on a date. My next thought was, what about Travis? My heartbeat sped up. Things could get complicated pretty quickly. I went through the motions of opening up the store, starting with turning on all the lights, and stepping to the cash register to count the money.

Jim was downstairs quickly with my purse in his hand. "You were right; it was right beside the door. Along with your keys." He waved the keys in the air. "I know it's convenient to hang them on a hook right there, but you are really making it easy for someone to take your purse and your car."

I snagged my purse from his hand and felt the heat of a blush rush up my cheeks. "Thanks for the advice, but I'm sure I'll be fine."

"I'll have someone drive your car back here," he said.

"Thank you," I said.

He dipped his head, put on his hat, and left through the back door. I stared at it for a full moment. Everett was back downstairs, and he jumped up on the counter and meowed.

"I know," I said with a sigh. "I don't know what I'm going to do about that." I turned, stashed my purse in the cabinet under the cash register, and finished opening. I'd given Porsche and Aunt Eloise both the day off. Porsche had things to do with her sick kids, and Aunt Eloise was preparing for tomorrow's UFO festival.

The mist clung to the morning air, driving away most shoppers. I played soft music in the empty store and cleaned shelves, taking note of the things I needed to make for the weekend traffic. It didn't bother me to have a quiet Tuesday. The damp, gray weather didn't make for fun shopping and most people seemed to stay away from the beach. I used the time to dust. I thought about washing the glass that was between the beehive and my customers, but movement in my right shoulder was still killing me.

Around noon, there was a ring at my back door. I headed back. Everett was curled up asleep in the front window, hoping for a ray of sunlight. It wasn't a long shot; the fog was burning off, and the ocean wind was hurrying the clouds toward the mountains.

I quickly peeked out the window and saw Officer Ashton. I opened the back door and let him in. "Hello, come on in," I said and stepped back.

He removed his hat and wiped his feet on the mat. "I brought your car back. We took a good look at it to make sure it was safe. I parked it in your regular slot. Here's your keys." He held out my keys.

"You took a good look at my car?" I blinked. Not that I had anything to hide, but it was a bit unnerving to think of the police going through my things.

"It was at a crime scene, so we went over it in general. Didn't take any fingerprints or anything like that," he tried to reassure me. "But Officer Hampton wanted to be sure it was safe to drive. You can never be too sure, with all the crazy people we have out and about these days."

"Sure . . . what exactly were you looking for?" I asked and took my keys.

"Bombs, broken brake lines, that kind of stuff," he said.

Everett came to greet him and was currently circling his legs.

"Bombs? Broken brake lines?" I repeated in horror. "You really think someone would go that far?"

"Ma'am, someone shot at you yesterday," he said. "We're just trying to make sure you're safe."

"Right," I said. "Thanks?"

"You're welcome. I should go now." He turned to go out the door, but I stopped him.

"Do you know how Mr. Reich is doing? I tried calling Sylvia, but she wasn't answering her phone."

"He's in intensive care," the officer said. "We've got security outside his room. The missus was inside the room, hasn't left his side since he got out of surgery. She's probably too tired and upset to answer phone texts."

"Right," I put my keys in the pocket of my work apron. "Thanks for bringing my car."

"You're most welcome," he said and tipped his hat before stepping outside. I closed and locked the door behind him.

"Well, our car doesn't have a bomb in it or the brake lines cut," I said to Everett.

Meow.

"Yes," I said as we walked into the store proper. "That is a good thing."

Chapter 13

Tuesday dragged on. I sent more flowers to Millie to make up for my absence at the funeral. Then I made a list of the shop's inventory. It was time for the early-summer displays. I liked to include bright essential oils in the candles and use pastel colors. The only problem was that my supply of beeswax was still at the Reichs' house. I was going to have to figure out a way to get more.

The bells on the store door rang, and Aunt Eloise came in. "Well, it's certainly a typical gray spring day," she said. "How's your shoulder?"

"It aches, but I was lucky, so I'm not going to complain. How was the funeral? I'm sorry to have missed it."

"The funeral was packed. I doubt Millie missed you. She was so heartbroken, poor thing. Besides, everyone knows you were shot at, and no one expected you to be there." Aunt Eloise looked around. "The place looks deserted," Aunt Eloise said and glanced at her watch. "It's almost closing time."

"It's been super quiet today. I spent the day working on inventory and accounting."

"Oh, good," Aunt Eloise said. "I went to the funeral and then spent the rest of the day on costumes for tomorrow's parade in McMinnville." She raised a paper bag. "I brought yours and Everett's."

Frowning I took the package. "What about the last one you gave me?"

"It was too crude. These are better."

"These? I told you I'm not wearing a costume this year. Besides, my arm hurts; I can barely lift it over my head. I think I wrenched it good."

"Then I brought the perfect costume for you," she said. "It's a sling for your arm made to look like silver metallic. See?" She pulled out a neatly stitched triangle of metallic fabric. "You just slip it around your arm to help stabilize it and tie it on the unharmed shoulder like so." She had me in the silver sling before I could protest.

"That's it?" I asked with narrowed eyes. "No antennae or crazy makeup?"

"No, dear, that's for me and for Everett." She reached into the bag and took out an elaborate cat costume, complete with silver antennae with fluffy crystal-look balls on the ends. "I expect you both to be dressed and ready by four p.m. tomorrow. If we play our cards right, we'll get there right in time for the parade." She rubbed her hands together with glee. "I can't wait."

"Don't you think a sling is a little over the top for a sore shoulder?"

"I think it's perfect. I made it for you especially. You will wear it, right?"

"Fine," I said. "Listen, I want to go check on Paul and Sylvia. Will you take me if I close the store early?"

"At this time of night? It's nearly eight-forty," Aunt Eloise said.

"They're not at the farm," I said. "The hospital visiting hours are until ten p.m."

"Well, then, let's close up fast and get a move on," Aunt Eloise said. "They are calling for harder rain tonight, so I doubt anyone will miss us if you close the store a bit early."

"Great," I said. "I haven't been upstairs since I came down this morning to talk to Officer Hampton. It hurt to come down, and I was hoping not to do it again until bedtime."

"Goodness, you should have called me. I could have helped. You do look a little pale, now that I take a closer look." She hovered over me and put her hand on my forehead. "No fever."

"I'm fine, really," I said. "But if you could be a doll and take Everett up to the apartment, fill up his bowl, and bring me the aspirin on the kitchen counter, that would be wonderful."

"Certainly," she said and picked up Everett, who had jumped up on the counter. "I'll be back shortly. Come on, sweet boy, let's go get you some dinner."

I watched as she moved to the back and disappeared up the stairwell. While she did that, I made a small sign explaining that we would close early on Wednesday and Thursday. Then I added an asterisk and noted that they could order from the website and pick up in the store on Friday.

"All right," Aunt Eloise said as she walked back into the shop. "I brought you a jacket—there's no way I'm letting you out in the cold and rain without one—and I'm taking you to dinner afterward. How did you eat today if you didn't go upstairs?"

"I had a sandwich and chips delivered," I explained, as I finished putting up the sign and closing the shop. There was no one on the streets as the rain beat down. I was grateful for Aunt Eloise, as I hadn't seen anyone in person since Jim had left this morning.

I put the jacket on, and we went out the back. Aunt Eloise drove a beautiful Subaru, and I carefully climbed into the passenger seat, groaning as quietly as possible as I adjusted the seat belt.

"So we'll go to the hospital first," Aunt Eloise said. "Then we can stop by and see Mr. McGregor, too."

"Wonderful," I said with a nod. She drove out of the alleyway, and I thought I spotted someone sitting in a car. I tried to look again, but it hurt to turn my head.

"What's the matter?" Aunt Eloise asked.

"Nothing," I said and stared straight ahead. "Just getting used to not moving my head like I like."

"You took an aspirin, didn't you?"

"I did," I said and chocked my suspicions up to the lingering effects of yesterday's shock. Besides, Aunt Eloise was right about the weather. The rain started pouring straight down, running in gushes in the ditches and along the streets with curbs.

We found a spot under cover in the hospital parking lot and hurried into the main entrance, where we learned that Paul was still in intensive care. We were led to the waiting room in that area to visit with Sylvia.

"Oh, Sylvia," I said and ran to give her a hug. I tried not to wince. At some point, she had showered and changed her clothes. "How is he?"

"He's unconscious," she said. "They've put him in a medically induced coma while he heals."

"Oh, dear, I'm sure the police aren't happy with that," I muttered.

"The police are so nice. Officer Hampton has been here so much, and when he's not, then there is a nice officer always near the door. They brought me clean clothes, and the nurses let me shower in the family showers down the hall."

"You must be exhausted," I said. "Can I get you some coffee? Have you eaten?"

"I'm not hungry," she said.

"You should eat," Aunt Eloise insisted. "Wren, take her down to the cafeteria. I hear they have a really good menu. I promise I'll stay here, and Wren has my cell phone number. I'll text the moment anything happens."

Sylvia wrung her hands. "Are you sure? I mean, they said they won't try to wake him until tomorrow, but what if something happens and I'm not here?"

"I'll be here for you," Aunt Eloise said. "You're not going that far."

"Something warm in your stomach will be good for you," I said and touched her elbow, gently guiding her out of the waiting room.

The cafeteria was an elevator ride down two floors and then a walk down a long corridor. We walked in companionable silence. I ordered soup, and she got a meal. I paid and carefully walked my tray to a table by the windows.

"I'm not really hungry," she said. "But I did need to get away from the waiting room. It's so depressing. I know they try, but the TV is all about health care, and the magazines are old."

I reached over and touched her hand. "You must be so worried."

"Yes," she said. "I am. Who would want to do this to Paul? To us?"

"Paul sent me an email reminder to pick up my supplies, but he also mentioned he might know something about Elias's murder," I said.

"You think this is related to Elias?" she said. "The only thing they had in common were the bees."

"I'm not sure who did this or why, but I find it odd that Paul wrote that he discovered something and then was shot before he could tell me. Do you know if he kept a journal or anything?"

"Why?"

"He might have written down whatever it was that he was going to tell me," I said.

"Oh, no, the police have his laptop as well as his files and such in case there was information in them," she said.

"Do you have his phone?" I asked.

"I do," she said. "The police cloned it and gave it back to me. Paul keeps it locked, but I know his password. We don't keep things from each other." She pulled a smartphone out of her purse. She put in a four-number PIN, and the phone screen unlocked. "He kept his email in here, and of course, his text messages and Google searches."

"Let's look at his email first," I said. "If you think he wouldn't mind."

"He won't mind," she said. "We keep no secrets from each other."

I took the phone while she ate and looked through the email account. I found the email he sent me and one from the beekeepers association chapter's board. I opened that message. In it, they talked about Elias's death and how they were looking for someone to take over Elias's bees. Paul had said he would do it.

"Sylvia," I said. "Did Paul pick up Elias's bees?"

"Yes," she said. "The association didn't want Klaus to have them because he was under suspicion. So Paul went over to Klaus's last weekend and picked up the three hives."

"I thought one hive was lost," I said as I frowned.

"The bees were, but Paul brought the box home. He was fixing it up and prepping it to introduce a new queen and start the colony again."

"Huh."

She looked at me with her big blue eyes. "Do you think that's the connection?"

"Maybe," I said and slowly scrolled through Paul's emails. There were just the usual requests for bee supplies and notes from his family and friends. "Did Paul do anything outside of beekeeping and the dairy?"

"What do you mean?" she asked.

"Did he have another occupation or hobby?"

"He worked for Brown's Market as a butcher," she said. "He also processed game for hunters during the fall hunting season."

"Wow, I didn't know that," I said.

"I work for the school district as a lunch lady, and the only thing my salary funds is our health insurance. Paul has a lot of jobs that allow us to have the farm, the dairy, and such."

"Yeah, health insurance is expensive when you own your own small business. I can send you my provider if you want. They are a collective of small businesses across the nation."

"Can you send me the information? If the insurance is

cheaper, we'll switch. I'm taking all my sick days to be with Paul as he recovers."

"Take family leave," I said. "Look into that. I think Oregon gives it to caregivers."

"I will," she said with a sigh.

I scrolled through Paul's texts. He mostly spoke to his buddies about sports and the beekeepers chapter, and responded to people inquiring about butchering or the upcoming fall's hunting season. Then I spotted it. A text from Barry Goldbloom.

Meet me at 4 this afternoon at my place. We have to talk.

"Paul knows Barry?" I muttered.

"Yes," she said. "They are both in the beekeepers association. Although Barry owns and runs several orchards as well. Why?"

"There's a text from Barry saying they need to meet," I turned the phone toward her so she could see. "Did they meet?"

"Not that I know of," she said and took the phone from me. "Strange."

"What's strange?"

"Paul didn't really like Barry," she said. "I wonder what they needed to talk about?"

I handed her the phone. "I'm sure it's nothing."

We finished our meal, and I walked her back up to the waiting room. "I'll check on Barry." I hugged her. "Call me when Paul can see visitors, okay?"

"Sure thing," Sylvia said. "Thanks for stopping by."

Aunt Eloise and I walked silently down the hall, took the elevator, and went out to the car. As soon as we got in, Aunt Eloise put on her seat belt and turned to me. "What did you find out?"

"He got Elias's beehives," I said as we rolled off. "This has to be something about the hives."

"Well, it's dark now," Aunt Eloise said. "We can't go out to the house and look at the hives today."

"We should stop by Mr. McGregor's," I said. "Let's get dinner and bring him something yummy. What do you think?"

"I thought you got dinner with Sylvia," she said.

"I bought soup so she would eat," I said. "But I know you haven't eaten. Let's go get barbeque."

We ordered meals to go and headed straight to Mr. McGregor's home. I knocked on the door and waited a moment. Then I knocked again. There was muttering on the other side of the door. "Go away," he said. "I don't want anything."

"Hi, Mr. McGregor," I shouted through the door. "It's Wren Johnson. I brought you dinner."

"No!" he said. "Last time I opened the door for food, I was darn near killed."

"He does have a point," Aunt Eloise said.

"Mr. McGregor, it's me, Wren. I'm not going to hurt you. My Aunt Eloise is here with me. We brought you barbeque for dinner."

There was no answer.

"Fine," I said and sat down on the stoop. "We'll just sit here and eat without you. I'm not leaving until you open the door." I tugged on Aunt Eloise's coat sleeve. She sat down on the damp porch steps with me. Luckily, we were under the porch roof. I pulled out a big bag containing takeaway containers and handed one to Aunt Eloise.

She took it and opened it. "Oh, burnt ends, yum!" she said. "What'd you get again?"

"Pulled-pork sandwich," I said and reached into the

bag. "And french fries. They make the best curly fries." I pulled out fries and began to eat them. "Too bad Mr. McGregor won't let us in. I'll have to take the meat sampler home to Everett."

The door opened a crack. "Who's Everett again?"

"My cat," I said. "The cat who saved your life."

The door shut closed, and we could hear him removing the chain. Then the door flew open, and Mr. McGregor stepped out, grabbed my bag from me, and hurried back inside, but Aunt Eloise was prepared. She had her foot in the door before he could close it behind us.

"Fine, come in," he grumbled. "Lock the door behind you." He walked over to his easy chair. I noticed he was wearing pajamas and an old striped bathrobe with dirty slippers. He sat in the chair and pulled his container from the bag. "Did you bring sauce?"

I reached into the bag. "There's hot, spicy, and sweet." I put the packets on the end table beside his chair. "How are you doing?"

"Glad to be out of that hospital. People die in hospitals, you know."

"I know," Aunt Eloise said and took a seat on the only other chair in the room. "You can catch your death there."

"Will you two stop," I said and stuffed fries in my mouth. I chewed thoughtfully and swallowed. "Now, tell me. Who hurt you? Do you remember?"

"I already told you and the cops," he said and stuffed sausage in his mouth.

"Do you remember anything new? I need to know," I said.

"Why?"

"Because I need to know if it was related to Elias's murder. I think it was. Do you know that someone shot

Paul Reich yesterday? He was out at his beehives. I was walking up to say hi, and someone in the woods opened fire on us."

Mr. McGregor swallowed and studied me with narrowed eyes. "Paul took Elias's hives and mixed them with his."

"He did," I said. "And he told me he had a clue as to who hurt Elias. So I went out to see him, and the next thing I know, I'm under fire."

"Are you hurt?" He pointed his chin at my shoulder.

"A bullet went through my jacket. It must have hit my shoulder hard; mostly it's stiff and sore." I said. "But Paul's in the ICU. What I need to know is if the person who stabbed you is related to this. I know you don't do bees, but I also know you keep an eye on Elias's place."

"The punk kid who stabbed me was wanting money or drugs," he said with a shrug. "I don't have that shit here."

"Why did they stab you?" I asked.

"I don't know," he shrugged. "I don't remember. As soon as the cops realized I didn't remember anything, they decided I was safe and took away my escort. Which is fine by me."

"I bet you didn't make it easy for your police escort," I said.

He shrugged. "They have better things to do with my tax dollars."

"I'm not convinced," I said. "I think you didn't want the police escort, so you told them you don't remember what happened. Well, you can tell me what happened. I'm not going to run to the police."

"I don't think you have to run to the police," he said. "Everyone knows Officer Hampton checks in on you on a regular basis."

I felt my cheeks flush hot with embarrassment. "I won't tell him. He still thinks Klaus has something to do with this, and I don't. I'm pretty sure your attacker wasn't Klaus, either. So can you help me save a man from being falsely accused?"

He sat back and ate brisket. "This is a good meal. Thank you for bringing it by."

"Our pleasure," Aunt Eloise said. "It's been a while since I've seen you."

"I've been busy," he muttered and wiped his mouth with the back of his hand. "I like my privacy."

"How are you feeling?" she asked offhandedly. I think we both knew that if we showed too much concern, we'd be out on our ear.

"I'm fine," he said with his mouth full of barbeque. "A little sore."

"I understand," I said and lowered my sweater to show him my bruise. It was deeply purple.

"Are you on pain pills?" he asked and stuffed pulled pork into his mouth.

"Over the counter," I said. "Pain pills make my brain fuzzy."

"Mine, too," he said and swallowed. "I flushed my pain pills. Don't want no punk kids breaking in looking for drugs. Might have been better just to leave them out on the porch."

"I see why you don't want to open the door," I said and sat back. "You don't remember anything?"

"No," he grumbled. "You think I don't want to remember? If I did, then those punks would go to jail for what they did."

I chewed on that thought for a moment. "Do you remember if anyone was hanging around Elias's bee-hives?"

"What do you mean?" he asked.

"You said you saw the blue sedan in the alley the day before Elias was killed."

"Yeah. So?"

"Did you notice anyone hanging around the beehives before that?" I asked.

"Who would hang around beehives?" he asked. "Darn bees are a nuisance. They sting you if you mess around with them. You've got to know what you're doing."

"Yes, you do," I said. "So you never saw anyone but Elias at his hives?"

"No . . ." He chewed thoughtfully. "Wait, come to think of it, there was one character a few weeks back. I was outside, getting something from my garage, when I saw a guy in a black hoodie standing near the hives. I called out to him. Told him to be careful. You get stung too many times and it can kill you."

"Did he answer?" Aunt Eloise asked.

"No," Mr. McGregor said. "I figured let him get stung then."

"Did you see his face?" I asked.

"Naw, he didn't budge when I called to him, so I just went inside. None of my business if he wanted to mess with the bees."

"Did you see him again?" I asked.

"I might have looked out my window a few times after that, but he wasn't there."

"How tall was he? Did he have any distinguishing characteristics?" I pressed.

"I don't know, he was average height, average build.

Wore a hoodie and blue jeans. Could have been anyone really. Except . . ."

"Except what?"

"Come to think of it, he did have a crowbar in his hand."

I pursed my lips. "Do you think he was going to pry open the beehives?"

"Naw, he didn't have a bee suit on. That would be madness," Mr. McGregor said.

But sane people don't usually commit murder. Do they?

Chapter 14

The next morning, I got word that Paul was out of the ICU. Porsche was in the shop by ten a.m.

"How are you feeling?" Porsche asked.

"I think I'm okay," I said. "Then if I move wrong, it hurts."

"Are you still going to the parade today?"

"I plan on it," I said. "Did you do something fun on your day off?"

"I made costumes for the boys," she said. "They can't wait to go to the UFO festival. They think ET might be there."

I laughed. "Ouch."

"Are you going?"

"I promised Aunt Eloise I would. So we're closing at four p.m. today and tomorrow."

"Yay, short shifts," Porsche did a happy dance. I laughed at her.

"You love working here, and you know it."

"I do," she said. "It's like my own shop. Which reminds me, we need more inventory if we want to be fully stocked for the weekend."

"Yes, boss," I teased her. "I'm going out to pick up supplies so that I can make product today. Just holler if you need anything."

"Oh, I will," she said and winked. "Oh, hey, I heard that Paul Reich was doing better."

"Sylvia texted me today, too," I said. "What a relief. I'm sure that Jim will be asking him a lot of questions."

"Aren't you going to look into it?"

I shrugged. "I'm not sure Paul saw anything. He stood up straight, and the gun shot went off, turning him to us, and then the second shot. He couldn't have seen anything."

"Maybe he saw something earlier," she suggested.

"And I'll ask him when I visit him in a few days."

"Are you putting off your investigation?" She seemed genuinely perplexed. "What about Klaus?"

"Klaus is still not talking to me, and Jim asked me to step down," I said. It sounded lame to my own ears. I wasn't going to get her involved in this investigation. People were being attacked, and Porsche had a husband and kids counting on her.

"Are you deliberately keeping me out of the loop?" She narrowed her almond-shaped eyes at me.

"People are getting shot." I waved at my sling and sucked in my breath at the pain it caused.

"So you're not going to tell me what you know." She

scowled at me. "Maybe my kids will be sick for the rest of the week."

"I love you, and I don't want you to get hurt," I said. Everett jumped up on the counter and meowed his agreement.

"I'm a big girl, and I can take good care of myself and you," she said, then leaned against the counter. "Tell me everything."

"But your boys—"

"—are going to be fine, and I'll be fine," she said. "Now, I heard you went to see Mr. McGregor last night. What does he know?"

I frowned. "He's not saying. I'm not sure he even knows. He was stabbed and beaten, and after surgery . . . well, sometimes they give you drugs to forget when you go into surgery."

"Why?" she asked.

"In case you wake up," I said.

"Yikes, yes, that would be a nightmare," she straightened. "So the meds they gave him keep him from remembering?"

"The incident," I said. "But I think he saw something before that."

"What do you mean?"

"I think this has something to do with Elias's hives. Paul was shot because he was working with Elias's hives."

"What are you going to do?" She narrowed her eyes.

"I don't know," I said honestly. "I'd go out there and look at the hives, but the police are guarding the Reichs' place. They won't let me near the hives."

"So what are you thinking?" she asked.

"I'm thinking that I need to make product and go to a parade today."

"How's that going to help with the investigation?" she asked.

"It's not," I said, "but sometimes if you give things a bit of time and space, they tend to fall into place."

"Okay, fine." She sounded disappointed.

"I know," I said and squeezed her hands. "But sometimes it's best to let things ruminate in the back of your mind."

"I hope you're right," Porsche said.

"So do I," I said. "Okay, I'm off." I went out the back, leaving Everett with Porsche. The first stop on my supplier list was Anderson's Bees. Doris Anderson worked with Klaus and Barry Goldbloom. Together, the three did a significant percentage of the bee business in the state of Oregon.

My cell phone rang. It was Aunt Eloise. "Hello?"

"Oh, good," Aunt Eloise said. "Are you at the store?"

"No, I'm headed toward Anderson's for a supply run. Why?"

"Because a call came into our Havana Brown rescue group. There is a report of a kitty mill. We're going now to check it out. Can you come?"

"To save kitties? Yes, of course," I said. "Send me the address. Do I need to pick up some carriers?"

"Do you have any?" she asked. "I filled my car with carriers, but we might need more."

"I don't have any with me," I said. "I don't need one with Everett."

"Hmm, stop by my place and grab some, please," she said. "I heard there might be close to fifty kitties."

"Oh, no, that's terrible," I said. "I'll run by your place." Aunt Eloise lived on the edge of town, near a bluff that had the most amazing walkway down to the beach. She had bred Havana Brown cats for years, and one day, it dawned on her that her time was better used rescuing Havana Browns. She had a comfortable shed behind her house. I teased her that it was her "she shed" because it had heat and light and was well decorated in cat motifs. I got out of my car and grabbed the spare key that I had and opened the shed. It was surprisingly empty. Aunt Eloise had had her last foster adopted last week.

She had her own kitties, of course, but they stayed in the main house with her. Fosters and rescues had to be acclimated to the she shed before she allowed them in the house. This meant Aunt Eloise spent a lot of time in her shed.

It had a small loft, and I climbed the ladder and brought down ten kitty carriers. Hopefully, that would be enough because I had a sedan, not an SUV, and I didn't want to stack them. I climbed back down and stopped when I thought I saw movement in the trees beside the shed. I went to the window and looked out. It must have been a trick of my eyes because there was nothing there.

Then I loaded up my car with the ten carriers. Four had to go in the trunk and six in the seat areas. Then I headed out to the country address Aunt Eloise had texted me. When I arrived, there were several cars lined up in front of the house. The door was wide open, and a policeman and an animal control officer stood on the porch and talked to a little old woman, who appeared confused.

"Oh, good, you're here," Aunt Eloise said as she came around the house with a cat carrier in each hand. "How many carriers did you bring?"

"I was able to fit ten in my car," I said. "What's going on?"

"This is Mrs. McDougal," Aunt Eloise said, pointing her head toward the old woman. "Her husband used to breed cats, but he died two years ago. No one's been out to check on her, and things have gotten out of hand."

"You said it was a kitty mill?"

"At first, that's what we thought, but it turns out it's just a cat collector who went too far," Aunt Eloise shrugged. "She kept the cats in her house and her barn. They weren't spayed or neutered, and she let them run wild. They are practically feral, especially the barn cats. Best count we can get is forty-nine kitties. I don't know what she was thinking."

"She looks confused," I said and grabbed two cat carriers.

"Yes, they've called the EMTs to evaluate her mental state." Aunt Eloise put the carriers in the back of her SUV and grabbed two more. "Come with me."

The smell hit me first as we drew closer to the house and barn. My eyes watered from the sulfur of cat urine. "Oh, poor things." There were five people, all members of the rescue group, wearing heavy gloves, chasing cats, and putting them into carriers. The place was filled with kitty meows and protests.

"Careful where you step," Aunt Eloise said.

The floors of the barn were covered in straw and cat poop and urine. Some of the kitties were just babies. Others were older, with torn and healed ears and battered tails. It was clear they had been through a lot.

"Did she let them out?" I asked.

"No," Aunt Eloise said and picked up a cat who

protested the action by biting Aunt Eloise's hand. My aunt wore thick leather gloves, so the bite didn't break her skin, and she placed the cat in the carrier. "Do you have gloves? These poor things are not taking well to being picked up, and it's a beast to get them in the carriers."

I pulled gloves out of one of the carriers I had. "I remember the last time we did a rescue," I said and put them on. I found a huddle of kittens in the back corner and carefully collected them. Kittens could go three to a carrier, and I hauled out the two carriers, deposited them in my car, and brought in two more.

We worked for three hours, right through lunch, and finally were able to collect nearly all the cats. Five rescue cars and vans full, plus those transported by animal control. It was a lot of hungry, anxious, sad cats. The racket was off the charts as they made their complaints.

Mrs. McDougal was taken away by ambulance. The word among the volunteers was that she was dehydrated and showed signs of dementia.

I stopped near my car full of kitties and studied Aunt Eloise's worried face. "Why didn't anyone find out about these poor cats?" I asked.

"Mrs. McDougal didn't have any children. Her husband died, and no one visited her."

"Oh, the poor thing was alone out here?"

"It happens sometimes," Aunt Eloise said. "She got depressed after Alfred died and gradually stopped going to church. She had food delivered, and once things started to get out of hand, she just worked harder to hide it."

"How did you find out about the cats?"

"Lucy Anderson from the church came out this morn-

ing for an annual welfare check. Mrs. McDougal wouldn't
let her inside. But a glance in the window gave her concern, so she called social services and the police. They
called animal welfare, who called the rescue group."

"What's going to happen to the cats?" I asked.

"I've got contacts with some shelters in Oregon and
Washington," Aunt Eloise said. "For now, we're going to
get them to shelters for veterinary care, spaying, and neu-
tering. Then the foster system will sort the more feral
ones from those who can get placement."

"It's a lot of cats," I said sadly. "What happens to the
feral cats?"

"Once they can't have kittens anymore, they will be
released to people who need barn cats," Aunt Eloise said
and touched my arm. "We will do everything we can to
save them all. Can you drive your cats to the Benton veterinary group? Doctor Benton said she can see some
today and tomorrow."

"I will," I said. "Then I need to go pick up supplies for
new product. I take it we aren't going to the parade?"

"Oh, we're going," Aunt Eloise said. "Don't think
you're getting out of it."

"But the cats?"

"I have been on the phone all morning. They will be
safe and warm and in vet care by four p.m. Just in time
for me to pick you and Everett up for the parade. Porsche
is still going, right?"

"Yes," I said. "She and her boys are looking forward
to it."

"Good, well, get on with taking those cats to the vet.
See you shortly." She waved her fingers at me, and I got
into the car. The kitties were protesting their containment

loudly. "Sorry, babies," I said in a soft, singsong voice. "But this is all for the best. You are going to be happy and healthy in no time."

I kept my fingers crossed that it was true. This many cats are known to overload the system. Maybe it was time to get a second cat. Everett could use the company, right?

Easy Baklava Bites

Ingredients:
½ cup finely chopped walnuts
1 tablespoon butter, cut into 8 cubes
1 tablespoon sugar
½ teaspoon cinnamon
¼ teaspoon vanilla
1 pinch salt
1 package of 15 mini phyllo shells
¼ cup water
¼ cup honey
3 tablespoons lemon juice

Directions:

Heat oven to 350°F. Mix walnuts, butter, sugar, cinnamon, vanilla, and salt. Mix until a ball forms. Place phyllo shells on a parchment-lined cookie sheet. Pack 1 heaping teaspoon of the mixture into each shell. Bake for 10 minutes. While that's baking, combine the water, honey, and lemon juice in a saucepan and bring to a boil. Simmer for 10 minutes to form a thin syrup. Remove shells from the oven, and carefully spoon the honey syrup over the baked baklava, letting it soak in. Refrigerate until ready to serve. Makes 15 bites. Enjoy!

Chapter 15

"You make an amazing alien!" Porsche said to Aunt Eloise. We stood on a corner in McMinnville, waiting for the parade to start. The skies had cleared, and the parade watchers would be able to stand outside without umbrellas or raincoats.

Aunt Eloise was dressed in a silver-lamé leotard, silver tights, silver boots, and gloves. Her face was covered with silver makeup, and her eyes had been drawn large to look like alien eyes. She wore her gray hair with silver sparkles in it along with two antennae attached to a head band. Her two kitties were leashed, one to each of her wrists, and wore silver alien suits.

"Thanks," she said. "I'm the pet to my cats."

"Ah, a twist," Porsche said. Porsche wore a white jumpsuit with a tool belt that had ray guns and various space necessities attached.

"Where are the boys?" I asked.

"I sent them off to get snacks," she said. "I'm holding our places here. Where's your costume, Wren?"

"Aunt Eloise made me this 'space suit sling,'" I said. "Everett loves his costume," I said and gathered my kitty into my arms, trying not to wince, to show off his metallic hat and cape. "Courtesy of Aunt Eloise."

"Everett, you look quite dashing," Porsche said and stroked his ears.

Meow.

"Oh, I heard about the massive kitty rescue," Porsche said to Aunt Eloise. "I hope they are all going to be all right."

"I'm sure the vets will do thorough exams," Aunt Eloise said. "I've been calling rescue groups in three states to ensure we have enough homes for them. Right now, I'm waiting for a call from Channel Five. I'm hoping putting this on the news will help raise awareness."

"You are such a dear," Porsche said and hugged Aunt Eloise.

"Oh, that reminds me," I said. "I printed up posters to put along the parade route." I dug through the bag I carried and pulled out twenty posters. "This is just to build awareness." The picture was of the group of kittens I had first pulled from the barn. The title was CAN YOU HELP? And I went on to explain, in as few words as possible, that kittens needed good homes and urged people to call the rescue hotline.

"These are wonderful!" Aunt Eloise said. "I'll take some and go to where the parade starts. Wren, you post them where it ends."

"Sorry, guys, but I have to stay near my boys," Porsche said and pointed to them in the line at the snack bar.

"It's okay," I said and gave her a quick hug. "You can hold our place. We need to hurry because the parade starts in fifteen minutes."

I followed behind the gathering crowd and stopped on every block to staple or tape a poster. I could hear the bands as they started to come down the parade route.

"Excuse me." A lady with a young girl stopped me. They were both dressed in costumes from the '90s and held a sign that said ROSWELL on it, along with a picture of the cast of the show from the '90s. "Are you giving away kittens?"

"I'm building awareness," I said. "We just rescued nearly fifty cats from an overcrowding situation. They'll be ready for adoption next week."

"I want a kitty, Mommy," the little girl with blond hair said.

"How do we get one of the cats?" the woman asked.

"Call the number on the sign, and the rescue group will give you more information."

"Wonderful," she said and took a picture of the poster with her cell phone. I stapled the last of my posters at the end of the parade route.

"Hey, aren't you the bee lady from Oceanview?"

I turned to see a group of three people, two women and one man, staring at me. "I'm Wren Johnson."

"You own that bee shop," one woman said. She was wearing a Star Trek uniform, and her face was painted half blue.

"Yes," I said. "I own Let It Bee."

"You worked with Elias, didn't you?" the man said. "You found him dead?"

"Yes," I said, slightly confused. "Can I help you?"

"I'm Atlas Annie," said the second woman, who was

dressed like Princess Leia. "This is Krystal Sage and Crash Waves."

"Hello," I said.

"We were friends of Elias," Atlas said. "He said if anything happened to him to talk to you."

"Oh," I said, still confused. "Did he think something would happen to him? Because he didn't mention anything to me."

"Can we get a beverage?" Atlas asked. "We really want to talk to you."

"Sure," I said and followed them to the coffee shop on the next block. We ordered drinks and sat down. "I can't stay long. I have friends waiting for me on the parade route."

"Yeah, we figured," Crash said. He was dressed as a red-shirted Star Trek character with orange skin and pale blue eyes. "We'll keep things brief. We belong to a watchdog group."

"A watchdog group?" I echoed.

"Yes, we meet once a week to look into mysteries. You know, things the press is overlooking, like the vandalism of beehives across the state," Krystal said. She wrapped her hands around her cup of coffee.

"Elias was one of our members. He brought the plight of the beehives to our attention," Crash said. "He said that if anything happened to him, we needed to find you and tell you what we know."

"What do you know?" I asked, my curiosity on edge.

"Elias was looking into the beehive vandalism up and down the coast," Atlas said.

"Yes, I know. I think that's why he was killed," I said.

"We think it's a government cover-up," Crash whispered as he glanced around the shop. "They don't want people to know that Bigfoot is stealing honey from bee-hives."

"Oh," I said and felt my heart sink.

"Well, some of us are divided on the whole Bigfoot issue," Krystal said. "But we're pretty sure there's a cover-up. Think about it. If we have no bees, then we have no produce. Without produce, we are all subject to dwindling food supplies."

"We will have to eat algae and fish," Atlas said. "There's a big push for farm-raised fish."

"No, no, no," Crash said. "Bigfoot is trying to dwindle our numbers because we are encroaching on their land."

"Is this what Elias thought?" I asked.

"No," Krystal said with a sigh. "Elias had this crazy idea that people were smuggling illegal substances inside beehives. I mean, the hives move around to various places, and no sane person is going to look inside."

"Except a beekeeper," I said softly.

"Or Bigfoot," Crash said.

"Thanks, guys," I said and stood up. "You've been a big help."

"You're welcome," they all said at once.

"Are you staying for the talk on detecting aliens among us?" Krystal asked.

"No," I said. "I've got people waiting for me."

"Keep in touch," Atlas said and slipped a business card in my hand. "We understand you solve mysteries. We can be a great resource."

"It's true," Crash said. "People come to us with all kinds of information."

"Thanks," I said. "Enjoy the festival."

I hurried out. The parade had caught up to the end of the route, and people were milling about, talking and laughing. Photographers were taking candid photos. I hurried through the crowd back to where I'd left Porsche.

The conspiracy theorists confirmed what I was already beginning to suspect. There was something hidden in Elias's hives. Something important enough to kill for.

"You missed the whole parade," Aunt Eloise said when I returned and took Everett's leash from Porsche. "What took so long? I was able to put up all my posters and still get back in time to see the floats. There was one where a Bigfoot was being abducted by aliens, and another full of people wearing shirts with the dates of their abductions."

"I ran into a group of conspiracy theorists," I said and pulled out the business card. "They said that Elias was a member of the group and told them if anything happened to him to find me."

"Odd that they found you here," Porsche said, "considering the crowd." Her boys were dressed as Jedi knights, complete with glowing swords. They fought each other nearby, plastic swords pinging off each other.

"I agree," I said, "but I was putting up the poster in front of a coffee shop when they spotted me. They knew who I was, and they knew Elias."

"Seems like a strange coincidence," Porsche said. "Do you think you can trust them?"

"Well, I won't be running off to Jim Hampton about their theories. One said he thought it was Bigfoot destroying the beehives."

Porsche giggled. "Why?"

I shrugged. "Something about dwindling food supplies making us all move out of their territory."

"And you believe these people?" Aunt Eloise asked.

"Not all of them," I said. "One said that Elias thought drug runners were smuggling drugs inside the beehives."

"Well," Porsche said. "That's more plausible. I mean, who's going to search beehives? But why not just sell drugs like everyone else. It's not like the hives leave the country."

"They move from farm to farm during the season," I said. "Clearly someone could be smuggling something."

"You're going to look into this, right?" Aunt Eloise asked.

"Of course. Come on," I said. "Let's all get dinner. There's this pub that is serving Baby Yoda cocktails."

"Baby Yoda?" Aunt Eloise repeated.

"From *The Mandalorian* on Disney+," Porsche said. "Really cute, and there are memes everywhere on social media." She pulled out her phone and scrolled until she found one. "See?"

"Oh, isn't that the cutest thing?" Aunt Eloise said. "I'm up for cocktails."

We locked arms and made a parade of our own with three cats on leashes, three women, and two small boys in tow. Luckily, the town was filled with crazy celebrators and celebrities talking about UFOs. So we didn't stand out that much.

We didn't stay long after dinner. Porsche had to put the boys to bed, and Aunt Eloise needed to check on the kitties. I took Everett home and went upstairs to make product.

For a couple of hours, I poured candles and made lip balm. While the items cooled, I designed labels for them. Customers liked kitschy names for lip balm and candles. Half of the labels featured a picture I had taken at the

UFO festival, and for the other half, I made up out-of-this-world names.

Everett meowed at me.

"What?" I asked him.

He jumped up on my desk and put his paw on the poster of the kittens and meowed again.

"Oh, that's a great idea," I said to him and spent the rest of the night designing labels encouraging cat adoption and donations.

By morning, I had my product displays restocked and a poster in the window asking people to adopt or make a donation for the kitties.

"You look exhausted," Aunt Eloise said as she came in the back for the morning shift. "Were you up all night?"

"I had to make product," I said. "Look, Everett suggested I make some product labels featuring cats and putting the adoption and donation number on them." I showed off the pillar candles and the kitty jars of honey.

"That's a wonderful idea," Aunt Eloise said. "I'll call the gal from Channel Five to come and maybe add them to her story about the kittens."

"Did the police charge Mrs. McDougal?" I asked.

"No," Aunt Eloise said with a shake of her head. "They put her in a nursing home. The poor thing has dementia very badly. Partly because she had a terrible bladder infection and partly because she was suffering from a broken heart. They hope that they can pull her out of it with some antibiotics. Otherwise, she'll be in a home for the rest of her life."

"Oh, no," I said. "Will they allow kitties to visit? I'm sure she'll miss her cats."

Aunt Eloise petted Everett, who sat on top of the register counter. "I think they might if the cat goes through a certified comfort-animal course."

"Do they have those for cats?" I asked.

"I'll check," she said. "And if they don't, then I'll make one happen. I'm sure Everett would make a great comfort cat."

"Yes," I said and poured us both a cup of coffee. "I think he would."

"What's the plan for today?" Aunt Eloise said. "Are we going to the UFO festival tonight? They are having a carnival."

"You and Porsche can go," I said and sipped my coffee. "I'm going to stay home and go to bed early." I yawned to prove my point.

"So you're keeping the store open for its usual hours?" she asked.

I glanced outside to see a soft mist was falling. "I think so," I said. Prepping to open the store, Aunt Eloise counted the register money. I straightened the shelves and then unlocked the door at ten a.m. The streets were quiet, probably due to the rain. In May, Oregon kids were still in school, and we didn't have much more than a trickle in the store unless the weather was good.

"Did you have a chance to look up that conspiracy theory group?" Aunt Eloise asked.

"I'm going to do that right now," I said and pulled up a stool and opened my laptop. I typed in the URL for the website listed on their business card. The website was well done, and the blog had a lot of followers. Listed as one of the members was Elias's name, along with Klaus's. "Huh."

"What?" my aunt asked.

"Klaus is a member of this group," I said.

"Did you ever get a chance to talk to him?" she asked.

"Not since he was taken in for questioning," I said. "I'm going to text him right now." I pulled out my phone and texted. *Hi, Klaus. How are you holding up? Can we talk?*

He texted back. *I'm fine. There's nothing to talk about.*

I ran into your conspiracy theorists group yesterday, I texted. *I would love to hear your take on why the bee-hives are being broken into.*

It's not Bigfoot, he texted back.

I sent a smiley face emoji. *I didn't think so. Can I buy you lunch?*

Fine, he texted. *I won't turn down a free meal.*

Great, I said. *I'll meet you at Mo's at noon.*

He texted back a thumbs-up emoji. I popped off my stool. "I'm meeting Klaus for lunch."

"That's great news," Aunt Eloise said. "Maybe he knows something but doesn't realize it."

"I certainly hope so," I said. "I'd hate to see him go to jail for a crime he didn't commit."

Chapter 16

I met Klaus at Mo's Seafood and Chowder. The place was packed, as usual. It was a damp, misty, rainy day, so it was nice to be inside in the warmth, surrounded by the bustle and the smell of chowder and fresh fish.

He sat at a table in the back corner, and I joined him. "Hi, and thanks for meeting me," I said and took off my hooded raincoat and hung it on the chair beside me.

"I don't turn down a free lunch," he said.

The waitress came and took our orders. I ordered chowder and coffee. He ordered the daily special.

"How are you holding up?" I asked.

"Better than you," he said and motioned toward my bandaged shoulder.

"Yeah, getting shot at wasn't the most fun," I said. "They shot Paul Reich."

"I know. I got a call and was asked for an alibi," he

frowned. "Lucky for me, I was with Jack Poleson, putting hives out in his orchard."

"I think it has to do with Elias's hives," I said and leaned forward. "It was suggested that people are smuggling things inside the beehives. Do you think that's possible?"

"Maybe," he said. "They'd have to be pretty darn desperate. Bees don't like to be disturbed."

"It's kind of ingenious," I said. "No one's going to open the hives and look."

"Not unless the bees are dwindling," Klaus said. "Then the keeper will look inside to see what's going on."

"I ran into Atlas, Krystal, and Crash yesterday at the UFO festival in McMinnville."

He sat back and gave a short bark of a laugh. "That must have been some meeting."

"I didn't know you and Elias were part of their conspiracy theorists group," I said.

He leaned forward. "We didn't really highlight our involvement. People would think we were nuts."

"Why did you two join?" I asked. "I mean, you don't seem like the government-conspiracy type."

"You mean paranoid and crazy?"

I winced. "I guess I watch too much television."

"So do Atlas, Krystal, and Crash," he said. "I got into it when I came across some things I couldn't explain."

"What things?"

"Logging patches in state parks," he said. "I don't say this lightly because logging is a long tradition here. Heck, I have relatives who work in logging, but our state parks are supposed to be off-limits."

"And they aren't?"

"Let's just say someone paid a pretty penny to local

congressmen for the chance to do some deep-forest logging."

"How did you find that out?"

"I fly drones as a hobby," he said. "I brought my photos to the state park commissioner but was told it was no big deal."

"And Elias? Why was he part of the group?"

"He thought it was cool. You know, looking into the unexplained," Klaus answered.

"Like Bigfoot?" I asked.

"Aliens, UFOs," he said with a shrug as the waiter brought our drinks. Then he leaned in. "Elias was convinced the beehive vandals were connected to something bigger."

"Like a government cover-up?" I asked and wrapped my hands around my coffee cup.

He laughed. "You really have been talking with Krystal and Atlas."

I felt my cheeks warm from embarrassment. "Maybe those notions are far-fetched, but the idea that someone is smuggling things in beehives holds some water. I mean, Elias died next to his hives. And when Paul got the beehives, he was shot."

"How is Paul doing?" Klaus asked as the waiter brought my chowder and his seafood platter.

"I haven't had the chance to check," I said. "Have you heard anything?"

"Nothing," he said. "I've reached out to Sylvia, but she replied that the police have asked her not to speak to me."

I winced. "They must still see you as a person of interest. I thought you had a clear alibi."

"So did I," he said and bit into his crab cake. "But Officer Hampton can be like a dog with a bone when he gets an idea in his head."

"I'll speak to him again," I said.

"Again?"

"Yes, I already told him you weren't the killer. I think the killer attacked Mr. McGregor."

"That old grouchy man who lives behind Elias? Why?"

"I think he saw something, but now he says he can't remember anything."

"You spoke to the old guy?" He sounded amazed.

"I did," I said. "He's a bit difficult to reach, but I think I'm building a nice rapport with him." I sipped my soup, letting the creamy taste of clam slide down my throat. "If someone were smuggling things in beehives, do you have any idea who they might be or why they're doing it?"

"Hives would be warm and moist inside," he said. "So whatever it is, it has to withstand the environment."

"Hmm, it would most likely be bagged, right? I suspect drugs."

"I don't know any beekeepers who would smuggle drugs. We're usually a nature-loving kind of people. You know, hard-working farmers' advocates. A real beekeeper would be worried about the health of the hive. Besides why smuggle drugs in bee hives? There are easier ways."

"Right," I said and thought about it. "So probably not a beekeeper but someone who is close to a beekeeper, and probably not drugs."

"And the vandalism has happened up and down the coast, so there's not just one beekeeper involved."

"True," I said and pursed my lips. "Elias suspected someone. I'm certain that's why he was murdered."

"Maybe he surprised whoever was trying to retrieve the stuff from his hives."

"If that's the case, then I must have interrupted them. I think they attacked Paul because they needed to get to Elias's hives." I finished my soup.

"Well, I don't know anyone who is into smuggling," Klaus said. "I suspect neither do you."

I blew out a long breath. "I don't. But there are a lot of beach people who might. You know, the ones who camp out on the beaches and move up and down the coast, depending on the weather."

"It's too cold and rainy right now to be camping on the beach," Klaus pointed out.

"Right," I sipped my coffee. "Maybe Aunt Eloise knows someone."

"Maybe you should talk to your police pal about it," Klaus said. "Anything to get him off my back. My farmers are balking about renting my hives because they don't want to work with a killer."

"Oh my gosh, I didn't even think of that," I said. "I'm so sorry."

We finished our meal, and Klaus let me buy some beeswax, honeycomb, and honey from him before he packed up his truck and headed out of town. I dialed Jim Hampton's phone number.

"This is Hampton," he said when he answered.

"Hi, Jim; it's Wren. Do you have time to talk?"

"I have a minute," he said. "What's going on?"

I explained about the theory of something being smuggled in beehives. When I was done, he was quiet for a long time. "Jim?"

"It's not a bad thought," he said. "I'll send someone out to the Reichs' to open their hives."

"It's raining," I pointed out.

"We need to check the hives before someone else gets hurt."

"Are you still sending patrols around to their farm?" I asked.

"Yes, we run through every couple of hours."

I frowned. "That leaves plenty of time for someone to get whatever from the hives."

"That's my thought exactly," he said. "I'm sending a patrol car out to check on them. If someone is taking something out of the hives, then they aren't caring about the bees, making it look like vandalism."

"So you would know if the hives have been touched," I said.

"Yeah," he said.

"Well, let me know if you need a bee wrangler."

"I've got my own sources, thanks," he said. "Stay home and stay safe."

"Right." I hung up the phone and parked behind my shop. I opened the trunk and pulled out the boxes of supplies and went in through the back.

"Wren?" Aunt Eloise called.

"Yes, it's me," I said as I unloaded the supplies at the bottom of the stairs. "How's it going?"

"It's been another slow day," she said. "Mrs. Zachary came in, and we put together a gift basket for her son's fiancé. Also, Olive Snook came in and bought four containers of honey for her latest batch of pies."

"Well, you can go to lunch," I said. "I'll take care of the store."

"Good. I have a meeting this afternoon," Aunt Eloise said. "Are you feeling better? Are you up for going back to the UFO festival? You can close at four, and I'll pick you up."

"Oh, I can't," I said. "I've got product to make, and my shoulder is killing me."

"How'd your lunch with Klaus go? Did he know anything more about the bee vandals?"

"It went okay," I said. "He agreed that they could be smuggling things in the hives, but he's pretty sure it wasn't any of the beekeepers doing it."

"I could see that," she said. "Do you want to go out to the Reichs' place and look in Elias's hives?"

"I doubt there's anything in Elias's hives. The beekeepers were inside them the day Elias died. I'm sure we would have found anything strange. But there are still several beehives at Paul's place, so I called Jim Hampton. He's going to send out a patrolman to see if the hives have been touched and to stay with them until a beekeeper comes."

"But you're a bee wrangler. He should just use you. After all, it was your idea."

"Anything I touch could hurt Klaus if he's arrested, since I'm his friend," I explained. "It's best if Jim brings in outside help. Which reminds me. You have your ear to the town gossip. Are there any new drugs making the rounds?"

"I've not heard," Aunt Eloise said and tapped her chin. "The usual beach bums haven't come up from California yet. It's still too cold."

"That's what I thought," I said. "Do let me know if you hear anything about who might be smuggling things into town. Whoever it is may have been running things up and down the coast using beehives. Just look at all the vandalisms."

"Poor bees," she said and gathered up her purse and her raincoat. "I tell you what, I'll do some discreet probing. If anyone in town knows anything, I'll call you."

"Thanks," I waved her goodbye and looked at Everett. He was curled up in his box on the counter behind the register. I made coffee and helped a pair of ladies who had stopped to browse on their afternoon break. Then I pulled out my laptop.

A quick Google search of new drugs in Oregon came up against a dead end. So I picked up my phone and called Sylvia.

"Hi, Wren," she answered.

"How are you doing?" I asked. "Are you still at the hospital?"

"We're getting ready to take Paul home," she said. "The doctors think he will heal faster in his own bed."

"That's great news," I said. "Have you been back to the house?"

"I have," she said. "I'm not going to lie. It was kind of creepy."

"Did Officer Hampton call you today?"

"He did," she said. "He said something about checking the hives for contraband. Do you really think someone would use beehives to smuggle?"

"I don't know," I said. "But it would make sense of the vandalisms."

"Maybe Elias found whatever they were smuggling," Sylvia said. "It could be why they searched his house."

"No one searched your house, did they?"

"Not that I was aware of," she said. "Everything seemed in its place. I locked the house well, and the police came by every couple of hours."

"That's great," I said. "Does Paul remember finding anything in the hives?"

"He said he was just heading over to Elias's hives to check on them when he got shot. So there's not a chance he found anything."

"I was thinking more about your hives," I said.

"Our hives? Oh, no, no one would mess with our hives," she sounded adamant.

"Okay, well, stay safe," I said.

"We will," she replied. "Thanks for all your help."

"You're welcome." I hung up and stared out the windows of the store. The drizzle began again in earnest, and a cool wind off the ocean sent it shooting sideways in waves.

I took another look at my computer browser, this time focusing on local news. I rarely watched the news these days, as I was so busy with the shop. I relied on Aunt Eloise and Porsche to give me any important information. The scrolling was disheartening as I read about missing children, school shootings, and the debate about genetically modified animals.

None of those things made any sense when it came to smuggling with bees. So besides people not likely to suspect beehives as a vehicle, the mobility of hives during the pollination season, and the inability to rob a hive readily, what else about bees would make it a good environment to smuggle things in?

I went over to my bee wall. The hive inside was busy at work, creating wax and chambers for new drones. Bees usually only lived five or six weeks. So the constant need to reproduce drove the hard work of the bees. The best time to harvest honey is usually late July and August.

Which means May was a great time for bees to gather pollen and make new honey and honeycomb. I put my hand on the glass as if I could somehow ask the bees what someone might smuggle.

Meow.

I looked down to see Everett circling my legs. Reaching down, I picked him up. He was soft and warm and a real snuggle bunny. "What are they smuggling with the bees?" I asked him.

Meow.

Standing there, staring at my hive and holding my kitty, it dawned on me that beehives were warm and moist. What needed to be kept relatively warm and moist? I walked back to my computer and put Everett down on the counter.

Farmers, I thought, are the ones who are receiving the beehives. What would farmers want? I went back to an article about animal husbandry. There was some debate about cloning and artificial insemination. My eyes widened at the price of successful animal husbandry. Then I noticed that it is actually illegal to clone animals and to artificially inseminate thoroughbred horses. Wait, could the smugglers be illegally smuggling semen for farm animals?

The thought was a tad ridiculous. I shut my laptop and stared at the growing darkness of the evening. It was probably drugs. Drugs made the most sense. People swallowed them all the time to carry them over borders.

I texted Jim. *Any discoveries over at the Reichs'?*

He texted back. *Someone vandalized Paul's hives. There's no telling who or why. I have a team dusting for prints.*

That's not going to help, I texted back. *Beekeepers usually wear gloves.*

Still have to try.

It was the last text. I frowned and texted my friend Bobby Smith. Bobby and his family had been raising organic farm animals for over a hundred and fifty years. They sold their meats and organic cheeses at farmers' markets and through online grocery clubs.

Hey, Bobby, how are you? I texted.

Good, he replied. *What's up?*

I have a strange question that you might be able to answer.

Go ahead, he texted.

Okay . . . Have you heard anything about clones or illegal animal breeding practices in the area?

We stay away from all that genetically modified stuff, he texted.

Yes, I know, but have there been any rumors about anyone doing weird things?

There was a long pause, and then the triple dots played while he wrote his text. Another pause, and then he sent it. *You didn't hear this from me, but the Appleton farm has been breeding award-winning cattle, and recently they have started a thoroughbred program.*

Sounds like they are spending a lot of money, I texted.

The thing is, they don't have a lot of money, he texted back. *Their livestock was pretty middle of the road until last fall. Suddenly they are producing a large number of stock that is extraordinary.*

I frowned. *Anyone else seeing these results?*

The Millers are, too, he texted. *The farmers' council asked them for their secret. They claim it's the new bull they have purchased and a new stallion."*

Okay, I texted. *That sounds reasonable.*

Except when you look at the animals they purchased, the breeding doesn't fit.

You think they're cheating?

Who knows? he texted. *Hard to say. Why?*

I think someone is smuggling something in beehives. There have been several vandalized hives, and now Elias has been murdered and Paul shot.

There was a pause. Then he texted, *You think it's illegal semen? Or heaven help us cloning eggs?*

I know it sounds silly, I texted. *It's probably something else like drugs, but so far we haven't found a drug connection. Then I thought about the fact that the hives go out to farms.*

No, it can't be that, he texted. *The temperatures in a hive are too warm for maintaining the type of things you need to create superior breeds.*

Okay, I texted back. *It was just a thought. Thanks.*

You didn't hear it from me, but I overheard some guys in the bar bragging about this new synthetic drug. It's supposed to come in a vial and makes you high without any side effects.

Do you know what they're calling it? I texted.

Vitality, I think, he texted.

Thanks for your help, I texted back.

Anytime.

I wasn't sure if I'd learned anything helpful, but at least I'd figured out that it wasn't semen or cloning material in the beehives. Now all I had to do was find someone who could tell me more about this new drug. The problem was, I wasn't into the drug scene, and neither were my friends.

Chapter 17

To prevent a hangover after a girl's night out,
simply add 3 teaspoons of honey to warm water.
Stir until combined, and drink before you go to
bed. The honey will help the body metabolize
the alcohol, minimizing your hangover.

"Come on, you're closing up shop," Aunt Eloise said
as she entered my customer-less shop. She locked
the door behind her and turned the sign to closed.

"Wait, why?"

"We're going to McMinnville," she said.

"But I told you that I had things to do tonight," I said.
Meow. Everett agreed with me.

"Yes, but I happen to know a certain hunky guy named
Travis who is going to be there. You should come with
me. We'll have some fun. You deserve a little fun in your
life."

"I don't know," I balked.

"Too late, it's happening," she insisted. "You close the
register, and I'll take Everett upstairs and feed him." She

picked up my cat and was up the stairs before I had time to protest.

The idea of seeing Travis again made me smile. Also, it made me wonder what he was doing in McMinnville. I thought his business was in Seattle. I counted out the money and locked the register. I thought briefly of Jim Hampton and his telling kiss. But it had been days since I'd seen him, and I wasn't sure if he was serious or simply trying to get me out of his hair.

"I brought your jacket," Aunt Eloise said. "It's raining."

I put on the jacket, grabbed my purse, and followed Aunt Eloise out the front to her car. When I locked up the store, I always kept one light on that illuminated the product in the front window and hopefully discouraged any thieves.

Getting into her Subaru and buckling my seat belt, I turned to my aunt. She was dolled up, with her hair in a poufy bun, and she wore her black jacket and a purple velvet dress underneath, along with tights and ankle boots. Her earrings were bells, and they twinkled whenever she turned her head.

"How do you know Travis is at the festival?" I asked.

"He texted me," she said. "He wanted to know if we were going. I said, yes, of course. There's a great lecture by one of the doctors who witnessed the alien autopsy. I got us tickets."

"You know those videos are fake, right?" I asked.

"Maybe," she countered. "But that doesn't mean the autopsy didn't happen. This doctor is very credible. I'm really curious about what it was like."

"He has to be ancient," I said. "Didn't the crash happen in the fifties?"

"He's in his nineties and still sharp as a tack," she countered.

"And Travis?"

"He wants to meet us for dinner afterward," she said.

"Why didn't he text me?" I asked.

"I think he wanted to talk about you, so I decided to bring you so he can talk about you to your face."

"Aunt Eloise! If we weren't already driving down the highway, I would make you stop and let me out."

"Oh, come on, dear," she said, keeping her eyes on the road. "Live a little."

I fell silent for a while. Then asked, "What do you think he wanted to talk about?"

"I don't know," she said. "How are you two getting along?"

"Okay, I guess," I said.

"Do you text? Does he call you late at night and chat?"

"Not that it's any of your business, but no. I've been busy getting shot at and trying to figure out who killed Elias."

"Uh-huh," she said.

"What does that mean?" I asked.

"It means you are not building a relationship," she said. "That's what's dating is for. How can you expect to fall in love and get married if you don't work at it?"

"Get married?" I think the spit in my mouth dried up. "To Travis?"

"And what's wrong with that?"

I blinked a few times. "Nothing, I guess. I just never thought about it."

"Well, I have to say, it's high time you did. You aren't getting any younger."

"I'm not even thirty," I said.

"Your twenties are prime baby-making years," she replied.

"Okay, now I don't want to see Travis," I said and crossed my arms over my chest.

"Too late," she said, with a touch too much cheer.

We parked outside the lecture hall and followed the crowd inside. I was handed a program and pointed to my seat, but my mind was on relationships. If I poured my life into my store, would I end up alone like Mr. McGregor?

The lecture was a lot of fun. The speaker was engaging and almost made me believe the autopsy really happened. Almost.

Travis found us as we came out of the lecture. "That was interesting," he said. "What did you think?"

"I thought it was informative," Aunt Eloise said.

"I found it entertaining," I said. "I'm surprised to see you here. I mean, Aunt Eloise said you were meeting us for dinner, but I thought your business was in Seattle." I wasn't sure, but it looked like he blushed.

"Let's go get some dinner," he said and put his hand on my back. "I made us reservations at the Kingpin."

"Good thing," Aunt Eloise said. "With the festival in town, every restaurant is going to be packed. It's why they bring in all the food trucks."

"I hope you don't mind that I took the liberty," he said. "I wanted the chance to have a nice conversation."

"We don't mind," Aunt Eloise said.

I murmured my agreement. Still, I was curious why he had connected with my aunt and hadn't simply called me. I guessed I would soon find out.

Chapter 18

The restaurant was three blocks up and off Main Street. It was inside what used to be a house built in 1910. We stepped up to the wide front porch, and in the foyer met a hostess at a stand.

"Welcome to the Kingpin," she said with a cheery smile. She wore her hair back in a bun. Her chocolate skin shone against her crisp white shirt and black skirt. "Do you have a reservation?"

"We do," Travis said. "It's under Hutton."

"Yes, please follow me."

We followed her through what must have been a front parlor to a cozy dining room. A fire was crackling in the fireplace. Our table was in a little alcove. The hostess pulled out a chair for Aunt Eloise, and Travis pulled out a chair for me. We sat.

"Your waiter is Scott. He'll be here shortly." The hostess turned and left. The restaurant was full, but still quiet enough that we could have a nice conversation. The menus were on the table, beside our plates.

"The prime rib is excellent here," Travis said.

"You're been here before?" I asked. McMinnville was a long way to come for dinner when you lived in Seattle.

"I had a business meeting in town, and we came here," Travis said as he examined the menu.

I tried not to goggle at the prices. "I think I'll have a soup and salad."

Travis looked up. "Dinner is on me, so please treat yourself. Try the prime rib."

"All right," I said. "Sounds good."

The waiter came over, and Travis ordered wine, appetizers, and prime rib for the entire table.

"I'm curious about why you didn't call me," I said and sipped my water. Sometimes I could be blunt, but it had been on my mind. I mean, this felt like a date, but he had asked Aunt Eloise. It didn't make any sense.

"Actually, I have a business proposition for you and your aunt," he said. "I'm sorry to spring it on you during the festival, but tonight was the only opportunity I had. I'm off to China tomorrow for a two-week business trip."

"A business opportunity?" Aunt Eloise said. "You certainly have my attention."

"Well, I know you've bred Havana Brown cats, and I was wondering if you would consider doing it again," he said.

"Oh, dear me," Aunt Eloise said. "I'm afraid I've given up on that hobby. You see, there are so many kitties that need good homes. I could no longer breed cats. Instead we help place homeless cats."

"Yes, in fact, just yesterday we rescued nearly fifty cats," I said. The waiter poured our wine and placed the appetizer of crab-filled endive in the center of the table. "Some will undoubtedly be feral, since the poor dears were barn cats, but some could transition to become house cats."

"I understand," he said. "And I know it costs money to spay and neuter rescue cats and see to their health issues. I'm proposing using the money from the sale of pure-bred cats to help rescue cats." He studied us both for a moment. "There is a place for pure breeds in the world. I'm proposing we carefully select the parents. Keep the breeding pairs to only two litters. Show them and use any winnings to help fund your rescues."

"Why?" I asked.

"What do you mean?" he asked.

"Why cat breeding? Why Aunt Eloise? Why me?" I replied. "Why now?"

"Well, I know your aunt has one of the highest-winning show cats in the nation," he said.

"But I'm not breeding him," she said. "He's too old, and I had him spayed."

"He doesn't have to breed," Travis said. "I'd like to take some stem cells from him and clone him."

"What?" I said.

"Is that even possible?" Aunt Eloise said.

"It is possible," Travis said. "It's why I'm going to China. I'm investing in a company that will clone favorite pets. If I can get some stem cells from your grand champion, then we can make a younger copy. I'll put him in some cat shows to see how he compares. Then we can breed him."

"But the World Cat Federation won't allow a clone to be shown," Aunt Eloise said. "And I'm pretty certain the Cat Fanciers Association won't either."

"I checked, and there is no wording about cloning," he said.

"That's not true; they need a pedigree," Aunt Eloise said.

"And that's what makes this brilliant," he said. "We'll use a surrogate mother with a solid pedigree and use your cat's pedigree. No one will question it."

"But I'll know," Aunt Eloise said as the waiter put down plates of prime rib in front of us and brought dishes of garlic mashed potatoes and brussels sprouts. "I can't do it."

"My investors are willing to pay you one million dollars for the stem cells from your cat. All you have to do is let us harvest some stem cells, and you can use that one million to help your rescue group. Think of the number of cats you can save with that money."

"I don't know," Aunt Eloise said with a shake of her head.

"How do you harvest stem cells?" I asked.

"We take a needle and gather cells from the bone marrow and from the fat. Don't worry, the cat will be under anesthesia and won't feel a thing." He dug into his meal as if he had just offered us the world.

I looked at my aunt. She seemed to be thinking things over. "You can't seriously do this," I said. "It's morally wrong."

"It's a cat," Travis said. "And a miracle, if you think about it."

"We could save a lot of cats with a million dollars," Aunt Eloise said.

I stared at her in horror. My stomach turned, and I pushed my plate away. "We are not making a decision tonight."

"Actually, it's not your decision," Travis said.

"Then why did you want me here?" I asked.

"Because I enjoy your company," he said and sent me a smile that would have melted any woman's heart. "I'm going out of town, and I was hoping to see you before I go."

"Oh," I said. "I wasn't sure. I mean, you haven't called or texted since our last dinner."

"Yeah, sorry about that. I have several deals in the works, and I've been working late. I didn't want to bother you late at night."

"Oh, yes, I can see that," I said. "I've been a bit busy with my anniversary sale and making product."

"Well, I'm glad you two get to have dinner tonight," Aunt Eloise said. "We all share a love of cats. Travis, how is your new kitty doing? Who's taking care of her when you go to China?"

The rest of the conversation was carried by Aunt Eloise and Travis. As I marveled at how well they got along, I also mulled over his offer of a million dollars to be able to take Elton's stem cells to clone. He wasn't wrong. A million dollars could go a long way to helping with cat rescues. I guessed I could see both sides of the equation.

"Can I ask a question?" I broke in after the waiter took away our plates and put dishes of crème brûlée in front of us, along with coffee.

"Sure," Travis said, studying me with his gorgeous gaze.

"Does the US have import laws around cloning? I mean, you're going to create your cat in China, correct?"

"Yes, the cloning procedures will be done in China. We can bring a pregnant cat back to the United States."

"So you just won't mention it's a carrying a clone?"

"It's not a question on the customs form," he said with a smile.

"Why are you wondering?" Aunt Eloise asked.

"I had a thought this afternoon that what is being smuggled in the beehives might have to do with livestock, but my expert thinks the hives are probably too warm."

"Something is being smuggled inside beehives?" Travis asked.

"I think so," I said. "I haven't found any evidence that they are smuggling drugs, so I was thinking about the heat inside a hive and the fact that the hives go from farm to farm."

"And you were thinking semen or cloned eggs?" he asked.

I winced. "I know it sounds crazy. In fact, it's probably the craziest idea I've ever had. I mean, whatever they are smuggling, it has to be worth killing people over. What if the hives aren't too warm?"

"I think it's an extreme idea," he said and frowned at me. He put his hand on my hand on top of the table. "Honey, you're working too hard and really reaching. I'm sorry. I shouldn't have tried to talk business."

I pulled my hand away. Emotions boiled up inside me, emotions I didn't want to express in front of my aunt and a room full of diners. I stood. "Thank you for dinner," my voice was too calm. "Aunt Eloise, I will see you tomorrow."

Grabbing my coat and my purse, I walked to the door. I heard a chair screech and someone follow me. I had to get out into the cool, damp night air before I exploded. Throwing on my coat, I stepped through the door and hurried down the stairs.

"Wren." It was Aunt Eloise, not Travis, who followed me.

"Go enjoy your dessert," I said and pulled out my phone.

"But we drove together."

"I've ordered a driver," I said.

She touched my arm. "I'm sure he didn't realize how he sounded."

"Don't make excuses for him," I said. "He was patronizing and controlling. I'm so mad right now I could spit nails."

The door to the restaurant opened, and Travis stepped out. "Wren—"

"That's my car," I said to my aunt and turned to wave down my driver.

"Wren!" He stepped to the edge of the porch. I walked around to the street side of the car and got in.

"Wren Johnson?" The driver asked.

"Yes," I said.

"For Oceanview?" He started driving, thankfully ignoring Travis.

"Yes, thank you," I said. We drove off, and I didn't look back. I was a grown woman with a successful business, and I was smart. It was all I could do not to slap the man. But I didn't want to go to jail for battery. Instead, I needed to go home and go for a long run.

Chapter 19

Feeling a little nauseous? Honey and ginger will help. Cut peeled ginger root into small pieces. Boil for 5 minutes, strain out the bits, and keep the liquid. Add a teaspoon or more of honey to taste. This tea should work wonders on your upset tummy.

There was something comforting about running in the dark, rainy night. I stayed on the sidewalk along Main Street and turned down the promenade. I would have run on the beach, but it was not illuminated, and I wasn't aware of the tide. What I was aware of was the anger boiling up inside me. No one patronized me and got away with it. The theory of smuggling breeding material and possibly cloning material seemed a little science fiction-y, I agreed, but that wasn't what had made me crazy.

I sped up and sprinted from one end of the mile-long promenade to the other and back. I liked the rain on my face, the steady beating of my heart, and the brisk wind off the ocean. It smelled of salt and ozone and spring.

Counting my breath—in two three four, and out two three four—became a meditation. On my second time up the promenade, a man joined me. It was Jim.

"You should wear more reflective gear when you jog at night," he said as he fell into step beside me.

"I don't need a lecture right now," I said.

"No, I guess you don't," he said. We jogged the length of the promenade south and turned back to the north and turned again before he spoke. "Your aunt texted me."

"Yeah, well, I'm fine," I said and picked up my pace.

"I can see that," he said and stretched his legs, so I had to push again. We raced to the south end of the promenade before I raised my hands in protest. By my count, I'd jogged over five miles. I was too tired to be mad at anyone.

"I think someone's been following me," I said as I stretched my calves.

"Any idea who?" he asked.

"No." I took off walking. "It started as a feeling. I'd catch a glimpse of someone out of the corner of my eye. I think it's a guy, but I can't tell you anything more than that."

"Have you seen him tonight?"

"No," I said. "Earlier today, but not tonight."

He stopped me by putting a hand on my arm. "How often do you feel the presence of this person?"

"Often enough," I said. "So far, they haven't scared me. But I worry that they are hurting the people I'm meeting with."

"You think that the killer or killers are following you and hurting people you are questioning about Elias." He had figured it out fast.

"Maybe," I said with a slight frown. "I can't say for

sure. It's why I didn't tell you before. It's more a feeling than anything I can prove."

"Listen, I know you want to help Klaus and get to the bottom of this mystery, but it makes me very nervous that you seem to be so involved with people who are getting hurt. And you were almost shot doing it."

"I know," I said. "But I was just bruised, and at this point you are a broken record."

"A broken record?" He looked confused.

"Oh, it's something Aunt Eloise says. Apparently, when they played vinyl records, sometimes they would get stuck in a spot, and you had to actually move the needle to get it to stop repeating itself."

"Huh," he said.

"I know," I said. "I could never get into vinyl records." We walked down darkened Main Street, our breath misting in the air as the fog settled in. "I have this crazy idea. I mean, I know it's crazy, and I wouldn't say anything, but—"

"I've been looking into drug smuggling in the bee-hives," he cut me off. "There isn't a new drug in the area, and the hives that have been vandalized aren't really near any drug dealers."

"So, I did have this other really out-there idea," I said.

"You just don't give up, do you?" he asked, his blue eyes twinkling in the glare of the streetlights.

"You like that," I teased. "It gives you something to complain about."

"What is this theory?"

We made it to the back of the shop, and I unlocked the door, opened it, and turned on the light. "Let's get some water first," I said. After I locked the door behind us, we went up to the apartment. The door was cracked open. "That's weird."

"Let me go in first," Jim said and motioned for me to stand aside. I wasn't going to argue. I never left my apartment unlocked. My heart started pounding, and my mouth dried up. My thoughts went immediately to Everett.

"Make sure Everett is okay," I said as he pushed the door open and flicked on the light.

I held my breath and listened to hear if anyone was inside.

Jim disappeared through the door. I stood there, tensely listening and trying to figure out what I would do if someone came running out of the apartment. There was a fire escape on the outside, but mostly people came and went through the door in front of me.

After what seemed forever, Jim called out. "It's clear."

I went inside. "Everett?" I called. The entire apartment was tossed. The kitchen cupboards and drawers were open, and dishes lay broken on the floor and the counters. The pillows had been thrown off the couch; the couch and coffee table were turned over, and the bottom of the couch was slashed. I went straight to the closet where Everett's favorite box was.

The closet was open, and the top shelf completely empty. The coats were in a pile on the floor, and Everett's box was missing. "Everett?" I heard panic in my voice.

"Found him," Jim said as he came out of the bedroom with Everett in his arms.

"Everett!" I raced to him.

Meow.

I pulled my kitty out of Jim's arms and held him to my heart. "Are you safe, my baby?" I said.

Meow.

"Whoever did this was looking for something," Jim said.

"I don't know what," I said. "Any idea how they got in? I keep the door locked and the windows closed when I'm not home."

He looked at my front door. "It looks like they broke in here."

"I didn't notice anything wrong with the back door. The only other way in is through the store front door. How did Porsche not hear them?"

"They must have come in through the front and waited for her to close up before they broke in," he surmised and pulled out his phone. "I'm calling the station and reporting this."

"Do you think it's connected to Elias's murder?" I asked.

"There's no telling, but they were certainly looking for something," he said. "Did you find anything in the hives?"

"I haven't been close enough to the hives," I said.

"Just the people who are getting attacked," he surmised.

"Yes," I said and kissed my kitty.

"Call your Aunt Eloise," he said. "It might be a good idea for you and Everett to spend the night at her house."

"She's in McMinnville," I said. "She and a friend invited me to dinner."

"You didn't go?" He tipped his head.

"I did, but I left and took a car service home."

"So she could be home by now," he said. "Call her or Porsche."

"I'll call Porsche," I said.

"Trouble in the family?" He raised an eyebrow.

"We had a disagreement," I said with a shrug. "But that reminds me what I wanted to tell you. What if they aren't smuggling drugs in the beehives. What if it's cloning or some sort of genetically modified animal husbandry? Think about it a minute. The bees keep the hives at a fairly constant temperature, and the hives move from farm to farm."

He studied me for a moment. "It's an interesting idea, but why smuggle?"

"Cloning isn't exactly approved, especially if the farm wants to meet the non-GMO label. Also, thoroughbreds cannot be artificially inseminated and maintain their label, but if a clone is grown, then they might not race it, but they could certainly use it as a stud, and it would bring in high dollars."

"I don't think anyone is going to use clones," he said. "That's crazy."

"Except that at dinner tonight, Travis Hutton asked my aunt if he could clone her grand-champion cat so he could use it for breeding purposes."

"I thought she wasn't breeding Havana Browns anymore and instead concentrating on rescues."

"That's the thing. Travis said he would keep the breeding highly selective and would pay my aunt's rescue a million dollars for the cells needed to start his cloning," I said.

"A million dollars is a lot of money," he said. "Why did you leave?"

"I disagree with cloning," I said and hugged Everett. "It's just too morally wrong for me. I don't care about the money."

"Maybe there's someone who agrees with you," Jim said.

I looked at him. "I hadn't thought about that. You think the killer is actually not trying to get what is being smuggled but to destroy it?"

"We need to look at all of the vandalized hives. There has to be at least one, if not two people who are connected."

"Don't tell me you're back to Klaus as a suspect," I said.

"No, Klaus has an alibi for all but Elias's murder and hive vandalism," he said. "It doesn't mean that I've ruled Klaus out for Elias's murder just yet, but it does put him lower on the suspect list."

There was a loud knock on the downstairs door, and I nearly jumped out of my skin. Everett jumped out of my arms and went down the stairs. The knock sounded again.

"Stay here," Jim said and went down the stairs.

"It's probably just the police," I said, standing on the landing at the top of the stairs. I was glad for the light above.

"Who is it?" Jim asked. I heard a muffled answer, and Jim opened the door. "Great, guys, come on in," he said.

"Don't let the cat out," I called out as I took the stairs down to find two uniformed policemen entering.

Jim turned and had Everett in his arms. "He's safe," he said to me. "Why don't you take him and stay down here while we investigate."

I took Everett and frowned. More strangers in my home.

"We'll be careful with your things," he said. "But we need to take pictures and prepare a report. Why don't you call Porsche?"

"Fine," I said as I watched him lead the police up to

my apartment. "Come on, Everett," I said. "Let's make some tea and call Porsche."

I filled the downstairs electric kettle with water and turned it on. Then I dialed Porsche and put her on speaker.

"Hey, girl, what's up?" Porsche said.

"Do you have room for Everett and me to come spend the night?" I asked her.

"Sure, always," she replied. "What's going on?"

"Someone broke into my apartment," I said.

"Oh, no. Are you okay?"

"I'm fine," I said. "I was out running."

"This late?" she said. "Well, thank goodness you weren't home. Did they go through the shop, too?"

I looked up. I hadn't thought about the store. "Oh, my goodness," I said.

"You haven't checked the store?" she asked. "Are you alone?"

"No, the police are upstairs. I was with Jim when we found the apartment."

"And he didn't check the shop?"

"Well, no," I said and looked around. There was always a low light on after we closed, just above the merchandise shelves, the door, and the register so anyone walking by could see if anyone is inside. The hope was that it would keep people from breaking and entering. I suppose I should have put in cameras, but I was a bit old school and hated to intrude on people's privacy.

"Turn on all the lights," Porsche said.

My kettle started whistling as I turned on all the lights. Nothing in the shop seemed out of place. "Lights are on," I said. "At first glance, it looks like whoever broke into the apartment didn't hurt the shop." I poured myself a cup of caffeine-free herbal tea. Everett circled my legs.

"Don't you find that strange?" Porsche asked. There was a knock at the back door. I went to the door and peered out. It was Porsche.

I opened the door. "You got here fast," I said and hung up my phone. Porsche stepped inside and shook off her jacket. The damp from the fog flew off her coat and made little puddles at her feet. "Come on inside. Can I get you a cup of tea?"

"Yes, please," she said, taking in my running outfit and damp hair. "You do realize it's eleven p.m." She made a sweeping glance around the shop.

I poured the tea, and Everett sat on the counter, his tail twitching. Porsche came over and took a cup of tea from my hand. "Why were you out running? I mean, it's good you weren't home when they broke in . . . wait, how did they get in? The back door didn't look busted." We both walked to the door and stared at the lock.

"I guess I could have left it unlocked," I said. My blood ran cold at the thought that I might have let them in. "But I carry my key when I run, so I don't think I did."

Porsche opened the door and examined it. "It doesn't look like it was busted, so they had to know how to pick a lock."

"Or they had a key," Jim said as he walked down the stairs toward us. "How many people have a key to your shop?"

"Just three," I said. "Four, if you count the landlord."

"I'm assuming you, Porsche, and Aunt Eloise are the three?" Jim said. He turned his gaze toward the fully lit shop. "Is anything down here missing?"

"Shouldn't you have checked that before leaving Wren

and Everett alone down here?" Porsche asked him. She gave him the stink eye.

He put his hands in the air. "Yes, I should have, but we saw the apartment first, and I was concentrating on that."

"Humph," Porsche said and took a sip of tea.

"Nothing seems touched down here," I said. "The register hasn't been tampered with. It's still locked up tight. It wouldn't matter anyway. We don't keep more than one hundred dollars in it at night."

The back door flung open, and Aunt Eloise came in dripping rain and curiosity. "What is going on? Why are all the lights on? Is that a police car outside?"

"My apartment was broken into while I was out on a run," I said. "They ransacked it."

"Oh, my goodness," she said and covered her mouth with her hands. She rushed to me and gave me a hug. "Are you all right?"

"Yes, I'm fine," I said. "Jim—Officer Hampton—was with me when I came home. My biggest concern was for Everett. We found him, and he seems to be safe."

"And they didn't steal from the store? That makes no sense." She opened her coat and strode around the store.

"We checked, and there doesn't seem to be anything missing," I said. Then I turned to Jim. "Can I go upstairs and pack an overnight case?"

"I'll go up with you," Aunt Eloise said. "I need to see how bad things are in your apartment."

"That's not necessary," I said. "Tomorrow I'm calling a security service so this never happens again. Besides, I'm spending the night at Porsche's place. Everett and I will be just fine."

"Porsche's place, not mine?" Aunt Eloise looked startled.

"I'm not sure how I feel about you making that deal with Travis, and until I come to grips with it, I'd rather not stay with you."

"Deal with Travis?" Porsche perked up.

"I'm not doing it," Aunt Eloise said with a wave of her hand. "We'll just have to find the money for the recue organization elsewhere."

"So you're turning down a million dollars," I said in disbelief.

"A million dollars?" Porsche repeated. "What? Why? How?"

"It was just a proposition, and I turned him down after you left," Aunt Eloise said. "Now don't be silly. You and Everett can stay in my guest room tonight."

"You'll be busy with your rescue kitties," I said. "Really, Porsche has room for us for tonight. We'll talk more tomorrow."

"Well," Aunt Eloise lifted her chin. "Then I'll talk to you tomorrow. I believe I have the evening shift."

"Great. See you then," I said and went upstairs to find the two policemen hard at work photographing my apartment. I gave them my version of events so they could write up an incident report. They gave me a case number, and then I packed an overnight case and escorted them out of my apartment and down the stairs.

Aunt Eloise had left, and Jim was talking to Porsche. Everett was in Jim's arms, purring up a storm. I took a deep breath, pasted on a smile, and stepped toward them.

"I think that's it for tonight," I said. "I've ensured all the windows and doors are locked."

"We should keep all the lights on in the shop," Porsche said. "It's nearly midnight. Let's get you to my place and settled in."

Jim handed Everett to me. "I'll be back tomorrow, and we can talk over theories on who broke into your apartment and what they might have been looking for."

He walked us out the back door, and I locked up. Jim jogged off toward his place, and I climbed into Porsche's SUV with Everett and my overnight bag.

"I don't like it that your apartment has been broken into twice this year," Porsche said. "You are going to get security in tomorrow, right?"

"I'll order one of those systems with motion-sensor lights and cameras online tonight," I said. "They'll deliver by tomorrow, or I'll go pick them up. So yes, if anyone breaks in again, I'll know."

"Good. This is scary, considering all the damage someone is doing to people around you."

"I know," I said with a sigh. "I need you and Aunt Eloise to be as safe as possible. It would kill me if either one of you were harmed."

"Don't worry about me," Porsche said. "Jason likes gadgets. We have the entire house run by voice control."

"You don't worry that people are spying on you through those machines?" I asked.

Porsche laughed. "No, we've set up all the precautions and privacy settings. The boys love that they can video-chat with my mom and ask the voice controller homework questions."

I sighed. "I agree. It's time I entered the modern era."

Chapter 20

I was up at six a.m., and Everett and I walked back to the shop. I liked a morning walk, and so did my cat. The sky was clear today and smelled like the ocean and spring. We went into the store through the front. I locked it behind me and took off Everett's leash. It was quiet in the shop. I did a quick walk-through to ensure that nothing had been touched. It seemed good until I passed my beehive.

Someone had taken something heavy and tried to smash the glass. The bees were agitated, but unharmed. The glass was safety glass, made to crack but not break. I swallowed the bile that rose in my throat. Whoever had broken in had left a clear message—that they hated my bees.

But why only touch the hive and my apartment? I pulled out my phone and dialed Jim's number.

"Hampton," he said, with the rasp of sleep in his voice.

"I'm sorry to wake you," I said.

It sounded like he sat up. "Wren, is everything okay?"

"No," I said. "I just came back to the store and was double-checking that we didn't miss anything last night."

"And?"

"Someone tried to smash the glass on my beehive," I said. "Looks like they used a hammer or something heavy. The bees are fine, but I think we need to add this to the report."

"I'll send a patrol over there to document it," he said. "Are you okay?"

"Yeah," I said. "I couldn't sleep."

"That's understandable," he said. "This is probably connected to Elias's murder, now that we know your bees were attacked. It's a good thing you called me. I'll make sure a patrol comes and checks on you every few hours."

"Do you really think that's necessary? I mean, clearly, they figured out I didn't have anything."

"I've got patrols on Mr. McGregor and the Reichs," he said. "I think it's sound practice to have patrols on you as well."

"I've ordered some security cameras and one of those connected-house things. They're supposed to arrive this morning around ten. I'm going to call the locksmith as soon as they open and have all the locks changed as well." I paced in front of my bees. "Now I have to call in replacement glass for the beehive, and that means I'm going to have to close the shop for a few hours while the glass store people replace it."

"We'll figure this out," Jim assured me. "Do you want me to come over and go through the place again? I can be there in five minutes."

I winced. "Could you?" I asked. "I mean, we didn't see that the glass was cracked last night, so someone could potentially be in the shop or my apartment, right?" I walked to the front door and leaned my back on it, in case I had to run.

"I'm on my way," he said. "Why don't you and Everett go down to the coffee shop and pick up some coffee and donuts. Then I'll meet you at the front door."

"Okay," I said and looked around the shop. "Thank you."

"My pleasure," he said.

I hung up the phone, grabbed Everett, put his harness and leash back on, went outside, locked the front door, and power-walked to the coffee shop. It was early, but the place was buzzing with people grabbing coffee and donuts before work. I felt safer in a small crowd. People oohed and aahed over Everett, and within ten minutes, I was carrying a bag of donuts and two cups of coffee. I had creamer and honey in my apartment.

"Wren, yoo hoo, Wren!"

I turned to see Mrs. Berber waving at me. She was dressed in yoga pants and an oversize, hooded sweatshirt. "Good morning," I said.

Meow. Everett had to greet her, too.

"I saw your store lights were on really early this morning. Is everything okay?" she asked and bent down to pet Everett.

"Yes, we're fine," I said. "There was an issue with my hive. But the bees are safe."

"Huh. I thought I saw a police car behind the shop last night," she said with a raised eyebrow.

"I'm sure it will be published in the police blotter," I

said with a sigh. "Someone broke into my apartment last night. But I'm fine. Everett is fine."

Meow.

"Well, Oceanview certainly has seen its fair share of crime lately," she said and crossed her arms. "Do you think it's because you're investigating Elias's death?"

"Wren, there you are," Jim called from across the street. "Are you letting my coffee get cold?"

"I've got go, Mrs. Berber," I said. "Have a great day." Everett and I hurried to Jim. I felt Mrs. Berber's interested gaze on my back. Oceanview was a small town. Very little went unnoticed.

"How's Mrs. Berber?" Jim asked and took the paper tray with the coffee cups from me.

"She's looking for firsthand information for the rumor mill." We walked back to the store, and I opened the door.

Officer Greer and Officer Hayes followed us inside and studied the cracked but not shattered glass in front of the hive.

"Sorry we missed this last night," Officer Greer said as he took pictures. "Are you sure it wasn't done after we left?"

"I didn't see any sign of a break-in," I said and let Everett off his leash and halter. "It does give me a chill to think someone might have done this while I was sleeping over at Porsche's." I glanced at my phone. It was now eight a.m. "I'm going to call a locksmith and change all the locks.

"That's a good idea," Jim said. "I'd like to have a patrol stop by here on the hour, at least for today."

"Any idea why they might have done this?" Officer Greer asked.

"No," I said with a shake of my head.

The front-door bells jangled, and Aunt Eloise walked in. "Good morning. What's going on now? Did you catch last night's vandal?"

"No," I said. "I came home to find this." I waved at the cracked glass. "I didn't see it last night."

Aunt Eloise took a look at the damage. "I didn't see it either, which means whoever broke into your apartment came back."

"That's why the police are here," I said. "I'm calling a locksmith right now."

"I'll call a security company," Aunt Eloise said. "I know you said you would order cameras, but I think this is important enough to get a professional out here to install things today."

I made a face.

"She's not wrong," Jim said as he opened the box of donuts.

"Fine," I said and looked at Jim. "Is there one you trust?"

"Call Dominic's Security," Officer Hayes said. "They respond quickly and will assess the situation, and their dispatch is local."

"Dispatch?" I asked.

"Yes, they are staffed twenty-four-seven in case an alarm is triggered," Officer Hayes said.

I looked at Aunt Eloise, who said, "Do it."

Leaving Jim to speak to the officers as they wrote up my second case, I dialed the number of the locksmith who had installed the locks for me before I'd opened. They agreed they could be over at my place by ten a.m. to change all the locks. I thanked them and turned back to my aunt.

"I asked Dominic's to put a rush on things," she said.

"They gave me a one o'clock appointment time. Now what are we going to do about the hive glass? Clearly, we can't have customers come in while it gets changed."

"I'll make a call to the glass store and have them come over and take a look. But no bees will be getting into the store, so I think we can open on time. We'll play it by ear then."

"You're going to have to call a bee wrangler to smoke your bees to keep them from swarming once the wall is opened," Aunt Eloise said.

"I know what to do," I said.

Officer Greer stepped up and handed me a form. "Here's a copy of your second case file. Officer Hayes and I have got to do our rounds."

"Thanks for coming by," I said.

"Thank you for the donuts," Officer Hayes said. He tipped his hat, and the two men left.

Jim stood, leaning on the counter and sipping his coffee. He wore a pair of jeans and a black T-shirt with the police logo on it.

"It's going to be a busy day," I said with a sigh. "And more shopping time lost."

"We can run a special online and see if we can't raise your profit numbers a bit," Aunt Eloise said.

"That's a good idea," I said. "I know I scheduled you to work the later shift, but since you're here, can you open the store? I need to go upstairs and shower and change and call the glass guys and find a bee wrangler. The ones I know are a bit busy with all the vandalisms."

"Do you need anything more from me?" Jim asked. "I can stay and watch the security guy for you."

I sent him a quick smile. "No, thanks. I know you have a murder to solve."

"Okay," he said and came over and brushed a kiss on my temple, causing a tingling sensation down my spine. "Call me anytime you think anything is funky, okay?"

"Of course," I said and watched him walk out the front door with his coffee cup in hand.

"Mmm-hmm," Aunt Eloise said with a nod. "So Travis is off the table."

"What do you mean?" I asked, drawing my eyebrows together.

"You and Jim Hampton," she said as she covered her phone with her hand.

"Are friends," I said. "Are you on hold?"

"Yes, she's checking their schedule to see if she can't get someone out here right away."

"Fine," I said. "I'm going upstairs. I've got to clean up my apartment and take a shower."

"Just text me if you need anything," Aunt Eloise said with a waggle of her fingers.

I rolled my eyes and went upstairs, unlocked my door, let Everett in, and locked it behind me. The place was a complete mess.

Meow.

"I know," I said. "I wonder if they were trying to annoy me or looking for something. If they were looking for something, what could it be?"

I grabbed my broom, my dustpan, a mop, and a dust rag and started from the door, moved into the kitchen, then the small living room, and then the den. Nothing seemed to be missing except my current murder board. I frowned. If it was the killer harassing me, he now had my murder board and everything I'd connected to Elias's murder.

I didn't think that was a good thing.

It took four hours to set my home to rights. I had ended in the bathroom, so I could shower, apply makeup, and get dressed in jeans and a Let It Bee T-shirt. I left Everett in his favorite box back in the closet and stepped out to find a big man in a white uniform coming up the steps. "Oh," I said and put my hand on my racing heart. "You startled me."

"Sorry," he said. "I'm Harry Stone, the locksmith working on changing your locks. I've already done the front and the back doors. I went ahead and added dead bolts so anyone who tries to break in has to go through two locks."

"Great!" I said.

He went to work on my apartment locks. "Do you want a chain on this door as well? And I see you don't have a peephole."

"Yes," I said. "That would be great."

I stood on the landing and watched him work. When he was done, he handed me a ring of keys. "That's two for each lock. See these colored dots on the key?"

"Yes."

"That's how you tell which key goes to which lock. I left a color-coded magnet with your aunt downstairs."

"Wonderful," I said. I locked the door to my apartment and followed him downstairs, where he wrote up his bill. I paid him with the store credit card.

"That should help keep you safe," he said. "You ladies have a nice day."

He left, and I saw that there were a couple of customers browsing candles, so I took Aunt Eloise by the arm and pulled her to the back corner, where I could keep an eye on things but we could talk privately.

"Have we been busy?" I asked.

"Mostly lookie-loos coming to see the cracked glass,

and to try to get me to talk about the break-in," Aunt Eloise said. "You were upstairs a long time."

"It took forever to clean the place up. They dumped out all my food and cat litter. What a mess." I frowned and shook my head. "But I did notice one thing that was taken."

"Oh, no, what?"

"My murder board," I said. "The one that held all the information we'd gathered so far on Elias's murder."

"Oh, that's not good," she echoed my sentiment. "We're going to have to find a new place to keep those things. You know, we could use my back shed."

"That might not be a bad idea," I agreed. "We should meet after closing and try to piece it back together."

The door bells chimed, and a man in a security uniform entered. "Can you keep an eye on things until Porsche gets here?"

"Sure thing," Aunt Eloise said.

I went up to the security guy, who was looking around at the windows and the ceiling. "Hello, I'm Wren Johnson, owner."

"Steve Smarsh, Dominic's Security," he said and shook my hand. "I've got an order to install a security package."

"Yes, we were broken into last night," I said with a shake of my head. "I'm going to need motion-sensor lights, cameras, window sensors, the works," I said.

"Sure thing," he said and spotted the beehive and took a step back. "Do you know that glass is cracked?"

"Yes, it happened last night. That's the reason we need security."

He made a face. "I'm allergic to bees. Can they get inside?"

"No," I reassured him. "It's the kind of glass that won't shatter. My insurance wouldn't let me have the hive without it."

"Okay," he said. "I'll look around down here and up-stairs, draw up a plan, and get your approval before I start setting up the system. I'm surprised you didn't have one before."

"Oceanview is a small town," I said. "I didn't think I needed it."

"Right," he said. "Walk me through the store."

I walked him through the inside and the outside, and even took him up to my apartment. He drew up a pretty aggressive plan that included motion sensors, cameras, and window and door alarms. I agreed to everything but cameras inside my apartment. I didn't like the idea of being watched in my own home; I didn't care how secure he promised me it would be.

When he left, there was a knock at the back door. I hurried back and peered out to see Porsche standing there. I opened the door to let her inside.

"My key didn't work," she complained as she came in-side.

"I changed all the locks," I said, "and we will soon have a new security system installed with cameras."

"That was fast," she said and took off her jacket and hung it up on the rack by the door.

"When I got home this morning, I discovered someone had tried to smash the beehive. Luckily, I had had them install shatterproof glass."

"Wow," Porsche said. "They had to have done that last night because I think I would have noticed it."

"I agree," I said. "I called Jim, and he said he thought someone had been in the store after we left last night. So, new locks and dead bolts." I held up the heavy key ring. "When we close up tonight, I'll distribute them and train you guys on how the security system works."

"Good," she said. "I think Jason will feel better knowing you've beefed up security."

We walked to the front to meet with Aunt Eloise. "Hey, Eloise," Porsche said. "Have we been busy?"

Aunt Eloise's mouth formed a thin line. "Mostly people coming in to see the damage and talk about the recent crime wave."

"Not a lot of buyers?" Porsche asked.

"I'm afraid not," Aunt Eloise said.

"That's fine," I said. "I need to go out to the Reichs' and pick up supplies. I hear Paul is out of the ICU, and Sylvia said to text her and she'll run home to get me the supplies out of the shed."

"Are you sure you want to go out there alone?" Aunt Eloise asked. "Last time you went, you were shot."

"I was bruised by a bullet, not shot. Besides, I need supplies," I said, "and they could certainly use the money. I'm pretty sure insurance won't pay for everything Paul has gone through."

"Call Jim Hampton and see if you can't get an escort out there," Porsche suggested. "It wouldn't hurt."

"I don't need to be watched over like a small child. Sylvia Reich has been back and forth by herself and been perfectly safe."

Aunt Eloise just looked at me and raised one eyebrow. "She is not looking for a killer."

I rolled my eyes and called Jim. Sometimes, Aunt Eloise did make a good point.

Easy Crustless Honey Cheesecake

Ingredients:
1½ cups plain Greek yogurt; 0% or 2% will work.
1 cup cream cheese
1 teaspoon vanilla
¼ cup lemon juice
⅓ cup honey
3 egg whites
¼ cup cornstarch
1 tablespoon lemon zest

Directions:
Preheat oven to 350°F. Whisk together the yogurt and cream cheese in a large bowl. Add the remaining ingredients and stir. (It's okay if it looks watery.) Pour the mixture into a greased 8- x 8-inch springform pan. Bake for 40 minutes. Remove from oven and chill in fridge for 8 hours or overnight. Remove from pan. Cut into 8 slices and serve. Enjoy!

Chapter 21

"Thanks for taking me out to the Reichs'," I said.

"I'm glad you called," Jim said. We were in his black pickup truck. He still wore dark jeans and his police T-shirt. Apparently, it was his day off. He picked me up fifteen minutes after I called him, and I let Sylvia know we were headed out to get the supplies.

We pulled up and got out of the truck.

"I don't see the car," I said.

"You said she was on her way?" Jim asked.

"Yes," I said. "She must just have not gotten here yet."

He knocked on the door twice, but there was no answer. He tried the screen door, but it was locked.

"She'll be here," I said and headed toward the barn.

"Where are you going?" he asked as he caught up with me.

"I'm going to check on the bees," I said. "I know no

one has looked after them since Paul was shot. And besides, I want to see how Elias's bees are doing."

"How will you know which hives are Elias's?" Jim asked.

"Elias liked to brand his logo on the hive before introducing the queen," I said.

"Huh," Jim said as we rounded the barn. "And you're just going to walk up to the hives with no protection and look for the brand?"

"Of course not," I said and opened the back entrance to the barn, where Paul kept gloves and his beekeeping hats. "I'll wear a netted hat and gloves. They don't want to hurt you, you know." I put on the hat and gloves, then walked slowly toward the hives.

"Wait," Jim said. "Let me walk the perimeter first."

"Why?" I asked. "There's no way anyone but Sylvia knows we're out here."

"Let's not take any chances," Jim said and walked off to the left.

I shook my head, crossed my arms, and frowned as I watched him play hero and walk to the tree line and then along the perimeter. When he was in line with the hives and still walking the perimeter, I figured it would be safe to head toward the hives. After all, if someone shot at me, Jim would be there to catch them.

I walked straight and steady toward the hives. Paul had six hives, and I counted nine hives. Which meant they must have brought even Elias's empty hive to Paul's place. Maybe Paul was going to try seeding a new colony.

As I got closer, I noticed that none of Elias's three hives had any bees around them. That made me sad. It meant Elias's two queens must have died or evacuated. Getting closer still, I saw it was more than three hives dormant. In fact, it appeared that all the hives, even Paul's, were lost. Complete colony collapse. It broke my heart.

"There's no one in the area," Jim called as he approached. "I don't see very many bees for all the hives."

I took off my hat. I counted maybe ten live bees. "Something happened to the bees. They don't just collapse this quickly. Not this number of bees."

Elias's hives were nearly gone. They were on the east end and completely without any live bees. There was one hive in the center around which a few bees flew. "It's almost as if someone poisoned them all."

"With what?" Jim asked.

"Maybe something aerosol," I said. "I don't know. We need to get a bee expert out here to find out what happened."

"You think this is related to Paul's being shot?"

"I don't think it was a coincidence," I said.

"Hello? Wren?"

I turned to see Sylvia walking toward us from her car, which was parked next to Jim's truck. "Hey, Sylvia," I waved. Jim and I met her beside the barn. "I borrowed some gear from the back of your barn so I could check on the bees. But the bees all seem to have disappeared. What happened?"

"They disappeared?" Sylvia looked and sounded as horrified as I did. She took off toward the hives. I followed her. "I don't understand. Where are all the bees?" Her eyes were wide. She covered her mouth with trembling fingers. "They could all be out gathering pollen, right?"

"No, you know that if they were out, there would be bees coming and going, dropping off the pollen."

She turned to me and Jim. "Who would have taken the bees and left the hive? Can you even do that?"

"When I was an apprentice bee wrangler, we would sometimes take out the frames, from the inside of the hive, to move the nurse bees to fortify a colony," I said. "So, yes, they could be moved."

"Why would anyone want to take our bees?" she asked. "I don't understand."

"I have no idea," I said. "But I think we need to call a couple of wranglers out here to see what's going on."

"I need to stay with Paul," she said. "I thought the police were patrolling the property."

"I doubt they would have come this far back," Jim said. "Usually, we watch the house and the barn. They may not have noticed fewer bees."

"I don't know what to do," she said. "I need to get back to Paul. Wren, the supplies you need are on the back porch. I'll open it up for you."

"Do we have permission to study what is going on with your hives?" Jim asked.

"Yes, of course, whatever, just don't tell Paul yet," she said. "He needs to think about healing, not bees."

"Of course," Jim said.

Sylvia walked away toward the house, and I turned to Jim. "If they moved the bees, they most likely moved the nurse bees in the middle of the day when most of the worker bees are out."

"Right," he said. "So whoever did this might have done it during the day. Which means the neighbors might have seen something."

"Or even the patrol," I said. "Ten acres is a lot of land to keep an eye on." He pulled out his cell phone to make calls, and I hurried after Sylvia. I needed my supplies, and she needed the check and to get back to Paul. All I could hope was that the bees had been moved and not poisoned.

After I loaded the supplies of beeswax, royal jelly, and raw honey into the back of the truck, I handed Sylvia a check, gave her a hug, and was waving her off as Jim walked up.

"I called in a few favors," Jim said. "I've got two bee experts from Oregon State heading this way, along with a poison specialist to see whether the bees had been killed or stolen. Some of the frames were missing."

"I know it seems weird to take the bees and leave the hives," I said. "Which means it's more likely someone destroyed the bees. I just couldn't tell her that. Did you see her face?"

"Maybe they took the bees to get whatever they're smuggling out of the hives without vandalizing the hives so that the patrols wouldn't realize anything was wrong."

"Until Paul is back up on his feet in a few weeks," I said. "That makes the most sense."

"I want to stay until the patrol car gets here. I want people out here around the clock until our specialists come. Can you stay that long?"

I looked at my phone. It was nearly four p.m. "Sure, I just need to call the glass company and set up an appointment to replace the glass on my hive."

"Great, you do that, and I'll take another walk around," he said.

I called and made the appointment for the next afternoon. I'd have to close the shop, smoke the bees to calm them while the new glass was installed by the glass company. This time I ordered double panes, so if anyone ever tried to break the glass again, it would be easier to repair.

When I had had the hive designed, I never imagined anyone would take a blunt-force object, like a hammer, to it. Now, I knew better.

I called the store.

"Let It Bee, this is Porsche. How can I help you?"

"Hey, Porsche. It's Wren," I said. "I'm going to be a little later than I thought." I filled her in on the findings and our wait for patrol.

"Who would do that to bees?" Porsche asked.

"Someone who is more interested in themselves than the world around them," I said.

"Well, maybe they did just move the bees," she said. "One can hope, right?"

"Yes," I replied.

"Oh, listen, call Aunt Eloise. She called and left a message for you to call her as soon as you can."

I frowned. "Okay, do you know why? I thought she was staying at the store until later so we can go over all the new security features."

"She left to get lunch and run some errands," Porsche said. "She called a few minutes ago. Which does seem odd. I mean, why didn't she call you?"

"That does seem odd," I said. "Did she sound okay?"

"No, she sounded strange. I asked her if she was all right, she said yes and that she was hoping to catch you at the store. Then she asked me to have you call her the minute you got back. But since it might be a while, you might want to give her a call."

"Thanks," I said. "I'll do that." A patrol car pulled into the driveway as I pressed END on my phone. The lights were flashing, but there was no siren. Jim went over and talked to the officers in the car.

They turned off the lights and got out. I stayed at the pickup and let Jim do his thing and called Aunt Eloise.

Her phone rang and rang and then went to voice mail. "Eloise Johnson. Please leave me a message, and I'll do my best to get back to you."

"Hey, Aunt Eloise, I'm running late, and Porsche said you wanted me to call. Please call me back or text. Love you." I pressed END.

A sedan pulled up, and inside was Bill Chechup, president of the Tillamook chapter of Beekeepers Association of America, followed by a crime-scene van. "Hello, Bill," I said and stuck out my hand. "Good to see you."

"Wren, I got a call that Paul's bees are missing?" He shook my hand.

"Yes," I said. "I stopped by to pick up some supplies and went to check on the bees. You know that Paul has been recovering for a few days, and Sylvia hasn't left his side except to come home, shower, and change clothes."

"Yes, I heard," he said and started walking to the hives, which were about fifty yards from the back of the barn. "Devastating tragedy. So you checked on the hives, and . . . ?"

I filled him in on the state in which we found them. "So we feel there are two options."

"Someone stole the bees, or someone poisoned the bees," he said with a nod.

"Yes, that's why the forensics guys are here as well as you," I said.

"And you're sure that these are Paul's hives?" he asked. "It could merely be that they took the live hives and left empty hives."

"I didn't think about that," I said. "I do know that Elias's hives are here. I saw his brand on the bottom corner."

"All three hives?" Bill asked. "I thought one hive collapsed after they were vandalized."

"Paul was trying to start a new colony in the hive."

We approached the hives. "Hang on," Jim said as he strode quickly toward us. "Let's have the forensics guys be the first to go in. We don't want to contaminate the place."

"Contaminate?" Bill asked.

"We might be able to get DNA samples and fingerprints, and we'll check for poison," a man in a crime-scene T-shirt and cargo pants said. He had brought his kit with him. First, he put on protective gear, then was led into the hive area. Only a small handful of bees buzzed around. He walked a grid, fingerprinting each hive, swabbing them, and then taking off the tops. "This hive is empty of all frames," he said. Then he moved to the next hive and the next as he meticulously checked each hive. None of them had frames inside.

Finally, after an hour, he stepped out and took off the protective gear and carefully labeled each bag with the number of the beehive in the grid.

"Do you think they were killed or just transplanted into new hives?" I asked.

"There are missing frames, so it looks like they were taken, but we'll let the lab go over the results," he said.

Bill and I walked over to the hives. The investigator had left the tops off of all the hives. A few bees buzzed around, looking for their colony. It was tragic to me.

Bill blew out a long breath. "This could be a new way to vandalize the hives."

"So it doesn't match the other vandalisms?" Jim asked.

"No," Bill replied. "The others were more smash and grab. Here they took the time to smoke the bees and move the frames."

I studied the ground around the bees; there were tracks from a car or, better yet, a pickup truck. I pointed them out to Jim. "I would guess that, with the Reichs gone, they simply drove up, smoked the bees, and transferred the frames into hives in their truck."

Jim shot pictures of the tire-tread impressions on the ground. He used his keys to indicate width.

"It does take some skill to do this kind of work if you want to keep the hives healthy," Bill said.

"Unless they didn't care what happened to the bees," I said. "They may have wanted the patrols not to notice that the bees were vandalized."

"Why would they do that?" Bill asked.

"I have a theory that they're smuggling something in the hives. You have to admit that police and police dogs don't check beehives," I said.

"Well, that's a creative theory," he said. His expression was a bit odd but only for a second. If I hadn't been watching, I might not have caught it. "I'm sure it's just kids messing with bees. The association received some angry threats. We believe the vandalism is a sort of protest over beekeepers making money off of bees. Tell her, Hampton."

I turned to Jim. "Protesters?"

"There is a group who are against farmed-out bee-hives. They blame them for colony collapse," Jim said. "It's an angle we've been pursuing."

"Why didn't you tell me?" I asked.

"It's just a theory," he said, "And it's an—"

"Ongoing investigation," I finished his sentence and narrowed my eyes. "I thought we were friends."

"You know I can't talk about investigations," he said.

"Right," I said. "I'll go wait in the pickup." I walked off.

"Wren, don't be like that," he called after me.

I turned back to face him while still walking backward toward the pickup. "I can be any way I want. In fact, I think I'll call a driver so you don't have to worry about me."

"Your supplies . . ."

"Will fit in the trunk," I said and pulled out my phone and scheduled a ride as I turned back toward the pickup. Lucky for me, there was a car fifteen minutes away. I grabbed my supplies and piled them at the end of the long driveway. Looked at my phone and saw it was still five minutes away. I hugged myself and paced. To distract myself, I texted Aunt Eloise.

Hey, are you okay? I texted.

There was no answer, and that made me frown. I tried calling, but only got her voice mail, so I hung up because my driver had arrived. We put my supplies in his trunk, and he took me back to town. I suppose it was a bit childish of me to be mad at Jim for not sharing about the group protesting. I used my phone to search for information on the group, but all I found were a couple of scientific articles on studies that concluded that many bee colonies were overworked.

I got back to the shop, and Porsche helped me bring in the supplies. The store was empty, which was not surprising because it had started to rain.

"Did you talk to Aunt Eloise?" Porsche asked as we brought the supplies in. There were no customers at the moment.

"I couldn't get ahold of her," I said. I looked at the

clock; it was after six p.m. "I thought we agreed to meet at six for a team training."

"That's kind of worrying," Porsche said.

"I'll try again," I said and put my phone on speaker as I entered Aunt Eloise's phone number and hit SEND. It rang and rang, and then suddenly it went to voice mail. "Aunt Eloise," I said, "Call me, please. You're missing the meeting, and I'm worried."

"Why don't you teach me the security and the keys," Porsche said. "If she isn't here after we finish, then we're going to go to her house and check on her."

"Sounds like a plan," I said. I proceeded to explain the color-coded keys and gave her her copies. Then I showed her the code to the security system and how to access it on the tablet and laptop. I could access it on my phone, but she didn't need that. After all that, I blew out a deep breath.

Everett meowed.

"I'm not paranoid, am I?"

Porsche hugged me. "You've been through a lot lately. It's good. This will help me sleep at night, knowing you're safe."

I looked at my watch. "It's after seven, and we haven't heard from Aunt Eloise. I'm going to go by her house."

"I don't think you should go alone," Porsche said. "I've got to go home and put my boys to bed. I think you should call Jim."

"I don't know; he really made me mad today," I said and raised my chin.

"What happened?"

I related the whole argument.

"Honey, I love you, but he's not wrong," she said, and I scowled.

"I know, but it doesn't seem fair," I knew I sounded pouty. Sighing, I called Jim.

"Hampton," he answered.

"Jim, it's Wren. I'm worried about Aunt Eloise," I said. Then I relayed what was going on. "I was wondering if you had time to go with me to her house and see if she's okay."

"I can do that," he said. "I'll be over at your place in ten minutes."

"Thanks," I said.

"Anytime," he answered. "You know that, right, Wren?"

"I do," I said. "See you soon."

Porsche hugged me, and Everett and I walked her out the back to her car. "See you tomorrow," she said. "Be safe."

"I'll try," I said and waved her on. The store was still empty. I should reconsider my store hours. It didn't seem to matter that I closed early unless it was a sale day. So I locked up the shop and set the alarm code, then took Everett for a short walk. This time I didn't feel as if anyone followed me. In part, it was a relief, but it also made me nervous that someone might have been following Aunt Eloise.

Chapter 22

Jim pulled up and rolled down his window. "Are you bringing Everett?"

"Do you mind?" I asked. "He's pretty good at sniffing out people. You know, in case Aunt Eloise has fallen and can't get up."

"Do you really think she's hurt?" he asked.

"I'm hoping not, but things have been nuts lately," I said. "She left a message with Porsche instead of calling me. That is really odd. Then I've been calling her and texting her, but she hasn't answered. Also odd."

"When did you last see her?"

"At the store. She worked the morning shift," I said.

"Maybe she misplaced her phone and called the shop because she knows the number," he suggested.

"Well, now, that does make sense," I said as I opened the back-passenger door and connected Everett's leash to the seat belt. Then I closed the door and entered the front passenger side, climbed in, closed the door, and buckled up.

Jim stared at me.

"What?"

"I'm surprised you didn't hold Everett in your arms."

I sighed. "A friend of mine did that once and got into a fender bender. It was just enough to pop the airbag, and the poor cat went face first into the air bag, and it snapped her neck. So Everett is always buckled into the back seat."

"I'm sorry to hear that about your friend," Jim said as he pulled away from the curb. "But glad you take care of your pets in the car."

The drive to Aunt Eloise's 1930s bungalow didn't take long. Oceanview was a small town, and we only lived three miles apart. Far enough that taking a car on a dark rainy evening was the smart choice. We pulled up, and the house was dark, which was odd. Usually the white clapboard bungalow with blue shutters and flower boxes at the windows seemed to glow with light and warmth.

"That's not good," Jim said as he put the car in park and turned it off. "If she were here, there'd be a light on, right?"

"Usually," I said and unbuckled and got out of the car. I pulled Everett from the back seat and put him on the ground. I didn't take hold of his leash. He'd been to Aunt Eloise's many times, and I trusted him to know where to go.

Jim came around the car with a flashlight in his hands. "Are we letting Everett go first?" he asked and nodded toward my cat, who jumped over the three-foot picket fence that surrounded my aunt's house.

"He has good instincts," I said and opened the gate.

Everett didn't go up the front porch steps. Instead, he took the stepping-stone walk around the side of the house. The rain pattered softly against my jacket and hood, but I followed Everett around the side.

Jim also wore a raincoat and hoodie. He stayed behind me, but used the flashlight to keep the walkway in front of me lit and Everett in clear sight.

Everett didn't go up the steps to the back screened-in porch as I thought he would. That meant that, most likely, Aunt Eloise was not inside the house. Which was a good thing, I thought, since all the lights were out.

He made a beeline straight for Aunt Eloise's cat house aka craft house aka she shed. There were no lights on in the little house with a gabled roof and a front porch. Everett scratched on the front door. Jim shone a light into the front two windows.

I checked the door and found it unlocked. I opened the door, and Everett went straight inside. Then I hit the light switch and was greeted by Aunt Eloise's cats Evangeline and Lug. I bent down to pet them. "Hey, babies," I said. "What are you two doing in here?"

Aunt Eloise used to breed Havana Browns, and she had built a comfortable one-room house, complete with bathroom, for the animals. But now that she did rescue, she usually kept all the cats in her house and used the shed for her arts and crafts.

Jim did a quick check of the room and the bathroom. "There's no one here," he said. "Maybe we should go back to the main house and check it out."

"We have to be missing something. Everett wouldn't come here just because the cats are in here."

Suddenly, there was a bang above us.

Jim frowned. "Does this thing have an attic?"

"A storage space," I said. "Yes, Auntie needs room for all of her crafting supplies and such."

There was another bang.

"How do you get up there?" he asked as he searched the ceiling.

"In the back corner," I said and walked to the corner opposite the bathroom. I jumped up, grabbed a short, dangling rope with a handle and pulled the trap open. Then Jim reached over me to pull down the ladder.

I stepped out of the way and picked up Everett, who was circling my legs. Jim climbed halfway up and stuck his head and shoulders into the space and turned on the flashlight.

"Who's there?" he asked.

I heard more movement and muffled sounds. Jim disappeared up the ladder. I put Everett down and hurried up behind him. When I got my head into the space, I saw tubs of supplies sitting on a wood-plank floor. Jim had stepped all the way up to the front of the of the space. Someone was sitting in front of him.

"Is it Aunt Eloise?" I asked.

Jim pulled a gag away from the person's mouth.

"Yes," Aunt Eloise croaked. "It's me."

I hurriedly pulled myself up.

"Don't come up here," Jim said. "There's not enough room."

"Aunt Eloise," I said as I crouched beside the trapdoor, ignoring Jim's request to go back down. "Are you okay? What happened? Who did this to you?"

"I'm fine," she said, but her throat sounded hoarse.

"Please, Wren," Jim said as he freed Aunt Eloise's arms and feet. "There's not enough room for three of us. Go back down and call 9-1-1."

I stepped back onto the ladder and thought I heard Aunt Eloise protest about 9-1-1, but I climbed down and pretended I didn't hear her.

"Nine-one-one, what's your emergency?"

"Hi, Josie," I said, recognizing my friend. "It's Wren Johnson. I'm at Aunt Eloise's, and she needs help."

"What's going on?" Josie asked.

"Jim Hampton and I found her tied up in the storage space above her she shed," I said. "She sounds hoarse, and we're not sure what kind of shape she's in."

"Got it," Josie said. "I've got an ambulance on the way. Did you say Jim Hampton was there? Officer Hampton?"

"Yes," I said. "He's helping her down from the attic. He told me to call 9-1-1."

"Okay," she said. "I've notified the patrol on duty."

I felt a sudden sense of embarrassment that I would be caught with Jim by his coworkers. They might make assumptions about us. They would be wrong, but I didn't want to have to explain.

Jim came down the ladder carrying Aunt Eloise. Luckily, she had a green velvet chaise lounge in the shed. He set her down on it.

Aunt Eloise's hair was a mess. Her face was pale, and her lips were drawn in a thin line. She had marks on her jaws from the gag and bruises on her wrists from the restraints.

"Who did this to you?" Jim Hampton asked.

The cats jumped up on the chaise to comfort her. I noted that my aunt was trembling. She didn't answer.

"I'll get you some water," I said and went to the tiny sink in the corner and poured her a glass of water.

Jim softened his tone. "Eloise, can you tell me what happened?"

I handed her the water. She took a trembling sip. "I thought he was a good guy."

"Who?" Jim asked.

"Travis Hutton," Aunt Eloise said.

"Travis did this to you?" I straightened. "I'm going to kill him."

Jim reached up and gently encircled my wrist to stop me. "Eloise, what happened?"

"I caught him trying to steal one of my retired prize champion cats," she said.

"Which one?" I asked, horrified.

"Elton," Aunt Eloise said, her voice trembled. "He took my Elton."

Elton was Everett's great-grandfather and recognized worldwide. He was also nearly twenty years old and hardly ever moved from his favorite spot in the sun, except to eat dinner and use the kitty litter.

"I'm really going to kill him," I said.

"I'm going to pretend I didn't hear that," Jim said. He turned to Aunt Eloise. "Did he do this by himself?"

"No," she said. "Bill Chechup helped him."

"The president of our local beekeepers association?" I was horrified.

"Yes," Aunt Eloise said and took another sip. "You were right, Wren. They are smuggling things in beehives."

"How do you know?" Jim asked as sirens drew closer.

"I overheard him talking about putting something in his hive," Eloise said. "I was going to call you, Wren. But then Travis grabbed me, bought me here, forced me to open my house and get Elton." She looked at me. "You know I would have died before I let them get Elton, but they took Evangeline and Lug and threatened to kill them if I didn't hand Elton over."

"Oh, honey, I'm sorry you went through that," I said. "It's not your fault. You did the best you could."

The door swung open, and the EMTs came in with their kits. Officers O'Riley and Morris entered behind them. I scooped up Lug and Evangeline and grabbed Everett's leash. We squeezed out of the crowded shed. I went to put Lug and Evangeline in the house when Officer O'Riley stopped me.

"Let us check that the house is empty first," he said and pulled out his gun. I stepped back and waited as he and Officer Morris cleared the bungalow. "All clear," I heard him shout.

So I stepped up into the small screened porch on the back of the house and then entered the kitchen. Aunt Eloise had strawberry wall paper in her kitchen to brighten it up and make it more homey. I put her two cats down, and they disappeared into their favorite spots. A glance toward Elton's regular spot told me that he was indeed missing.

Sadly, I went out to sit with Everett on the back stairs. The back-porch light created a warm circle around us. After a while, the EMTs helped Aunt Eloise out of the shed and into the house. I followed after them and watched them put her in a comfortable chair and place a throw over her lap.

"How is she?" I asked EMT Sarah Ritter.

"She's dehydrated and a bit in shock, but there doesn't appear to be anything wrong other than ligature marks on her wrists and ankles."

"What can I do?" I asked.

"Make her some tea and some dinner, and it would probably be best if you could spend the night with her."

"Okay," I said. "Should we follow up?"

"It probably wouldn't hurt to have her doctor check her over tomorrow."

"I'll call them in the morning and see if I can make an appointment for her," I said.

Jim entered the kitchen and took off his shoes. He spoke in a low voice with the other officers as the EMTs and ambulance left. The officers then left. I let go of Everett so he could go keep Aunt Eloise company, but I wanted to talk to Jim in the kitchen.

"I figured you were waiting for me," he said. "Why don't you put on a kettle for tea and then have a seat?" He waved toward the dinette chair that sat under the double window in the kitchen.

I put on the teakettle, pulled out three mugs and a selection of teas, then took a seat. Jim ran his hand over his face as if he were tired. "I suppose you want to say, I told you so," he said.

"Not really," I said. "Have you put out a 'bolo' for Travis and Bill yet?"

"Yes, but only Travis," he said.

"What do you mean?" My eyes narrowed.

"Right now, all we have on Travis is kidnapping. If we want to really connect him to the smuggling and to Elias's murder, we'll need more concrete proof he and Bill are connected."

"But Travis took Elton and tied up Aunt Eloise," I said.

"Yes," Jim said. "And that's it. So I'm going to talk to

the chief and see if we can't create some way to catch these guys in the act of vandalizing the beehives. We need to get to the bottom of this thing"

"Okay, but how do we link them to Elias's murder?" I asked.

"Leave it to me," Jim said. "I've got an idea."

"Right," I said.

"You have to trust me sometimes, Wren," Jim said and gently pushed a wayward piece of hair behind my ear.

My heartbeat sped up. "Um," I said. "I'll go see to Aunt Eloise and get her started talking to her friends."

"I'll work on the rest of the sting," Jim said. "I suggest you spend the night with your aunt. I don't think either of you should be alone." He got up and headed toward the back door.

"I agree," I said. "Good night." I followed him to the back door as the police offers left and locked the screen door and the main door behind me. Then I called Porsche, gave her the lowdown and asked her to take the morning shift. Luckily for me, she agreed.

Then I brought Aunt Eloise a nice hot cup of bedtime tea, hoping things would look better in the morning.

I slept restlessly; my brain couldn't turn off. How could we convince them to trust us to show us their smuggling?

"You look like something the cat dragged in," Aunt Eloise said.

"Good morning," I said and poured us both cups of coffee. "How are you feeling?"

"I'm mostly mad as heck," she replied and put two slices of bread in the toaster. "Plus I've got bruises everywhere to remind me about what happened, and that makes me even madder."

"I talked to Jim last night. He's worried that if he didn't have more evidence that Travis and Bill tampered with the hives, any trial would end up being only about kidnapping you. Which, I'm sorry to say, doesn't prove anything about Elias's murder."

"Well, doesn't that just take the cake," she said and buttered her toast in a stiff, angry manner.

I touched her arm. "We can prove this," I said. "We just need to think of some good way to trap them."

Aunt Eloise turned to me, and her eyes lit up. "We could do a sting. You could start up more beekeeping. You could let Bill know you are taking over Elias's hives and ask him to move them to a farm for you."

"Won't he know that I know about him?"

"No," Aunt Eloise said. "Bill doesn't know I know about him."

"Wait, what?" I asked. "How did you know it was him?"

"When Travis put me up in the attic, Bill was down below me. I heard him come in, and what they don't know is that I can hear perfectly in the attic. Also, there's a small window up there, you know."

"Oh, right, the portal," I said. "So you both saw and heard him. That makes you a witness."

"Like Jim said, being a witness isn't really nailing down the killer," she said with a sigh.

"Right," I said. "We need to set up a sting. I'll call Bill this morning and tell him that I have inherited Elias's hives and ask him if he will take them and rent them out for me."

"But first," Aunt Eloise said, "we need to put a camera and a tracker inside them."

"Yes," I said. "That way, we can see if they put anything in the hives and where they take them."

So we bundled up. I left Everett with Evangeline and Lug at Aunt Eloise's home. We went thirty miles back to McMinnville to order tiny cameras with Bluetooth signals and possibly tracking devices.

The town was still crowded with alien lovers and conspiracy theorists. We passed groups of people dressed as aliens from various science-fiction shows, and when we reached the camera shop, I opened the door. Aunt Eloise went inside first.

Our favorite conspiracy theorist was working the counter. "Hello, ladies, please come in," Crash said.

"Thanks," I said.

"What can I help you with today?" he asked.

"We need spy cameras that will work normally in moist and humid areas," Aunt Eloise said.

"Even better if it's the size of a bee," I said.

He leaned his elbows on the counter and looked at us. "So, what's going on?"

"We believe that certain people are smuggling illegal substances in beehives," I whispered.

His eyes lit up with interest. "Oh, that's a great idea, as long as you're not afraid of bees. What, pray tell, are they smuggling?"

"We don't know for sure," Aunt Eloise said. "But if we put cameras in beehives, we should be able to find out."

"I have the perfect item for you," he said and came around the corner and walked to a shelf in the back corner labeled CAPSULE CAMERAS. "These are pill-sized video cameras that will give you a three-hundred-and-sixty-degree view and send the video to your cell phone via an app. It's black, so it should not be too obvious."

"We'll take four," I said.

"Hold on. They are kind of expensive," he said.

"We still need four," Aunt Eloise said.

He broke out into a wide smile. "Of course. Is there anything else you need?"

"Do you have any tracking devices?" I asked.

"I'm currently out of stock but I'm expecting a shipment on Friday," he replied.

"No, I need them now," I said and paid for the cameras.

"You will let me know if the cameras discover your smugglers, won't you?" he asked.

I leaned in toward him. "We will, but for now you need to keep this between us. We wouldn't want our smugglers to figure us out."

"Mum's the word," he said and made the hand gesture of zipping his lip.

We left the shop and the aliens behind and went out to the Reichs' farm. While Aunt Eloise drove, I opened the packages and connected each camera to my cell phone. I pointed a camera at Aunt Eloise and looked at my phone. The picture was sharp and clear and in full color.

"These are great," I said and showed her my phone screen.

"Perfect," she said as she took a quick glance.

We pulled into the Reichs' long driveway and got out of the car. The barn was quiet, and no one was outdoors. So we went to the back porch and knocked on the kitchen door. The curtain moved, and we waved at Sylvia. She opened the back door.

"Hello," she said and put down a rifle, leaning it

against the kitchen counter. "Sorry, but I'm a bit skittish these days. Come on in. I'll make some coffee."

"How is Paul doing?" I asked as we slipped off our shoes and took a seat at the kitchen table.

"He's doing much better since he's been home," she said as she made coffee.

"How are you holding up?" Aunt Eloise asked.

Sylvia busied herself by pulling small plates from the cupboard, along with spoons and forks. "I'm as good as can be," she said and set the table. "I have a coffee cake. Please do me a favor and help me eat it." She brought out a glass cake stand and uncovered a gorgeous coffee cake, then cut us all pieces and plated them. Then she gathered the coffee pot and a cream pitcher and sugar bowl, placed them on the table, and took a seat. She wiped her hand on her apron.

I took the coffee pot and filled all the cups, then put creamer in mine and passed the cream and sugar around. "I can't believe you had time to bake."

"I can't take the credit. Harriet Van Nyes stopped by last night and brought it," she said.

"Well, it's quite good," Aunt Eloise said as she chewed.

"You should eat," I said to Sylvia. "You look like you've lost weight."

She sighed. "Stress does that to me."

We visited a little longer, talking about Paul, the UFO festival winding down, and other mundane things.

Finally, Sylvia pushed her half-eaten cake away from her and picked up her coffee cup. "Okay, ladies, tell me why you're really here. Have they learned more about who shot Paul?"

"Not yet," I said. "But we'd like to ask you for a favor."

"Certainly," she said. "What do you need? You know I can't leave Paul here, so whatever it is, I may not be able to help."

"We want to borrow four of the beehives," Aunt Eloise said.

"Particularly three that belonged to Elias, as well as one from you," I said.

"Whatever for?" she asked.

"We want to set up a sting," Aunt Eloise said.

"A sting," she parroted.

"Yes," I said. "Without involving you too much. We hope to catch this killer."

Chapter 23

Plant wildflowers in your front yard instead of grass. Not only will they look lovely and not have to be mowed, but it will help local bee colonies to grow strong. Don't want to lose your lawn? Plant wildflowers in your flowerbeds. Natural wildflowers in your area will be the best way to feed the bees.

Sylvia put up her hand, making a "stop" sign. "I don't want or need to know anything more. You can take the hives. The bees are lost anyway."

"Thank you," I said.

"Do you have a pickup? Because they won't fit in a car."

"I have my Subaru," Aunt Eloise said. "I've had hives in there before."

Sylvia finished her coffee and shook her head. "Paul is going to be so devastated over the loss of his bees."

"You haven't told him yet?" I asked.

"I need him to take care of himself first, and not worry about the bees."

We thanked her and helped her clean up the table before leaving. Aunt Eloise and I walked quietly to the beehives. The sun was out, and it was about sixty degrees, beautiful weather for beekeeping.

It took us about thirty minutes to carry the four hives to the car and place them inside. Sylvia watched us from the kitchen window. We waved goodbye to her as we pulled away.

My heart was heavy at the loss of so many hives. We didn't speak for a while.

"Well, this gives me the perfect excuse to contact Bill," I said. "I'll clean the hives and then ask him to place new colonies in them for me. When I pay him for it, I'll sneak a peek inside and place the cameras, then I'll see if he knows anyone who needs the bees for their crops. That should be enough to get him to use the hives. He'll think I'm too naïve to notice if they put anything inside."

"Will he?" Aunt Eloise asked.

"Are you having doubts?" I asked.

"No," she said, with a shake of her head, and pulled into the shop's back parking lot. "No, it's just hard to see Sylvia like that. It could be me if anything happens to you."

"I won't let anything happen," I said. "I'll act dumb. He'll buy it because he thinks most women are."

"Well, then, we have work to do," Aunt Eloise said.

We took the hives out of her Subaru SUV and placed them in the sun. I went inside the shop to check on Porsche and catch her up on the plan. She seemed to think it would work.

I changed into old jeans and a T-shirt and went back outside to take the hives apart. I had a hive tool, a long metal arm with a curved end that is used to pry tops off hives and also to scrape out gunk. I started with cleaning the bottoms of the hives of dead bees. Then I pulled out the center boards that were left and cleaned out any odd shapes of comb, scraped off dead bees, and left a bit of good comb and clean honey so the new colony would have something to start with.

It took me two hours, but the hives were ready. I set them in the sun on the opposite side of the parking lot. The plan was to let Bill introduce new bee packs, and then I would add the cameras, or vice versa, depending on how it worked out best. The relatively new hives should entice the smugglers to use them since it would be easy to insert something since there were so few bees. That was my hope anyway.

I went upstairs to my apartment to find Everett back and greeting me at the door. "I thought you might miss him," Aunt Eloise said as I picked him up and gave him pets.

"I did." I gave him a kiss and a treat and then put him down to go about his day. He went into his closet, to his favorite box on the top shelf. I imagined he was quite tired after spending the night with Aunt Eloise's cats.

"Okay, I'm ready to call Bill," I said. "The hives are ready for new bees."

"Put him on speaker," she said as she poured us both a cup of coffee. "Don't let him know I'm here, of course, but we need witnesses from now on."

"I can record it. I have an app on my phone for that, and it's not illegal as long as one party is aware."

"Wonderful! What won't they think of next?" she asked.

"Okay, I'm doing it," I said and motioned for her to be

silent. I went into my contacts, found his number, and hit SEND.

"Hello?"

"Hi, Bill, how are you?" I asked.

"Okay . . ."

"It's Wren Johnson," I said. "You know I inherited Elias's hives, but when I went to collect them from the Reichs, the bees were gone. So Sylvia let me take the three from Elias and one from them to try and restart them."

"What happened to the bees?" he asked. "Was it mites?"

"I didn't see any mites when I was cleaning," I said. "Honestly, it looked like someone stole them. Some of the center boards were missing. It's like they stole the queen and the nurse bees."

"Who would do that?"

"I have no idea," I said. "But the hives are empty, and they are mine. So, I was wondering if I could bring the hives to you and you could put in new bee packs. I'd like to use the bees to help farmers."

"Oh, huh, sure thing," he said. "It's why we have the association—to help beekeepers. How's your hive, by the way? I heard through the grapevine that your glass was smashed?"

"The hive is fine," I said. "Luckily, the glass I used was safety glass, so it didn't shatter. We were able to replace it with new glass that has even more strength and clear visibility for the customers to watch the bees."

"That's great," he said. "I'll be in town around five this afternoon if you want me to pick up the empty hives."

"Sure thing," I said. "Oh, how much for the service?"

"Well a two-pound packet of bees costs around a hundred and twenty dollars, and then I charge for time and care until the hive matures enough to rent out. How many hives did you say?"

"Four."

"So, I'd give a rough estimate of a thousand dollars."

"Okay," I said slowly. "I can do half up front, to pay for the bees, and then when they're ready to rent, I'll pay the second half."

"Sounds fair," he said. "So I'll see you at five?"

"Yes, the hives are behind the shop."

"Great."

I pressed END and looked at Aunt Eloise. Her face was pale, with two red spots on her cheeks. "Are you okay?" I asked her.

"Yes," she said. "I just need a moment. Hearing his voice was harder than I thought it would be."

I gave her a hug. "You've been through a trauma. You should go talk to a counselor."

"Maybe later," she said. "I'm pretty angry right now. I'd better avoid them both, or I can't promise I won't do something awful."

"Anger is a natural reaction," I said and patted her back. "Maybe we should switch you from coffee to tea."

Suddenly, tears welled up in her eyes. "What if I don't get Elton back? He's been with me most of your life. I love Evangeline and Lug, but I'm not ready to lose Elton."

"We'll get him back," I said. "Don't you worry. Jim is on the hunt for Elton. He told me so himself last night."

"Can you call him and see what is going on?" she asked and grabbed a tissue and wiped her eyes and blew her nose.

"Of course," I said. I dialed Jim's number.

"Hampton," he answered.

"Hi Jim, it's Wren. Aunt Eloise is with me, and she is hoping you might have heard something about Elton?"

"That's the cat Travis stole from her last night," Jim stated.

"Yes," I said.

"We've been to Travis's hotel room, but he checked out last night. I've got the patrols looking out for a Havana Brown."

"Isn't there anything else you can do?" I asked and drew my eyebrows together.

"I've got the Washington State Police on alert. I need Aunt Eloise to come down and fill out an assault-and-battery and theft complaint. That way, the Washington State and Seattle police will know to bring him in if he crosses their path."

"Okay," I said, "I'll have her come down to the station. We would have done it sooner, but last night you said to wait."

"Yes, but if the cat hasn't gotten away from him and found its way home yet and we find him with the cat in his possession, we can get him on theft. How much is Elton worth?"

I looked at Aunt Eloise. "How much is Elton worth in terms of dollars."

"He's priceless as far as I'm concerned," she replied with a tremor in her voice.

"Tell her if he's worth more than a thousand dollars, we can charge Travis with a felony," Jim said.

"Right," I covered the phone with my hand. "If he's worth more than a thousand dollars, then they can charge Travis with a felony."

"The last time I showed him, he was worth twenty-five

thousand," she said and sniffed. "He's older now, and I had him neutered, so he is most likely worth only about five hundred dollars."

"But Travis wanted his stem cells, right?" I said. "Didn't he offer you a million dollars for them?"

"He did." Aunt Eloise perked up.

"Then he's worth more than five hundred dollars," I said. Then I removed my hand from the phone. "Elton's blood and stem cells are worth a million dollars."

"Then it's felony theft," Jim said. "Send her down, and I'll get the paperwork started."

"Perfect," I said and hit END. "He wants you to go to the station and sign paperwork for assault and battery and felony theft."

"It should be kidnapping," she said. "Elton is a person."

"I understand," I said. "Do you need someone to go with you?"

"No, I'm fine. I can walk a half mile on my own," she said. "Besides, you have to stay here and give Bill the hive boxes to start our sting."

"Don't mention that to Jim, okay?" I asked.

"Don't worry. I won't say a thing."

Porsche was with me when Bill showed up. He had a giant, red king-cab pickup truck. Porsche watched the store and monitored the back-door camera as I stepped out to meet him.

"Hi, Bill," I said and held out my hand to shake hi. He had a firm, meaty grip. "Thanks for doing this."

"It's my pleasure to help another beekeeper," he said.

He wore a blue-plaid flannel shirt, jeans, and work boots. "I'm glad to see someone taking care of Elias's hives. Where are they?"

"Over here," I said and walked him to the back of the parking lot while I tried to stay within camera distance. "I cleaned them up and left some bits of good honey and comb for the new bees to clean up and use."

He walked to the hives and opened the tops to look inside. "You did a good job," he said. His gaze was on the task of opening all the hives one by one and checking them.

"I can help you put them in the back of your truck," I said.

"Great," he reached down and picked up one hive. I followed suit with another, and we quickly put them in the back of his truck. The truck was so big that I had to step up on the bumper to put the hive box in the back.

We silently put all the boxes in the back of the truck. He slammed the tailgate closed and turned to me. "I should have these ready for you by tomorrow."

"Great," I said and handed him a check. "This is the first half. Once I see the bees are healthy and getting to work, I'll pay the second half."

He took the check and nodded once, putting it in his back pocket. "They'll be done in a jiffy. Take care." He climbed up into his big truck and drove down the alley, turning onto Main Street. I waved, turned, and went inside.

"Did he take the bait?" Porsche half whispered.

"He did," I said and pulled out my cell phone and turned the cameras on. They gave us a shaky, full-color picture of the inside of the hive, both front and back. I'd hidden the camera in the good comb. If anyone tried to smuggle things in the hive, I would know. I showed Porsche my cell phone.

"Oh, man, that's slick," she said.

The bells on the front door jangled, and Jim strode in. "What's slick?" he asked.

I put my phone away. "Nothing," I lied. "Just a new game I found for my phone. What brings you here?"

"I tried calling your Aunt Eloise, but she didn't answer," he said. "I might have a lead on Elton, but I really need her to come down to the station and start the paperwork."

"Wait," I said with a frown. "She left to go to the station over an hour ago."

"Well, she hasn't been there yet," he said.

"Should I be worried?" I asked as I grabbed my phone and quickly dialed Aunt Eloise's number. It picked up, but all I got was a voice recording, saying leave a name and number and "I'll get back to you." "She's not answering. Have you found Travis yet?"

"No," Jim said. "We haven't found Travis yet. We've got a 'bolo' out on him from here to Seattle, but, you know, once he leaves the state, there's a chance that he will go unnoticed by the Washington police."

"But he practically kidnapped my aunt," I said.

"I know, but he didn't cross state lines with her so we can't do anything but ask the Washington State police to arrest him. It's out of their jurisdiction," Jim said.

"Goodness, this crime work is so complicated," I said.

"The system does have some flaws," he agreed. "It's not perfect because people aren't perfect, but it's this way to keep people safe and ensure innocent people don't go to jail."

"I went to jail, and I was innocent," I muttered.

Jim blew out a long breath and opened his mouth to say something when the camera app on my phone started beeping. I lifted my phone up, and Porsche and I stared at the face of the smuggler.

"What is that?" Jim asked.

I jumped because I hadn't realized he'd moved so close he could see my phone screen. "It's a camera feed."

"From where? It looks like a box?" he said.

"Oh, this is the coolest idea that Wren has ever had," Porsche said. She slapped my forearm in excitement. "Tell him what you did."

"Wren?" Jim seemed a trifle unhappy.

"I got permission from the Reichs to go pick up Elias's hives from their place and use one of theirs, so I would have four hives."

"Then," an excited Porsche said, "she cleaned them up and put tiny, three-hundred-and-sixty-degree cameras in the good honeycomb that you leave to help feed the new pack of bees."

"You put cameras in four beehives," he echoed.

"Yes," I said. "They are my hives."

"Where are these hives right now?" he asked, as we all watched Travis place bags with white powder and one bag with what appeared to be a vial of blood in it inside the hive.

"I'm not exactly sure," I said. "But I hired Bill Chechup to start new colonies in them. He left about thirty minutes ago, so I have to assume it's his place."

"You wouldn't happen to have placed a GPS locator on those little cameras, would you?" he asked.

"No," I said with a shake of my head. "They were out

of tracking devices. But Bill said I could come check the hives out tomorrow. So they are most likely at his place."

"Are you going to go arrest him?" Porsche asked.

"Wait," I said. "We need to wait until someone picks up the stuff or we can't prove smuggling or any motive to kill Elias, right?"

"Yes," Jim said.

"And if we go pick him up now, that deal might not go through," I pointed out.

"I can send out a car to surveil the premises," he said. "Probably unmarked."

"Why?" Porsche asked. "Wouldn't that tip our hand?"

"We could pick up Travis if he leaves," Jim said.

"Wouldn't Bill get suspicious if you pick up Travis?" I asked.

"Now that you have the cameras installed, we can hold him for assault on your aunt," Jim said. "We can keep those little videos of yours under wraps until we see who else might be involved."

I smiled wide. "See, I do have some good ideas sometimes." The phone dinged again, and we watched as Bill added a packet of bees to each hive. A package of bees is roughly two to five pounds, or six thousand to twenty-five thousand bees, plus a queen.

"Have you heard from your aunt yet?" Jim asked.

I put my phone away. "No, and after last night, that worries me."

"I'll go with you to your aunt's house again," he said.

"Porsche, are you okay with closing?" I asked.

"You kids go and find that wayward aunt of yours. I'm good here," Porsche said. I grabbed my coat and left with Jim through the front door. He was in uniform, and he looked good in it. Sheesh, I might be weak from hunger. When did I last eat?

He opened the passenger door, and I got into his cruiser and watched him walk around it, his gaze touching on everything around him, assessing for danger. I guess if you were a cop long enough, you didn't even realize you were doing it. Climbing into the cruiser, he buckled his seat belt and started the engine, put it into REVERSE, then DRIVE, and headed toward Aunt Eloise's house.

I dialed her number. This time she did pick up. "Wren, good. I'm glad you called."

"Aunt Eloise," I said, and Jim and I shared a glance. "Where are you? Are you okay?"

"Oh, I'm okay, but Travis Hutton is not," she said.

"I'm in the car with Officer Hampton, I just put you on speaker. Can you say that again?"

"I said, I'm okay, but Travis is not."

"Where are you?" I asked.

"I'm just off Seascape Drive," she said. "Better come quick." She hung up before I could get any more out of her.

Jim turned on his lights and sirens, and we left town, took Highway 101, then Els Street, which would take us to Seascape. The winding roads ran through thick forest. We turned onto Seascape, and Jim slowed as he studied his side of the road and I studied mine. We were like tourists looking for Bigfoot in the forest. Instead, we were looking for my aunt.

"There's her car," I said and pointed to the side of the road.

"Are you sure?" he asked.

"Yes, she has a Tardis sticker in her back window."

"Tardis?" He glanced at me.

"Dr. Who," I said.

"Huh," he pulled over and kept his lights flashing. "Stay here." He got out with his flashlight and looked the car over.

Meanwhile, I studied where she was parked, looking for clues. I noticed the mouth of a long driveway. It was not marked by a mailbox, so it would be hard to see. I got out of the car, but didn't shut the door, so Jim wouldn't hear me. I walked carefully to the mouth of the drive and used my phone light to illuminate it.

"There's someone standing in the drive a few yards ahead," I said in a low voice.

Suddenly, Jim was beside me. "I told you not to get out of the car."

"I'm not a very good listener," I said. Then I thought I heard a cat meow, so I took a few steps closer to whoever stood in the middle of the drive. "Aunt Eloise?" I called. It echoed for a moment as I felt the weight of Jim's disappointment on the side of my face.

"Wren? Come on down," I heard Aunt Eloise call.

Jim and I both took off toward her voice. This time, he had his gun out as he swung the flashlight from side to side. We came upon a sight to behold.

Standing in the center of the driveway was Aunt Eloise in boots, a long skirt, and a gray hoodie, holding a rifle in her hand that was pointed to a figure facedown on the gravel. Elton was wrapped over her shoulders.

Meow. He welcomed us.

"Aunt Eloise?"

"Put the gun down!" Jim shouted the order.

"Not until you point your gun at this jerk!" I didn't

know if the two men knew, but Aunt Eloise was a darn good shot.

"Put the gun down, Auntie," I said.

"Hampton, do you have your gun on this guy?" she said, without looking at us.

"I do," he replied. "Now put your rifle away."

She took a moment to look at us and verify that he did indeed have his gun pointed at Travis. Good, it's about time you got here," she said and tucked the rifle under her arm, the barrel pointed at the ground.

"Travis Hutton," Jim said as he straddled Travis and handcuffed him. "You are under arrest for assault and theft." Jim pulled Travis to his feet; he was wearing a puffy vest and jeans. His entire front was smeared with mud from lying in the driveway.

"Aunt Eloise, are you okay?" I asked and put my arm around her.

She had tears in her eyes and stroked Elton's fur. "He took my baby."

Jim dragged Travis toward the cop car.

I took the rifle out of Aunt Eloise's hands and walked with her toward her car. "What happened? How did you find Travis?"

"Well, I was going to go down to the police station," she said, her voice shaking with relief. "To fill out that paperwork."

"Yes . . ."

"And I got a text message from the company that I bought Elton's microchip from. You see, I'd notified them that Elton had been stolen. Anyway, they texted me that Elton had a GPS tracker in his chip. All I had to do was download the app onto my phone, and then I could follow the GPS."

"That's brilliant!" I said as we got to the mouth of the driveway and watched as Jim stuck Travis into the back seat.

"Huh, the older chip didn't do this. I wish I had known about it sooner," she said. "But it all turned out okay, didn't it, my baby?" She purred at the cat around her shoulders

"I think he took a vile of blood and stem cells from Elton for cloning," I said.

"Why do you think that? I mean, other than that's what he asked us for?"

"Because I have video of Travis putting what appears to be semen and a vial of blood inside the beehives." I waggled my phone.

"Then we have the Travis on multiple things, right?" she asked.

"Ladies, let's go down to the station," Jim said as the rain started again in earnest. "I'll follow you, Eloise. Wren, you drive her, but, please, I need you to go straight to the station and nowhere else."

"Why would we go anywhere else?" Aunt Eloise asked as she gave me her car keys.

"Who knows, with you two," Jim said.

Chapter 24

Porsche met us at the police station after she closed the shop. On her way there, I filled her in by phone about how Aunt Eloise had found Elton and captured Travis.

"Aunt Eloise, can I be you when I grow up?" Porsche asked as she handed us cups of coffee she'd brought from the coffee shop.

"So smart," I said. "To track him by his microchip. I didn't know you could do that."

"I bought the most expensive microchip because Elton was worth so much money," she said.

"I wonder if I can upgrade Everett's chip," I muttered. "Someone took him last fall. I'd love to have GPS on it."

"You know, you can put a GPS collar on him," Porsche said. "I think that might be easier."

"As long as it's a fancy collar," I said with a smile.

"Everett likes smart, fancy collars . . . you know, the kind with bow ties?"

"I know the kind," Porsche said. "Listen, I've got to go home and make the boys go to bed. See you in the morning?"

"Sure thing," I said and gave her a hug.

Jim came out to see us. No one else was in the lobby of the police station. Oceanview was a small town and usually didn't see a lot of crime, except maybe during tourist season, when we had a few shoplifters and pickpockets.

"Ladies, thanks for your statements. Travis will be in custody until we have a bond hearing, and then either he'll make bond or the judge will have him remain in custody."

"He better not make bond," Aunt Eloise said. "That man kidnapped me and stole my Elton."

"I can't believe I went on a date with him. I should have known better."

"How could you possibly know? We were both duped by the thief."

"And most likely murderer if he was involved in Elias's death, Mr. McGregor being stabbed, and Paul being shot, not to mention all the hives being vandalized," I said.

"It will depend on the lawyers and how big of a flight risk he might be," Jim said. "But for now, we have him."

"What about my bees?" I asked him.

"I have a plan worked out," he said. "Tomorrow, I want you to call Bill and see if he has your hives ready. Then, when you bring him his check, I want you to ask him to rent them out for you. I'll take it from there."

"You're not planning on doing this alone, are you?" I asked.

"No. I won't be alone. Now ladies, go home and get some rest. A lot happened today, and you're going to need it for what's coming."

The next morning, I called Bill at seven a.m. Because it was Sunday, the store didn't open until ten, so I had time to swing by, see how my bees were doing, and then give him his final payment.

"Good morning." Bill answered his phone cheerfully. He must not have heard about Travis, and I wasn't about to tell him.

"Hi," I said. "It's Wren. I know it's only been twenty-four hours, but how are the bee colonies doing?"

"I checked them this morning," he said. "It looks like each package took to the hives. Great job on keeping some of the comb and honey. It gives them something to eat and gets them started out strong."

"Can I run out and take a look?" I asked. "I'll bring the check for the last half of payment."

"Sure, come on by as soon as you can. I've got to get on the road soon."

"I'll be right there." I pushed END and grabbed my purse and a jacket to keep the drizzle off.

Meow.

"No, Everett," I said. "Not today."

Meow.

I poured some dry kibble in his bowl and grabbed my purse, locked the door, and ran to my car. It took me ten minutes to get out to Bill's house. The traffic was light at seven a.m. I figured it would take me longer to get back to the store. I might have to speed a little as I didn't have Porsche or Aunt Eloise scheduled for the morning shift, even though Porsche said she would see me in the morning. It didn't mean she was coming in to work.

I arrived, parked, and got out of my car. Bill met me on his back steps.

"Morning, Wren, how are things with you?"

"Good," I said. "Can I see the bees?" I noticed he had a flatbed trailer set up on his king-cab truck. It had some hives already loaded for transport.

"Sure, come on back," he said. "I started them behind the barn."

My heart rate went up at the idea of going a hundred yards from the driveway and into the wooded area behind his barn. "Oh, I thought you would have kept them closer to the house since you just filled them."

"I like to give the bees some space from humans walking around and from barn animals," he said, sounding very reasonable. "Until they get settled in."

"Oh, that makes sense," I said, glad my cell phone was in my pocket. Jim was on the line listening to everything and recording it just in case things went bad.

"I checked on your bees this morning, and like I said, they really took to the hives," he said. "With all the vandalism this season, bees are really needed by the orchards and fruit farmers. If you like, I'd be happy to put your hives on the trailer today. I think I could easily find a nice farm that would love to have them."

"I was thinking about renting them out," I said slowly, as if I was just now thinking about it. "But I thought the colonies would have to be established longer."

"Oh, no," he said. "They would be fine to go today, if you want. It can net you around a hundred dollars a hive this time of year. It would help with paying for the bees."

"Wow. Is that for the season?" I asked.

"For each blooming season," he said.

"And you'll transport them for me?"

"It would be my pleasure," he said and handed me gloves and a beekeepers' netted hat. "Take a look. I'm sure all your new colonies are buzzing."

I put on the equipment and headed toward the hives.

"Oh, one more thing," he said. "Don't open the lids too far, we want to keep the queen and as many nurse bees as possible from being spooked."

"Right . . . ," I said. I turned to the bees and muttered, ". . . and keep me from finding more than bees in the hives."

"Did you say something?" he asked.

"No," I said, and cracked the first hive. The bees did indeed seem to be taking to it very nicely. I carefully checked all four hives, minding that he had asked me not to crack them too far open. Then I walked back to him and took off the equipment. "You're right, they all look healthy. If you think renting them out is a good idea, then I say, sure, why not?"

"Exactly," he said as I dug out the check for him. "Why don't you keep that half, and then you'll already be paid for the renting."

"But I still owe you a hundred dollars," I said.

"Consider it a friends and family discount."

"Wow," I said as we walked back. "Thanks." I tucked the check in my pocket. We both stopped at my car. "Thank you for doing this for me," I said. "I'm so glad I called you."

"My pleasure," he said. "See you at the next chapter meeting."

"Okay," I said, got into my car and drove off. As soon as I was out of sight of his farm, I pulled my phone out of my pocket and synced it to my car. "Well, I'd say that went well," I said.

"You did a good job," Jim said.

"So, you think he's not on to us?"

"If he is, he hid it well," Jim said. "Now, come straight back to your store. I've got men who will be watching where he takes the bees and who picks them up."

"I hope they don't vandalize the hives," I said. "Those bees looked so happy to have a brand-new place."

"I doubt they will be vandalized. I'm certain he's told whoever picks up the stuff that we are watching the vandalized hives."

"Right," I said, satisfied. "Of course."

"Thanks for your help, Wren," he said. "Now it's time for you to go back to being a honey store owner."

"Do you think all of this will lead you to Elias's murderer?"

"I certainly hope so," he said. "Talk later."

"Keep me updated!"

He disconnected, and I went back to open my shop. So far, so good. Surely, when the sting was over, we'd have pictures of the smuggler and have a better idea who murdered Elias.

Porsche came in at one p.m. "Hey, girl," she said, as she hung up her jacket on the hook by the back door and put on the bee apron over skinny jeans and a sweater. Her long black hair cascaded down her shoulder. "What's going on?"

There were two tourists in the shop, browsing. "They've been going over every bit of product with a fine-tooth comb for the last hour," I said in a low voice.

"Are you due for a Health Inspection?" Porsche glanced at them and then turned back at me.

"No," I said. "I went up to them twice to talk about ingredients, but they gave me a 'back off' look. So, I'm here, backing off. How was your morning?"

"Great. With the kids away at my mom's, I took a nap!"

"Sounds delightful," I said as the two women left. "What do you think that was all about?" I nodded toward the door.

"Just tourists," Porsche shrugged. "Any news today on the sting?"

"I've been watching for pictures," I said and pulled out my phone. "I shared the link with Jim, but so far no one has opened the lids besides me."

"You?"

"When I went to Bill's place this morning," I said and explained what I did.

"Well, I imagine it will be after dark before anyone tries to take stuff out of the hives," Porsche said.

"I kind of agree with you," I said. "All we can do now is wait. I'm going to go upstairs and get some lunch, then get started on some candles. Our inventory is getting low."

"Well, I'll be here," Porsche said.

"Buzz me if you get swamped." I had installed a button under the counter near the cash register. When someone manning the shop pushed it, that meant I needed to come downstairs and help out. Picking up Everett, I went upstairs.

Around six p.m., I looked up from my candle work. I had four dozen candles made, along with some bath bombs.

A glance out the window told me that the sun was low in the sky. Sunset was officially eight twenty-four p.m., but it was already getting low. I checked my phone and saw that the cameras had left me a notice that something had triggered them an hour earlier.

Frowning, I opened the app and saw that someone had reached in and picked up the baggies of white powder and the vial of blood. Unfortunately, they were wearing a beekeeper's, hat, gloves, and netting. It was difficult to get a good look at the face. I put the candles in a basket and opened my apartment door. Everett ran out, meowing. I followed him down the stairs. "I made candles and bath bombs," I said as I stepped into the store. "And we got some video, but it's hard to tell much about it with all the protective equipment the person was wearing."

"A video of what?"

I looked up to see Millie Brown standing just inside the door, with a gun in her hand. "Millie? What's going on?"

She locked the front door and turned the sign to CLOSED while keeping her gaze and her gun trained on Porsche and me. "Tell me about the videos."

"Listen, I have security cameras in each corner," I pointed out. "I really think you should put that gun down."

She grinned at me. "If you check your security app, you'll see I have them blocked."

"I don't believe you," I said, with my hands in the air. "Show me."

"I don't care what you believe." She tossed one of the mini cams from the beehives onto the counter. "I am assuming this is yours."

"What is it?" I lied.

She took a step closer and pointed the gun at Porsche.

"Don't play games with me. I will kill her, and it will be your fault. Now, where is the video stored?"

I swallowed hard. "Don't hurt her."

"Where . . . is . . . the . . . video . . . stored?" She took another step closer, until the gun was three feet away from Porsche. I'm sure it would have been closer if we hadn't been on the other side of the cashier's counter.

"It's in the cloud," I said. "I saved it via the app on my phone."

"Then you will pick up your phone and delete the video and then the app," she said. "Or she's dead. Now, slowly pick up the phone."

I did what she said. "Now, put in your password." I exchanged a glance with Porsche and slowly opened my phone.

Porsche did the most amazing thing. She dropped to her knees behind the counter. Millie let out a shot that lodged in the wall behind where Porsche had just been. Then she rushed around the counter. I stepped back as she grabbed Porsche by the arm.

"I should shoot you just for trying that," she said as she dragged Porsche to her feet. In the meantime, I'd managed to hit the emergency number and muted my phone, so it could all be heard by 9-1-1 without Millie knowing.

"Please don't hurt Porsche," I said. "I need her to run Let It Bee."

"Shut up," Millie said and dragged Porsche back. She put her arm around Porsche's neck and put the gun to her head. "Did you open your phone?"

"Yes," I said.

"Give it to me," she said. "Move it slowly toward me and step back. Don't try anything, or she's toast."

I put the phone on the counter. She saw that the screen had gone black. "You said you opened it."

"I have it on a short screen time," I said.

"Tell me your password, and I'll open it," she said.

"It's set on facial recognition."

"Open it!" she ordered and shot at my feet.

I jumped back. "Okay, okay." I opened my phone, and hit END on the call so that she couldn't see. All I could do was hope 9-1-1 had gotten enough information to send help. I slid the phone face up toward Millie. She grabbed it and put her arm around Porsche's shoulders. "You should let me delete it. Your hands are a bit full, and I have the app password-protected."

Her gaze narrowed, and she put the phone down. "Do it."

I slowly reached for the phone.

"I want you to show me exactly what app and then bring up the videos."

"Okay," I said and picked up the phone. I opened the app and showed her that I had opened it.

"Delete all the videos," she ordered.

I deleted them and showed her the cleared-out inbox.

"Now delete the app."

I deleted the app and showed her the screen. She grabbed the phone out of my hand and threw it to the floor, stomping it with her booted foot.

"Now what?" I asked, as my heart pounded in my throat.

"Now, Porsche and I are going out the back. You are going to go first, open the door, and stay in the doorway until you can't see us. Or I will kill her, and you don't want her kids to grow up without a mother, do you?"

I swallowed. "No, I do not," I said.

"Go!"

My legs shook as I walked down the short hall toward the back door. Everett sat on the steps to my apartment; he was being unusually quiet. I prayed he would keep quiet and not catch anyone's attention. I opened the door and took one step out. There was movement in my peripheral vision, and I saw that Jim and Officer Hinze were waiting on either side of the door, with guns pointed. I tried not to show that I'd noticed. "The door is open," I said, turning sideways in the doorway to motion toward the outdoors.

Millie narrowed her gaze. "Is anyone out there?"

"I didn't see anyone," I said and worked like heck not to let it show that I was lying. I knew I was the worst liar, but this was life or death. "Do you want to stick your head out?"

Millie blew out a disgusted breath. "Step out," she ordered.

I did and could feel Jim behind me.

Then she shoved Porsche out the door with the gun to her back. "You better not be lying," Millie said. "I will kill her." She took a step out of the door.

"Duck!" I ordered Porsche and dropped to my knees.

"Police! Freeze!" both cops said.

I had my eyes closed tight and hugged myself into a small ball.

I heard Millie utter a nasty word.

"Drop your weapon now!" Jim ordered.

I heard the gun hit the ground, as gravel flew up to hit my arm. Then there was a short scuffle as Officer Hinze took down Millie.

"She's cuffed," Officer Hinze said and pushed the gun away with his foot.

Then Jim was beside me, his hand on my elbow. "It's okay," he said soothingly. "You can stand up now."

I opened my eyes to see his blue gaze looking at me with concern. Standing, I noticed that a third policeman was helping Porsche to her feet as well. "Nobody got shot," I said with relief.

"Nobody got shot," Jim said as Officer Hinze put Millie into a police cruiser. "Are you two okay?"

"I think so," I said and looked at Porsche, who ran to me and hugged me.

"Good," Jim said.

"Was it Millie who killed Elias?" I asked.

"I know it's hard to believe, but I think so. We found Millie's prints in Elias's house, but dismissed them as she was his girlfriend."

"They found the cameras in the beehives," I said. "She made me delete the videos."

"It's okay. We have copies," he said. "You shared the files with me." He gently put his hand on my back. "Why don't we go inside."

"Right," I said, and Porsche didn't let go of me as we crowded through the door. Everett moved off the stairs at the sight of us, and Porsche picked him up. "Let's go upstairs. I'll make a calming tea."

"I'll get your statements," Jim said behind us. "By the way, Wren, great idea to hit 9-1-1 when you did. It's how we were able to move here so quickly."

"Thank you," I said. "I tried to buy time, but she was too smart."

"What about Bill?" Porsche asked. "Did you arrest him?"

"We got him," Jim said. "It was hard to identify the person who picked up the blood and put money in the hive.

But now we can get a warrant to search Millie's home. I suspect we may find more information there, and possibly a match to the gun that shot Paul."

"It's too bad the videos weren't clear so you could be absolutely certain who picked up the biologicals," I said as I went to the stove to heat up a kettle of water.

"I had guys with eyes on the hives," he said. "Remember? They saw Millie. As soon as she gathered the stuff, they went to the hives to find the money. They tried following her, but she slipped their tail. Millie and Travis had been delivering illegal semen and cloning materials up and down the state. We have the feds on it now."

"Is that they were going to do with Elton's blood? Sell it to clone?"

"Not sure," Jim said. "But most likely."

"Is all this enough to put Millie and Travis away?" I asked.

"Hopefully, Bill made a deal with the district attorney. He's going to testify that Millie had Elias killed because he got too close to figuring out about the smugglings. It seems he'd met with Bill and explained that he'd figured out about the vandalizing and wanted Bill's help to catch the smugglers."

"And Bill told Millie," I said. "She must have planted notes about Klaus in Elias's home, then hired the boys in the blue car to kill Elias."

"Do you know who the boys were?" Porsche asked.

"You were right," Jim said. "It was the pizza delivery kid and his buddy. They started talking the minute we brought them in for an interview. They told us that Millie paid them twenty-five thousand dollars to kill Elias and make it look like bee vandals."

"What about Mr. McGregor?" I asked.

"They did that unpaid because they found out he was talking to you and could implicate them," Jim said.

I was quiet as I poured hot water into three tea mugs prepared with calming lavender tea. I put them on a tray with a bottle of honey and some milk, then took the tray to the living area, where Porsche sat on the couch petting Everett and Jim sat in the side chair.

I relaxed back into the couch with tea and honey in my hands and took a sip. "The thing I can't figure out is why Millie came to us about Elias suspecting the beehive vandals. She practically told on herself."

"Not sure why, unless she planned on implicating the boys and things got out of hand."

"Well, thank goodness the sting worked."

"Do me a favor next time, will you?" Jim asked.

"What's that?"

"Include me in your sting before, not after you do it, okay?"

I smiled and Porsche and I exchanged glances. "I will. Just understand that once I put a plan in place, I won't stop just because you say no."

"Yeah," he said, "I figured." He sipped his tea. "Seems like you two ladies are going to keep me on my toes."

"And you're going to love every minute of it," I said. He shook his head but I knew I was right. After Travis, I was done dating. Maybe it was time to let this thing between Jim and me happen. I thought of the kiss we'd shared. It wouldn't be a bad thing to date an officer. Especially one who understood when I *meddled* in an investigation.

Acknowledgments

Every book is a team effort. I'd like to thank the great team at Kensington, my wonderful editor, Michaela Hamilton, the copy editor, the cover artist, the publicist, and the entire team who work hard to produce the best quality books for you. I'd like to thank my Oregon friends who help me with my research, and please note that any mistakes are my own. I'd like to thank my agent, Paige Wheeler, and my family and friends who support me. None of this could happen without every single one of you.

In case you missed the first book in the Oregon Honeycomb Mystery series, keep reading to enjoy a sample excerpt.

DEATH BEE COMES HER

Available from Kensington Publishing Corp.

Chapter 1

The people who live on the Oregon coast are a bit . . . shall we say quirky? Hippies, grunge fans, and hipsters have melded into a colorful and interesting community. That's the way I like to think of us, anyway. When you think of the West Coast, you might think of sun, surf, and sand, right? That doesn't always apply here. We have fog, cool breezes, and rocky shores. Did you ever see that movie, *Twilight*? It's more like that. In fact, parts of it were filmed nearby.

Now, I've lived here a while and I've never seen a vampire, but I have seen a few sparkly people. One was Emma Jean Baily, who owns a gift shop near the beach. She was out sweeping in front of her shop.

"Glitter is the herpes of the craft world," she'd told me. "Once it's on you, it will never truly go away. I still find it in the most interesting places."

"Hi, Mrs. Baily," I said and smiled at her glittered T-shirt. Her shop was sided with rugged, stained redwood. The porch rose up from the sidewalk and invited people inside.

"Hello, Wren, how are you and Everett doing today?" Emma Jean asked. She was a small woman with a cap of blonde hair and bright blue eyes in a pixie face. She was my mother's age, but looked youthful in jeans and T-shirt.

"We're well," I said. Everett's my cat and constant companion. He purred his reply. Everett is a Havana Brown and his breed is known for their propensity to talk. "We're going for a walk on the beach."

"Good day for it," she said and gestured toward the beach. "I'd stroll with you, but I'm setting up for next week's Halloweentown extravaganza. Lots to do. Is your shop doing anything?"

"I'm making honey taffy. And we're dressing up, of course."

"Of course," she said and leaned against her broom. "This year I'm going as Little Red Riding Hood. What are you going to be?"

"Everett is going as a warlock and I'm going as his familiar." Everett meowed his approval.

Emma Jean laughed.

"I'm just kidding," I laughed. "As much as Everett might like that, I don't know yet what I'm doing exactly . . . maybe a *Wizard of Oz* theme."

"Oh, there's a lot you can do with that," Emma Jean said, her eyes twinkling. "If you need any help, I've got supplies. It would be fun to do Glinda the Good Witch, in glitter."

"I just might take you up on that offer," I said and Everett agreed.

"Well, if you need my help or not, I can't wait to see you both at the costume parade on Halloween."

"Bye." We continued toward the beach, which was only a block or two from my shop. Most people didn't look twice when they saw me walking my cat on a leash. Everett loved going for walks. He was a social cat with slick, chocolate brown, short hair and bright green eyes. My Aunt Eloise was a cat fancier and bred Havana Browns. Everett was the great-grandson of her best show cat, Elton, and just as handsome, if I say so myself.

Aunt Eloise loved Havana Browns because they were charming, outgoing, and playful. Everett fit the bill to a T.

"Hi, Wren," Barbara Miller said as she stepped out of Books and More. "Hello, Everett. Are you two off to the beach?"

"I thought we'd walk the shore for a bit," I said. "I've been making candy all morning and I needed to stretch my legs."

"Are you making honey taffy for the Halloweentown celebration?"

"It is a favorite for Halloweentown," I said. "Funny how people like the taffy for Halloweentown but prefer the dark chocolate for the Big Foot Festival." Halloweentown was a series of Disney movies that were filmed on the coast of Oregon. In honor of the movies, Oceanview celebrated all things magical and scary every year for an entire week in October.

"Everything in your shop is wonderful," she said. "I don't know how people choose. Now that I think of it, I need a couple of new candles. Is someone minding the store?"

"Porsche is there," I said. "She can help you pick out the best beeswax candles for the season."

"Oh, good," Barbara said. "I'm on my way over there now. Tootles." I watched her walk off. Barbara Miller was my grandmother's neighbor. They had grown up together. While my grandma had to use a walker, Barbara still got around quite well in her athletic shoes, jeans, and jacket. Her short hair went from gray in the back to white in the front, but it framed her wide face well.

Everett and I headed down the nearly empty street. Since it was October, most of the large crowds of tourists had left the coast, leaving the die-hards and the locals. It was my favorite time of year. I loved the colors of fall when the ocean was a deep cold blue. The trees had begun to turn red and yellow while the pines were dark green. Orange pumpkins dotted the sidewalks along with autumnal wreathes and Halloween decorations.

The thing about Everett was he was a bit of a talker. He liked to comment on things we saw on our walks. I talked to him often without even realizing that most people didn't understand talking to a cat. "Want to go down to the beach?" I asked him.

"Are you talking to that cat?" Mildred Woolright said as she passed by.

"Oh, hello," I said. "Yes, I guess I was."

She blinked at me. "You're a bit too young to be a crazy cat lady."

"I'm not crazy," I said with a smile. "But I'll admit to being a cat lady."

Mildred rolled her eyes and continued down the street as I winked at Everett. "Shall we go to the beach?" Cats don't usually care too much for water, but Everett had grown up beside the ocean and as long as we didn't get too close to the water's edge, he didn't mind the sand.

He meowed his agreement and we left the promenade.

There were a few slight dunes where the wind had blown the sand between the promenade and the Pacific Ocean. They rolled gently no more than a yard high and were covered with waving beach grass. Everett loved the feel of the grass against his fur.

Bonfires were allowed on the beach and the evidence of them crunched under our feet. Black charcoal spread out in piles large and small. Pieces of charred wood scattered about. The beach was a deep stretch of sand that narrowed during high tide and stretched out during low tide. I was enjoying the sound of the ocean and searching the waves for evidence of whales when I felt Everett pull on his leash. "What?" I asked as I followed him past a clump of dune grass. He led me over to a woman sleeping in the sand. "Hello?" I picked the cat up and looked at the woman. Sometimes people camped on the beach, but rarely in the rounded dunes.

Who was she? Why was she here?

The woman wore nice clothes and didn't look like someone who regularly slept on the beach. "Ma'am?" I squatted down and shook her shoulder, but she was stiff and cold. I put my fingers on the base of her neck. There was no pulse. "Oh, boy." I jumped back and wiped my hand on my long skirt.

I grabbed my phone and dialed 9-1-1.

"Nine-one-one, how can I help you?"

"I think there's a dead woman on the beach." My voice trembled and came out barely audible. My face felt a little numb and my thoughts tumbled.

"This is the nine-one-one operator. Can you please repeat that?"

"Josie?" I recognized my friend's voice through the jumble of emotions.

"Wren?" she asked. "Are you okay? Did you say there's a dead woman on the beach?"

"When did you start working as a dispatch operator?" I asked because I was in shock and not thinking clearly.

"It's my first day," she said with what sounded like nervous pride. "You're my first call. Where are you? Are you okay?"

"Oh," I said. "I'm okay, yes, I'm fine. I think. There's a woman on the beach and I think she's dead. I guess that would make her a dead body?"

"Where are you exactly?"

"I, um." I glanced around. "I'm about fifty yards from the beach entrance on Main Street."

"Okay, good, an ambulance and police officers are on their way. Are you in danger?"

"No, I seem to be alone on the shore. Should I stay on the line?" I asked.

"Yes," she said. "Please stay on the line. You're sure you're safe?"

"I'm sure," I said.

After a pause that stretched out for what seemed like forever, she said, "the police are on their way."

"Great."

"Please stay on the line so that I know you are safe."

"Okay," I said and waited a couple of long moments in silence. The wind blew against my face and the ocean roared. I felt as stiff as the woman at my feet. "Maybe we should keep talking."

"I can do that. Why don't you tell me what she looks like," Josie asked. "Anyone we know?"

I leaned down closer. "She's dressed like a country club woman. Nice shoes, expensive dress slacks in a swirl pattern, and a tunic-style black top, blonde hair," I said. "She might be in her sixties. Strange, though . . ."

"What?"

"The sun is out, but you know the wind off the ocean . . ."

"Brisk, I bet," she said. "Why?"

"She isn't wearing a jacket."

"Weird," Josie said. "Most ladies that age would be wearing a puffy coat."

"Maybe the killer took it," I said and squatted down to take a closer look.

"Does it look like a mugging? Is she disheveled?"

"No, I don't think so. She still has her wedding ring on and what looks like large single diamond earrings."

"Does she look familiar?"

"There's something familiar, but her face is hidden," I said with some relief.

The woman was on her belly facedown. There didn't appear to be any wounds, but she did have sand stuck in her hair.

"Any idea how she died?"

"I don't see any obvious signs of trauma," I said. "There's some goop in her hair, you know, sand and such."

"And no one else is nearby?"

I glanced around. "There are a couple of kids walking down the shore toward me."

"Keep them away," she said.

"Right." I stood and watched them. "If they get too close, I'll wave them off. I'm just afraid that if I wave now, they will come see what's going on."

"Oh, okay," Josie said. "Can you hear sirens yet?"

I held my breath and listened to my heart beat in my ears. "Not yet," I said.

"Don't worry, they are on the way," she said. "Boy, this job is stressful. I mean, I never imagined anyone dying on my first call . . . you know what, I'll check again."

I looked down at the dead woman at my feet. Everett was lying nearby watching everything from a rise in the dunes. The grass sprung up around him like the vegetation surrounding a lion on the Serengeti. It struck me that I should keep an eye out for tracks or other evidence and make sure no one stepped too close. I glanced around and saw indentations that must have been the woman's original tracks in the sand. Just hers. It didn't look like anyone else had been there.

Her hands were curled into fists. They were drawn against her at the waist. A piece of paper fluttered from the edge of one of her hands, so I took a closer look. She was clutching something. I knew enough to grab a tissue out of the pocket of my skirt and carefully turned her hand to reveal the paper. It whipped about in the breeze. I wanted to take it, but I didn't want to upset a crime scene. Still, it might just blow away in the wind. Thinking quickly, I grabbed my phone and took a few pictures. Then I used the tissue to pry the paper from her fist.

It was a label. A familiar label.

"What's going on, Wren?"

I turned at the sound of a deep, male voice. It was Jim Hampton, a regular on the promenade, a beat cop, and a noticeably handsome man. He reminded me of the actor Paul Newman. My Aunt Eloise raised me on old movies, and I remember he played a cop in one of them. Jim's blue eyes were guarded and unreadable.

I felt a flash of guilt and I think he picked up on it. "Josie, Jim Hampton's here. I'm going to hang up now."

"Okay," she said. "Call me later?"

"I will."

"Wren?" He raised an eyebrow, looking from me to the body. "What's going on?"

"Everett found her," I said.

Jim was a tall man, maybe six foot, with square shoulders and an athletic frame. He hunkered down and felt for a pulse. "She's dead."

"I know, I called nine-one-one," I said and raised my phone. "Josie said she called the police. I'm glad you're here, but I didn't hear a siren."

Then I heard the siren in the distance coming closer. He looked up at me. "I was walking on the promenade and saw you. You looked . . . upset." He rubbed the back of his neck, his gaze falling to the poor woman.

"I guess I am," I said and hugged my waist. "It's not every day you find a dead body."

"Everett seems to be handling it well," he said glancing toward my cat, who rolled in the sand.

"He's used to dead things," I said, stating the obvious. "He's a cat."

"What's that in your hand?"

"My phone?"

"No, the paper you were looking at."

"Oh, I found it in her hand," I said and held it out. "It's the label off one of my lip balms." He took it from me.

"You mean it belonged to you?"

"No, it's from my store. I make it and sell it. It's beeswax, coconut oil, and honey. My recipe. I also designed the label. That's why I recognized it."

"Yes, well, it's evidence and you moved it," he said and stood.

"I have a picture of her holding it," I said as if to prove

my limited prowess in evidence collecting. "I watch crime shows."

He made a dismissive sound. "I'm not sure that will hold up in court."

The siren went silent as an ambulance stopped at the edge of the promenade. Two EMTs hopped out and went in the back for their gear. Jim stood. "Better call the morgue. This woman is long dead."

"That's what I told Josie," I said and picked up Everett. He took an interest in the vehicle's flashing lights.

"Neither one of you are doctors," the female EMT said. Her shirt tag read RITTER. She was five foot ten with short brown hair and serious brown eyes. Built for power, she hauled a stretcher out. Her partner was a young guy about my height with bleached blond hair and a thin build. He had a surfer's tan and winked at me.

"Gotta let Ritter check her out," surfer EMT said. "We'll call the morgue if she's—"

"Oh, she's dead," Ritter confirmed as she knelt beside the body. "She's stiff. Fender, call Dr. Murphy and let him know that we've got a dead body for him."

"Will do," the younger man said. He grabbed his radio and started talking.

Jim took pictures with his cell phone. Then, he and Ritter turned the body. I saw her face and gasped.

Even without color to her skin, I would know her anywhere. It was Agnes Snow.

"You recognize her?" Ritter studied me.

"It's Agnes," I said. "Agnes Snow." Agnes was my aunt's rival at the local craft fair. They had been feuding over who got the grand champion ribbon for decades. It didn't matter which craft my aunt picked up, Agnes was always there with an award-winning entry.

Aunt Eloise had been acting secretively, hiding her latest craft, certain that Agnes was spying on her. She'd even gone so far as driving all the way to Portland to buy her materials on the off chance that Agnes was somehow keeping track of what my aunt bought at the local craft store.

I should have known Agnes from the way she was dressed. Agnes always wore high-end boutique clothes. She looked like a woman who came down to spend two weekends a year in her million-dollar beach house, but, in fact, Agnes had lived in Oceanview her whole life. She had married into a local family with political clout. Bernie, her husband of nearly forty years, was mayor of Oceanview for over half those years. They never had children. Instead, Agnes had gotten good, very good, at every craft known to man.

"Wait, is she the ex-mayor's wife?" Ritter asked.

"Yes," Jim said. "Bernie Snow's wife and Eloise Johnson's biggest rival." He glanced at me, his blue eyes squinting in the bright autumn light. "Might explain the label you found in her hand."

"Could I see that?" Ritter asked, stepping closer.

"It's from one of my lip balms," I said. "I own Let It Bee. The honey store in town. I make handcrafted lip balms, lotions, candles, and—"

"Candy," Fender said. I turned to him.

"Yes, candy."

"The best candy," he said, grinned a smile worthy of a toothpaste ad, and leaned in. "The honey salted caramel is to die for."

"Let's hope Agnes didn't agree," Jim said.

"I'm sure there's no connection," I said. "Besides, it was a lip balm label, not one from candy."

"You have to admit that it still doesn't look that good for you," Jim said his face suddenly sober.

"Wait, you think I had something to do with Agnes's death? That's nuts. Why would I call nine-one-one if I killed her?"

"You watch crime shows," Jim said. "You know the answer."

"Because I want to involve myself in the investigation?" My voice crept up two octaves. "That's crazy. It doesn't happen in real life. Does it?"

Jim raised an eyebrow. "It happens often enough that they put it in a television show."

"Well." I hugged Everett. "It's silly to think I could hurt anyone."

"Any idea how she died?" Fender asked. He leaned over the dead woman and studied her. "I don't see any obvious trauma."

"Cause of death is for the coroner to determine," Ritter said.

"Stand back," said a woman my age as she walked up with a black bag in her hand. She wore a blue shirt that was marked with CSU. "You all are muddying up my crime scene. Is that a cat?"

"Yes, his name is Everett," I said. "He found the body."

She stepped over to me. "Hello there, handsome," she practically purred and scratched Everett behind the ears. He purred back at her. "Is he wearing a leash?"

"He loves to go for walks and the leash keeps him safe," I said and patted his head.

"Okay," she said and turned on her heel. "All of you, do not move! I need to see where you all have come in and messed up the crime scene." She put down her bag, opened it, then pulled on a pair of gloves. Frowning, she took a large camera out of her kit. "Really, Officer Hampton, you know better."

"We moved the body," he said. "Needed to see if she was hurt."

"I have pictures," I said and held up my phone.

"Someone is smart," she said as she snapped away with her camera. "I'm Alison McGovern."

"Wren Johnson," I said.

"Wren, like the bird?"

"Yes," I said. I was used to the question. "My mom loved the name."

"It's cool," Alison said. "Okay, you two can remove the body." I watched in fascination as she continued to bully the EMTs and Jim and work the crime scene. I swear she bullied the grass into giving up its secrets. But she did it in a slow and methodical way.

After a while, Jim stood beside me and watched her work.

"She's good," I said.

"Thorough," he agreed. "I'm surprised that cat is letting you hold him so long."

"Everett? He loves to be held."

"That is not my experience with cats," he said. "My experience is they lure you in to pet their belly only to scratch and bite and run to hide under the bed for the next day and a half."

I laughed. "Yes, that also sounds like a cat. They're all different, you know. Just like people."

"So where were you for the last twelve hours?"

I turned to him. "Are you still thinking I'm a suspect?"

"Can you answer the question?"

"Can you?" I asked him. "I mean, twelve hours is a lot of time to account for."

"I've been working for the last six," he said.

"That doesn't mean you didn't kill someone," I countered. "Did anyone see you every minute of the last twelve hours?"

He narrowed his eyes. "I'm not a person of interest."

"I'm not either."

"Not yet," he admitted and took out his notepad. "That could change at any minute." He started writing in his pad. "Let's start from the beginning, you found the body?"

"Yes."

"How?"

I went over how I found Agnes step by step right up until the time I pulled the label out of her fist.

"I see," he said as he took notes. "And you know Agnes, how?"

"Like I said—and you know—Agnes and my aunt have this informal competition going."

"Can you explain what you mean by informal competition?"

"The two of them have been competing against each other my entire life," I said. "I think it started when they were in grammar school."

"What kind of competition?"

"Everything," I said, knowing that was the truth. "Most recently it's been about crafts."

"Such as?"

"Quilting, scrapbooking, knitting, crocheting, flower arranging, jelly making . . ."

"Right," he said. "And how do you do any of that competitively?"

"Oh, there are all kinds of contests," I said. "Church contests, county fairs, senior center contests . . ."

"I get it," he said. "I think. So they were rivals."

"Yes, everyone knows that. You even said it yourself."

"Do you think your aunt killed her?"

"What? No, no," I said and hugged Everett just a bit too tight. He squeaked. "She would never. Besides, she was in Portland last night."

"Why was she in Portland?"

"She had a date," I said. "I assume she has an alibi for every minute of her night."

"Did you have a date?" he asked.

"Is that relevant to this case?" I replied, eyebrow raised.

"If it provides you an alibi."

"No, I did not have a date," I said and studied the outgoing tide. "I was home alone making candy and a batch of hand and body scrub."

"Best candy ever," Fender said as he came back from putting the body in the ambulance. He bent down and picked up his bag, then held out his hand. "Rick Fender."

"Hi, Rick, Wren Johnson." I shook his hand.

"Nice to meet you, Wren," he said and grinned. "Can I get a discount on the candy?"

"Come in while I'm there and I'll see what I can do," I said.

"Perfect." He walked back to the ambulance and climbed in the passenger side while Ritter closed the door and walked over to the driver's side. The two EMTs made an odd couple as Ritter was a large woman with square shoulders and Rick was lanky.

"Well, I've got to get back to the store," I said to Jim. "You know where to find me?"

"Wait while I check if they want you to come down to the station," he said.

"Are you kidding me?" I asked, somewhat unnerved by the idea. He held up his palm to quiet me while he turned and spoke to someone on his radio.

I'd been by the police station so I knew where it was, but I'd never been inside. In fact, Jim was the first police officer I'd ever spoken to—it was at a chamber of commerce meeting. I was lucky enough to never have run afoul of the law. Until today.

"You can go for now and take the cat home," he said. "He would be too big a distraction at the station, anyway." He reached over and scratched Everett behind the ears.

Everett meowed as if he agreed.

Relief washed over me. "Then, we're going home."

"I'd advise you not to go anywhere. Right now you're my only lead and it would be better if you didn't do anything suspicious."

"Right." Everett and I left the beach. The wind was colder than I remembered. I felt like the business owners were watching me as I walked by. Suzy from Suzy's Flowers stared. I turned my sweater collar up. Mrs. Beasley, of Beasley's Gifts, watched me from across the street. I waved my hand and she stepped back.

Wallace Hornsby, owner of Hornsby Tailor Shop, peered at me from behind his small round glasses and I sent him an uncomfortable smile. Everett meowed so I hugged him. "It's okay," I said. "They're just curious." I paused and decided I was going to act as natural as possible. I put Everett down, straightened my sweater, and we walked the rest of the way back to my shop. The last thing I wanted to do was act like a murder suspect. No, really, the last thing I ever wanted to do was find a dead body. I guess I needed a new last thing.

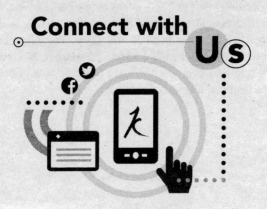

Grab These Cozy Mysteries
from
Kensington Books